2

SNAKE OIL

A PATRICK FLINT NOVEL

PAMELA FAGAN HUTCHINS

SKIPJACK PUBLISHING

FREE PFH EBOOKS

Before you begin reading, you can snag a free Pamela Fagan Hutchins ebook starter library by joining her mailing list at https://www.subscribepage.com/PFHSuperstars.

CHAPTER ONE: DRIVE

SHOSHONI, WYOMING
SUNDAY, DECEMBER 19, 1976, TEN A.M.

Patrick

The 1960 International Harvester Travelall accelerated out of the Wind River Canyon and into an angry churn of steely clouds. Patrick thought the canyon drive had been hairy—twists, turns, dips, and drop-offs—ever since the Wedding of the Waters, back where the Wind River flowed north and uphill from Boysen Reservoir and became the Bighorn River near Thermopolis. Beautiful, if sobering, even in December with snow clinging to the faces of the towering red sandstone, limestone, and Bighorn dolomite cliffs. One patch of black ice, and it was all over but the screaming on the way down. So, this unexpected wall of weather made him tighten his belly and his grip on the arm rest. They had seventy-five miles left in their drive through the barren Wind River Reservation to the Fort Washakie Health Center.

"That's a storm there, Doc." Wes Braten grinned under the coppery walrus mustache that didn't match his blond hair. Wes was Patrick's best friend and sometimes-favorite co-worker at the hospital in Buffalo, Wyoming. He'd been growing the mustache all fall, and it was his pride and joy. Patrick rubbed his own upper lip. Susanne had threatened him with his life if he even thought about one.

The gray wall enveloped them in a burst of wind that rattled the windows and forced its way inside. The temperature drop was instantaneous. Patrick rubbed his arms. Visibility dropped to about ten feet as snowflakes seemed to converge from all directions, like the center of a snow globe. Wes turned on the windshield wipers. They scraped and screeched across dry glass as they tossed the snow off, only to have the wind blow it right back on. Patrick reached in the rear seat for his thick plaid jacket and wrestled his way into it, adding snow gloves and a wool cap with ear flaps. He looked at his feet. Hiking boots. Not exactly snow gear, but all he'd brought, except for his running shoes, which would be even worse.

He turned up the heater. It spit out a burning smell, and he heard a terrible rattle in the belly of the beast. "Is that okay?"

"Oh, sure. But turn it to defrost for me. On high. Otherwise our breath will ice up the inside of this glass pretty quick."

Patrick did as Wes asked, then huddled over the dash. "The forecast called for unseasonably warm weather."

"Haven't you lived here long enough to know that's a load of horse nuggets?"

"Where do you get your forecast?"

"You don't need one if you're always prepared for anything."

After nearly two years in Wyoming, Patrick did know this. But a lifetime in Texas had made him winter soft. The big vehicle shimmied, then felt like it was surfing a Gulf Coast wave, absent the sand, sun, and water, telling him they had already run into accumulated snow. Patrick leaned to the windshield for a closer look. There had to be a foot or more on the road. His breath fogged the glass, and, as Wes had predicted, it started to crystallize in a flash.

Patrick scraped at the condensation and ice with the forearm of his coat, mostly just smearing it. "Where did all of this snow come from?"

Wes shrugged. "The sky, most likely."

Patrick wouldn't be surprised if Wes met an early death someday, a few seconds after one of his smartass remarks to the wrong person. Right now, though, he could say whatever he liked as long as he kept the vehicle between the lines and moving forward. Being stuck in a blizzard wasn't on his schedule.

A shadow and two yellow dots like headlights materialized in the road. Wes mashed the brakes.

Patrick clutched the arm rest. "What is it?"

"Damn prairie wolf." The Travelall stopped, and Wes honked.

"Prairie wolf?" Patrick fancied himself something of an amateur wildlife biologist, but he wasn't familiar with the term.

"Coyote."

Patrick squinted into the storm. Sure enough, a coyote stared back at him before loping off and disappearing in the blinding white. Wes grumbled and pressed the accelerator, slowly picking up speed. The two men rode in a tense silence for about fifteen minutes. Patrick's eyes burned from strain. Snow pelted the undercarriage of the vehicle. It reminded him of mudding in the Brazos River bottoms in the family truck, then washing it until it gleamed in the moonlight so his dad wouldn't figure out what he'd been up to.

The snow grew deeper. Wes slowed, and the high clearance Travelall soldiered through it without faltering, the noise from its knobby tires in competition with the whistling wind and laboring defrost. The interior temperature dropped further.

Patrick touched the side window. It was bitterly, excruciatingly cold. "What do you think the temperature is out there?"

"I don't think. I know, Doc. It's minus 10, not counting the wind chill." Wes pointed at his sideview mirror. "I rigged a thermometer. Works like a charm."

"That's chilly." Patrick tried to get a look at the thermometer but couldn't get the right angle. "With all this snow, we're going to be late."

"Late isn't usually an issue on the reservation." Wes tapped his instrument panel. "Now that doesn't look right." He decelerated, then flipped on his right blinker. "Damn thing doesn't work." He turned it back off.

"What are we doing?"

"Pulling over, of course."

"I can see that. I meant *why*. Do you need to take a leak?"

"Nah. Not that I ever pass on the opportunity. But we're overheating."

"In this weather?"

"Yep."

Patrick felt a moment of rising panic. His time at the clinic was limited as it was, without a delay. Worse, his wife would be worried sick if he didn't call her with news of his safe arrival at Fort Washakie, roughly on time. "Are we breaking down?"

Susanne hadn't been happy about this trip to begin with. Less than a week before Christmas and only hours before the mass arrival of her Texas family on their first visit to Wyoming, all before the calendar flipped over to 1977. He was skipping out on the house cleaning, the kid wrangling, and the last-minute runs as Santa's main helper. Plus, they were down to the wire on negotiations for her dream house. She thought his absence might sour the deal, if he wasn't available to help resolve any last-minute issues. But wasn't that what phones were for?

He believed in the work he and Wes were doing in Fremont County, though. The Indian health care promised by treaty with the U.S. government was perpetually underfunded and underserved, and the health care centers for the Eastern Shoshone and Northern Arapaho on the Wind River Reservation were no exception. Even if Indian Health Service clinics had the funds, it was next to impossible to recruit qualified medical personnel to the reservation. Faced with extreme weather, isolation, poverty, and a crime rate five times higher than the national average, most declined the opportunity, or left quickly if they came at all. So, he'd been volunteering at Fort Washakie once a month for the last year, and there was no other aspect of his medical practice he found more rewarding. The people needed him. The average life expectancy for an American Indian on the reservation was fifty years, twenty less than the rest of the state. If he could help improve those numbers, he'd have done something good to justify the cushy salary and lifestyle being a physician afforded him.

Susanne didn't see things his way. While she supported his desire to help out, it was the timing of this trip that had them at odds. And when it came to his safety—watch out. She was a bear. With good reason. He'd worried her before when he was unreachable. It had triggered her intuition and sent her running pell-mell into the mountains to find him and the kids. They'd been in serious trouble and needed her help, too. She'd give him a few hours grace on his arrival time at the clinic before she sounded an alarm this time, but then she'd be on the horn to their next-door neighbor Ronnie Harcourt, a Johnson County Deputy. Which he supposed wasn't a bad thing, given that the Travelall was not going to be traveling all that much longer, apparently.

Wes turned off the highway. "Gussie's the best winter weather vehicle in the state, I'd wager, but she's not as young as she once was." He crept along a mostly white road, his eyes cutting back and forth between fence posts on either side, then jammed on the brakes. Gussie slid a few inches downhill and sideways. "Well, that wouldn't have been good."

Patrick peered into the gloom. A sign announced a boat ramp, into the reservoir which they had almost just slid into. "Shit."

"On a stick." Wes donned his winter wear, then hopped out with a flashlight in his hand. His size extra-lean body didn't block much weather, even with the five inches he had on Patrick's six feet. He leaned back in. Snow blew past him and splatted in the seat. "Let me check the radiator fluid. I'll be right back."

Patrick wasn't sending his friend out into the elements alone. He took a deep breath and pulled his cap flaps lower over his ears. Then he was out, in the middle of the blizzard, with the wind howling across the lake and blowing him up the ramp. Icy snowflakes pelted his cheeks. Wes had popped the hood open, and Patrick shuffled toward him, using Gussie to steady himself as he walked. The hood didn't block all of the wind, but the warm engine drew him in as if it was a crackling fire. Snow sizzled, melted, and steamed back upward from it.

Wes put the cap back on the radiator. "It's empty."

This was bad. No auto parts stores or tow trucks for miles, and no one on the roads in this weather. "You're kidding."

"Don't worry. I've got an idea what's wrong."

Patrick followed him to Gussie's rear, sliding along the length of the Travelall. The ramp was like a ski slope. Wes opened the back doors and selected a snow shovel, his toolbox, and a length of hose from an assortment of carefully arranged and secured emergency gear.

He handed the shovel to Patrick. "Can you dig me under?"

Patrick answered by getting to work scraping snow out from under and away from Gussie's front end. Wes scooted headfirst beneath the vehicle on his back.

"I knew it," he shouted.

"Knew what?"

"Frozen radiator hose. So frozen, it burst. All the water leaked out through the burst hose, so nothing getting to the engine to keep it cool. I can fix this right up."

"What happened to the anti-freeze?"

"I don't use it. Water is cheaper."

Until you break down in the middle of nowhere in a blizzard. Then it's a really expensive choice. Patrick pictured the snowy, cold miles ahead of them. "What if it freezes again?"

Wes grunted, and his voice was muffled. "I've got some anti-freeze in the back. I'll add a little this time, and that should take care of it. But if all else fails, I've got more hose."

"Okay."

"There's a water hauler in the back end. Can you fill 'er up with some nice, cool reservoir water?"

"Sure thing."

Patrick retrieved a ten-gallon hauler from the back end. Once filled, it would weigh—he calculated quickly in his head—more than eighty pounds. Quite a load to carry in this weather and terrain. He shook his head and walked to the side of the ramp until he found a more level approach down to the reservoir. Trudging through snow, he placed his feet carefully, still somehow finding rocks and holes that robbed him of his balance with every step. He skidded the last few inches to the lake, grimacing, expecting icy cold water to seep through his boots, but it didn't come. He lowered the container on its side. It met resistance. Ice. He smacked it with the container, and it broke apart, splashing water up his arm.

The cold grabbed his full attention. "Holy mackerel." Cursing euphemisms were something Susanne had talked him into once they'd had kids.

He submerged the container in the opening. Water flowed in the mouth as ice gushed on small ripples, knocking against the plastic. When it seemed like the jug was full, he tilted it and screwed on its attached cap. He lifted the water. The weight, the wind, the snow, the rocks – they were all too much. He stumbled into the reservoir up to his knees. The container became a handheld flotation device and kept him upright. The icy water was like a thousand cactus needles stabbing his feet and legs, something he was very familiar with after his horse, Reno, spooked at a rattlesnake the summer before, tossing him into a cactus patch on his tush.

"God bless America." Euphemisms weren't good enough now, though. He needed more and shouted, "Son of a bitch!"

He turned, planning to scramble out quickly, but the slick rocks made it rough going. Bracing on the container for leverage, he struggled out, then hugged it to his abdomen to stabilize his center of gravity. He cursed the storm and Gussie and the water and the big, trouble-making jug. Inching his way along, wobbling and sliding, he reached the snowy bank. When he stepped out, the wind whipped around his legs and feet, making him even colder. He tried to gauge the distance to the vehicle and could barely see Gussie's lights. A burst of air escaped his lips, like a horse's laugh. He wasn't going to let himself die thirty feet from safety, but that's exactly what would happen if he stayed out too long. *Time to do this.* He waded uphill through snow that clung to his wet jeans in icy crusts. What had seemed like a short walk down felt like a hike up Mount Everest, and what was slick and wobbly before was twice that now. He fell to his knees three times before he reached Wes at Gussie's hood, where his teeth chattered so hard he worried he'd break one.

Wes took the water from him, one eyebrow raised. "Looks like you took a polar bear plunge. Do you have spare socks and gloves?"

"S-s-s-socks." Patrick knew he had to get out of the wind, so he nodded at Wes and hurried away.

The inside of the Travelall was blessedly warm. He ripped off his gloves. After laying them to dry in the heated breeze from the defrost, he reached over into the back and dragged his duffel to the center of the seat. He unzipped it. Clothes fell to the floorboard as he dug for wool socks, tennis shoes, and two pairs of clean underwear. He stacked the haul in his lap while he fumbled with his hiking boots. His cold fingers didn't want to cooperate with the laces, but with a lot of struggling, he got them loose enough to pull off, followed by his sopping socks. He chunked all of them into the back, careful to avoid the dry garments. Then he propped his icy feet on the dash for a moment, groaning. The warm air hurt so good. Drawing in a deep breath, he forced himself to pull his feet away from the heater and put his socks on. His wet skin gripped the dry wool, and he was out of breath by the time he'd forced his feet in. He cuffed his jeans and rolled them to the top of his calf to get the wet material away from his legs, then pulled the socks the rest of the way up. Next, he put on his shoes. His feet tingled and burned more every second, which was a good sign. No frost bite. Finally, he wrapped his red, stiff fingers in the dry underpants.

What seemed like a painful eternity passed. He wondered what was holding Wes up. A few minutes later, he heard him at the back of the

Travelall, putting away his tools and supplies. Then the rear doors shut, and, moments later, Wes jumped into the driver's seat. He, too, took off his gloves and put them on the dash, then rubbed his hands briskly together.

He grinned at Patrick. "And I thought I was wet."

"What t-t-took you so long?"

"I got another container of water, in case we need it on down the road."

Patrick was grateful that Wes didn't rub it in that he hadn't taken a dunking, too. "Good idea."

"Let's get gone." Wes shifted the vehicle into reverse, leaving one foot on the brake and accelerating gently with the other. The tires spun for a heart-stopping second, then caught, and the Travelall backed up the incline. "Thank the good Lord for four-wheel drive."

Patrick was still thinking about his dip in the icy lake water. Stupid. He hadn't been careful enough, and he could have drowned or died of hypothermia.

"Whatcha talking about over there to yourself, Doc?"

Patrick pressed his lips together. No matter how hard he tried, he couldn't keep from moving his lips when he talked to himself, which, according to his friends, family, and co-workers, was a lot. "Ha ha."

Back on the highway, they got lucky. While they'd been doctoring Gussie, a snowplow had made a pass down their side of the road. For now, at least, their new radiator hose wouldn't be submerged. The Travelall surged over the shallow snow like a Coast Guard cutter, and the map dot towns passed slowly but steadily. Shoshoni. A right turn, then on to Pavilion. A left to Kinnear. Meanwhile, the snow continued to fall, and the sun refused to shine. On 132, past Johnstown and halfway to Ethete, Wes hit the brakes.

Patrick sat up with a jerk. He'd dozed off. Ahead, he saw an old crew cab Dodge pickup broadside in the road with its nose off one edge and its hazards flashing. A man in head-to-toe puffy black winter wear waved both arms over his head. Wes pulled Gussie to a stop as they approached the truck. Wes and Patrick looked at each other.

"How about you stay behind the wheel," Patrick said. "I'll go see what he wants." He wanted to have faith in his fellow man. He also didn't want to walk the rest of the way to Fort Washakie if this was a hold up.

"Are you armed?"

Patrick got his holster from his doctor's bag and buckled it around his waist. He checked his .357 Magnum, then re-holstered it. "Loaded."

He patted his hip, feeling the reassuring hardness of his backup weapon. Wes had given him the six-inch pocketknife his last birthday, the one with SAWBONES engraved in the handle. The one that he'd rammed into the throat of Chester, the man who had kidnapped and sexually assaulted his daughter. He shuddered. As a doctor, it was his mission to save lives, not take them, and he hoped he was never in a position where he had to choose to end a human life again. He opened the door, and the full force of the north wind blasted him in the face.

"Aren't you going to roll your pants down, Doc?"

Patrick glanced at his legs. Knee high gray and red wool socks, Adidas running shoes, and pedal pusher jeans. It was the kind of look that got a fellow's ass kicked. "Thanks." He grinned and rolled them down. "If I'm not back in five minutes, send the cavalry." He reconsidered. "That sounds bad, given our location."

"Don't worry. I've got your back."

Patrick slammed the door and ducked into the wind. He buttoned his jacket on his way to the truck. *Wyoming's not for sissies*, he thought. One of the things he loved best about it.

The man in black met him at the door to the back seat of his truck. With the hood pulled close around his face, Patrick saw smooth, dark skin, pupils dilated in brown eyes, and white, chapped lips. "My wife is in labor. I was taking her to the hospital in Buffalo." His expression turned almost apologetic. "The medical care on the reservation isn't so good. But the snow got too deep. I was trying to turn around, and we got stuck. Now she says the baby is coming."

As if on cue, there was a long, piercing scream from inside the back seat.

The man winced, drawing heavy eyebrows together. "I don't know what to do to help her. My mother delivered all the babies in our family, but she passed on three years ago."

Patrick patted his shoulder. "Buffalo has come to you. I'm a doctor there. I was just on my way to the health center in Fort Washakie to lend a hand. Would you mind if I checked on her? If she's okay to travel, we could at least get her there where she'd be warmer and more comfortable. Maybe you and my buddy can get your truck unstuck while I see to your wife."

Tears sprang to the man's eyes. "Thank you. Yes. Yes. That would be great."

Patrick reached for the man's gloved hand and shook it. "I'm Dr. Flint. What's your wife's name?"

"Eleanor. Eleanor Manning. And I'm Junior."

"Is this her first child?"

He nodded.

"Okay, then, why don't you tell her who I am before I crawl in there with her?" Patrick smiled at him.

Junior laughed, a nervous, brittle sound. "Okay." He opened the door, releasing a sweet spicy scent that reminded Patrick of berries. He knelt on the floorboard, whispering in the ear of a black-haired woman whose body was covered by a mound of colorful blankets. He kissed her forehead as she wailed again, then backed out. He nodded at Patrick.

Patrick moved into the spot Junior had vacated, taking in Eleanor's ruddy cheeks and strained face. Long, jet black hair was stuck to her lips and sweaty neck. "Eleanor? I'm Dr. Flint. How are you doing?"

Her scream was like a punch to the eardrums.

"I'm going around to the other side of the truck. I need to check on the baby. Will that be okay?"

Her eyes were wide and long-lashed. She bit chapped lips and nodded in short, rapid jerks.

"Okay. Give me just a second." To Junior, he said, "Why don't you stay here for a minute and see if she'll let you hold her hand. Talk to her, keep her distracted."

Junior dove back into the truck, ripped off a glove, and took Eleanor's hand. Patrick ran to the other side. He hated letting the wicked north wind in, but he had no choice. He wrenched the door open and his gloves off, jammed the gloves in his pocket, and then touched Eleanor's ankle.

"I'm right here, and I'm going to lift the blankets back so I can see what's going on. It's going to be cold, and I'm sorry for that. You just relax the best you can."

Behind him, a voice said, "I brought your bag of snake oil." Wes. Referring to Patrick's doctor's bag. "Need a hand, Doc?"

"Thanks. I'm good. But this is Junior, and he needs his truck dug out and pointed toward Fort Washakie."

"No problem. Junior, I'm Wes." He held up his shovel. "I brought this, too. And I've had a lot of practice digging." He grinned.

"Thank you, Wes." Junior whispered to his wife again, then backed out to get to work with Wes.

Patrick set his bag on the ground, then dug around in it. Bandages. Antibiotics. Pain killers. Valium. Phenobarbitol for seizures. Muscle relaxants. Syringes. Tape. Activated Charcoal. A stethoscope, which he put around his neck. A pair of medical gloves. And a flashlight. He snatched the gloves and the flashlight, scrubbed his hands in the snow, then folded the blankets up to Eleanor's waist. He eased her knees up and apart and switched the flashlight on. He couldn't see the baby's head, which was a good thing.

As he put on his glove, he was happy that he didn't wear a ring so that he didn't have to take it off now and risk losing it. Once, right after he and Susanne had married, he'd caught his wedding band on a nail. He'd come close to ripping his finger off, and he'd never worn the ring since. To Eleanor he said, "I'm reaching in to see how far the baby has to go, Eleanor."

In the background, he heard Wes and Junior grunting and talking.

All he could see of the woman's head from this vantage point was her hair, but it was shaking like she was nodding. Patrick probed up the birth canal. His fingers found the baby's head. It wasn't breech. The woman was nearly fully dilated, though. He removed his hand and then the gloves, guided Eleanor's knees back together, and pulled the blanket back over her feet.

"Can I have your wrist to take your pulse?"

She pulled it from under the blankets and held it out to him. He counted beats with his eyes on his wristwatch. When he was done, he leaned over her.

"And now I'm going to listen to your heart. Just peel those blankets down a few inches, okay?"

She spoke for the first time. A young voice, almost childlike with fright and pain. "Okay." She folded the blanket down.

"This is going to be a little cold." He rubbed the stethoscope back and forth on his hand to warm it. Then he slipped it down the front of her blouse to her heart. It beat a steady whump-whump-whump in his ear. Healthy and strong.

"Good. Now, last thing. I'm going to press on your belly. It might be uncomfortable, but I just want to check on the baby."

She nodded. "Okay."

Patrick slid his hands under the side edge of the blanket. He palpated her belly until he had a fix on the baby's location, position, and movement. Then he searched for its heartbeat with his stethoscope, found it, and again counted beats against time on his watch. He couldn't help a sigh of relief. All was as it should be, other than the fact that they were stuck in the middle of the road in a blizzard far from a hospital with a birth imminent.

"Good job, Eleanor. Everything looks just fine."

She gave him a weak smile.

"Can I turn the truck?" Junior asked over his wife's head.

"Yes, I'm done. Eleanor, I'll talk to you more in a second." He kept his stethoscope around his neck but put his doctor's bag in the floorboard and shut the door. Again, he scrubbed his hands with snow.

Junior got in the driver's seat, then eased the truck back onto the road, turning it as he went.

Wes came to stand beside Patrick, leaning on his shovel and panting. "Well?"

"She's fully effaced and her cervix is dilated to about eight centimeters. But this is her first baby, so I think we can make it to the clinic, if we hurry. I should ride with them, though."

"Sounds good. See you there." Wes disappeared into the storm.

Junior pulled back around and stopped. He got out and went to hold his wife's hand again.

Patrick joined him. "Are you okay, Eleanor?"

She nodded, and this time she smiled for a moment, before another groan escaped her lips, then escalated into a long shriek. Patrick glanced at his watch. Her contractions were about five minutes apart, maybe a little less. This baby was coming soon.

When Eleanor's contraction had passed, Patrick said, "Junior, Eleanor, everything looks just fine, and I think we can make it into the health center. How about I ride with you?"

They agreed, with Junior looking giddy about it.

Patrick settled into the front seat. Junior drove faster than Patrick was comfortable with, but he didn't say a word. He did look behind them every so often, shocked each time he confirmed Wes was keeping up. Patrick checked on Eleanor and reassured her. A few times he tried to make small talk with Junior, but the soon-to-be father seemed too nervous to carry on a conversation. Fifteen minutes later, the truck arrived at a one-story stucco building. It was a relic, the oldest IHS clinic in existence, built by the U.S. Army in 1814 as a cavalry commissary.

Junior had his pick of the spaces in the parking lot in front of it. Gussie barreled into the parking lot, too, spewing up snow as Wes parked the Travelall beside the Dodge truck.

"We're here. It will be just a minute now, Eleanor," Patrick said.

Wes ran ahead inside, then re-emerged at the other end of a stretcher from the tall, athletic looking Constance Teton. An Army medic and trained nurse now in the Reserves, she ran the clinic. Her hair was braided back from her face and hung down her back, showcasing magnificent bone structure in her cheeks, chin, and brow line. But it was her eyes that were her best feature. Like a fawn, brown, limpid, and thick lashed.

Patrick got out. "Hi, Constance. Thanks."

She winked at him. The woman was outgoing and confident in addition to beautiful, and, in the informal environment of the clinic, they'd become friends with a shared mission. Last time he was at the clinic, she'd told him over lunch in the staff room that she'd dreamed of running off to Hollywood as a teen but didn't have the money to make the trip. Her back-up plan was a college basketball scholarship. Then she'd wrecked her knee, something that Indian healthcare didn't cover. That hope dashed, she signed a contract for the military. "Next stop, Vietnam," she'd said. "Two tours. One wedding when I was home on R&R."

Constance opened the back door to the truck. The cheery expression drained from her face. "Oh. Hello, Eleanor. Junior." Her voice was chilly.

Junior nodded at her without speaking.

Patrick frowned. Before he could ponder the reason for the awkward interchange, it was time to transfer Eleanor to the stretcher. Wes took her shoulders. Patrick supported her mid-section. Constance brought the Mannings' blankets and tucked them around the woman. Within seconds, snowflakes dotted the blanket and Eleanor's hair. The woman was tiny, save for her labor-bloated face and belly.

A snowmobile parked beside them and a figure in all white gear climbed off, looking and moving like the Abominable Snowman. As he deposited the helmet on the machine's seat, Patrick saw angry, red burn scars on his right cheek and jawline.

"Dr. Flint." Riley Pearson lifted a hand in greeting without meeting Patrick's eyes, then unzipped his fur-trimmed hunting parka. Riley did janitorial and grounds work at the center. Introverted, but nice, and helpful. Whether the social awkwardness was a result of his injuries or was his personality, Patrick wasn't sure, just like he wasn't sure if Riley was Indian or not, with light brown hair and green eyes paired with high cheekbones and a hook nose.

Patrick said, "Hello, Riley. You made it in." Riley normally drove an antique of a motorcycle. Not the ideal vehicle for the conditions.

Riley nodded. "Need a hand?"

Constance waved him over. "Take my end. I'll prep the room."

"Okay." Riley stashed his gloves in his pockets and gripped one end of the stretcher.

He and Wes set off for the clinic, Junior on their heels.

"We've got Eleanor under control, Dr. Flint, if you want to get your-self ready." Constance walked backwards toward the door as she spoke.

"Thanks."

She turned and went inside. Patrick grabbed his doctor's bag from the Dodge. As he neared the door to the clinic, he noticed a rusted, dented truck parked on the far side of the building. The driver's door was ajar, one long booted leg hanging out.

"Hello?" he shouted.

There was no movement and no answer.

Careful not to slip and fall in his running shoes, Patrick trotted over to the truck. The engine was shut off, but he still smelled a hint of exhaust, like it had been on not too long before. "Hello?" He peered in. A man. "Sir?"

The big man was slumped over the steering wheel, his weathered brown cheek pressed against it, mouth open and a shock of hair over one glazed eye while the other stared into nothingness. His gray felt cowboy hat was balanced over the gap between the floorboard and the slightly open door, an eagle feather in the brow band erect but buffeted by the wind. Fuzzy dice swayed in the wind from the rearview mirror. Patrick laid two fingers on his carotid artery, feeling for a pulse.

None. The man was dead. Cold dead. For a moment, he considered performing CPR, but it was clear he'd been there a while.

There was nothing worse than someone dying in his care, even if this man wasn't his patient yet. Maybe if he'd had a chance to treat him, the man would have lived. But Patrick knew he had to shake it off, get inside, and deliver a baby. He didn't have time to examine him yet and figure out what had gone wrong. One person dies, another is born. The circle of life, with Patrick's first duty to the living. So, he lifted the man's foot back inside his truck. It was undignified to leave him half in, half out of his vehicle. He wasn't going anywhere, and it was deep freeze cold outside. He'd have to be fine until after the baby. Then Patrick would get help bringing him inside and call the police.

"Sorry, my friend." He shut the door and hustled the length of the building to the door of the clinic.

CHAPTER TWO: SPIFF

Susanne

S usanne Flint cradled the phone between her ear and shoulder as she spun herself out of the cord. She'd tangled herself, and good. That's what she got for cleaning and conversing at the same time. But she couldn't help herself. She was too worked up. "I understand he's helping people. I really do. But just this once, couldn't he have helped me instead?"

In her ear, Vangie Sibley's Tennessee accent was soothing. "Isn't the old saying, 'charity begins at home?'"

"Exactly." Susanne pushed her scarf back on her head, then applied some elbow grease and furniture polish to her slab table in circular strokes. It had a nice lemon scent. She'd been boiling Red Hots and cinnamon sticks on the stove for the last hour, and the lemon added just the right zest. When she started baking later, it would smell like heaven in here. Just right for Christmas guests.

Ferdinand, the goofy Irish Wolfhound who had adopted the Flints their first week in Wyoming, propped his head on the table, right where she'd just polished.

"No, Ferdie! Bad dog!"

He backed away, furniture polish darkening his long chin hairs. Now he was going to lie down and get it on the shag carpet. Not on her watch. She opened the backdoor. "Out."

He slunk out with his long, curved tail between his even longer legs.

To Vangie, she said, "My parents, my sister and her husband and kids. All of them. Their first visit to Wyoming, and they're arriving tonight. Six people, staying for a week. And Patrick's off saving the world again."

"When will he be back?"

"Mid-day on the twenty-third. Or late on the twenty-second. He's going to let me know. Come to think of it, he should have called by now. Which means he won't until tonight." She made a rumbly noise low in her throat. "It's a good thing he's so handsome, or I might be downright angry at him." And he was. Handsome, that is. Tall, with arresting blue eyes, and a little less light brown hair on top than he used to have. But still in great shape, without the beer belly so many men in their early thirties started to get.

Vangie's voice grew thoughtful. "I remember my mother explaining to me the meaning of the expression."

Susanne heard barking at the front door. *That dog.*

"What expression?"

"'Charity begins at home'. She said it meant that since you shared love at home, those in your home became better equipped to share love with others outside the home."

The front door opened and closed.

She heard the voice of Perry, her twelve-year old son. "Good boy, Ferdie. Good boy."

Susanne ignored Vangie's unwelcome clarification. She'd been taught that, too, but right now, she needed her husband sharing his love at home. He could share it outside the home later. So to speak. "Anyway, I have half a day, and I still have to run to the store, cook dinner, finish cleaning, wrap presents, and deal with the kids."

Ugh, the kids.

"How is teen love these days?"

Susanne moved on to the beloved hutch that matched her table. As she stretched to reach the high sides, she huffed and puffed, which matched her feelings on the subject of fifteen-year old Trish and her seventeen-year old boyfriend, Brandon Lewis. "Well, you know we're not crazy about this relationship."

"Brandon's family did kidnap Trish and try to kill all of you."

Susanne tried not to dwell on the fact that Brandon's relatives on his mother's side had kidnapped Trish to punish Patrick for the death of their matriarch, Bethany Jones, when they'd brought her in too late for him to save her. They'd dragged Trish into Cloud Peak Wilderness, and it had taken Patrick, Perry, Susanne, and their neighbor Ronnie to rescue her. Only Brandon's uncle, Billy Kemecke, had survived the encounter, and he was facing a death penalty trial for multiple murders. Something Brandon's mother blamed on the Flints, and resented. A lot. Susanne just hoped that Brandon's genetics leaned heavily toward his father's side of the family.

"Is it too much to ask that your kids don't date in families who want you dead?"

"Seems rational, except that you're talking about teenagers. Where are the lovebirds now?"

"Up at the church, supposedly. Where Perry was kicked out of Sunday school this morning for fighting, believe it or not." *What is happening to my sweet little boy?* She hoped he hadn't developed an aggressive streak playing football. "It's the one place we'll let Brandon drive her to and from."

"I used to tell my mother I was going to church with my high school boyfriend, too. Then we'd—"

"I don't want to hear this." Susanne stretched the cord as far as it would go and leaned over to dust the TV and coffee table in the living room. She remembered being that age, too, dating Patrick, and eloping with him when they were eighteen. All Patrick had on his mind at that age was sex. Roughly the same age Brandon was now. "The only thing we have going for us is that Trish is so bossy with him that they fight half the time."

"Making up is awful sweet."

"Stop!" She'd cry if Vangie wasn't so funny. And right. "We just have to keep them apart when they're getting along. Speaking of love, though, I have good news on the house."

Susanne and Patrick had been house hunting all fall. She'd agreed to continue living in Wyoming if they could buy a house on Clear Creek. He'd jumped at her offer. She'd finally found one she wanted. More than wanted. It was gorgeous and perfect and in their price range. Four

bedrooms, three baths, with an entry on the same level as the parking —
a big deal in rugged terrain where often the entrance was on the lowest
level and the main living area one story above it. And it met Patrick's
requirements, too. Twenty acres, a barn, horse fencing, and less than ten
minutes from the hospital.

"That dreamy one on the creek?"

"Yes. We made an offer, and the sellers countered. Then we did,
because Patrick is so incredibly cheap."

"That man could pinch a penny into a dime between his cheeks."

Susanne laughed. "He could. Anyway, they came down ten thousand dollars today after our counter-offer. If I can get Patrick to agree to
it and sign the papers, we're going to be moving next month."

"Yay! You do realize you'll be moving during the coldest month of
the year, right?"

"It has two massive fireplaces. I'll keep it snug as a bug in a rug all
winter."

"If by winter, you mean until it warms up in June, then that sounds
wonderful."

"It also has brand new deadbolt locks on all the doors."

"After the ordeal you went through with Billy Kemecke, I can only
imagine how that appeals to you. Did you see in the paper this morning
his trial in Big Horn County has been set for March?"

From downstairs, Susanne heard a crash, a yelp, and then big feet
scrambling up the staircase.

"Mom," Perry yelled. "Ferdie knocked over the plant stand."

"Oh, spit," Susanne said. "Catastrophe. I'll have to go in a second.
But, quick, tell me how you're feeling." After several first trimester
miscarriages, Vangie was pregnant again and halfway to term.

"Middle trimester is still a breeze. None of my clothes fit, and I love
it. We've decided to name it Hank if it's a boy, and Laura if it's a girl."

"Those are perfect names."

"We're getting excited."

Ferdinand loped up the stairs and into the living room, shaking
potting soil from his long, thin nose.

Feeling a little déjà vu, Susanne said, "Bad dog, Ferdie. Bad!"

Vangie laughed. "Call me later this week and let me know you've
survived."

"I will. Bye." Susanne hung up.

Ferdinand ducked his head and tiptoed toward her.

"What did you do, you clumsy oaf?" She knew she shouldn't, but she fondled his ears instead of giving him a swat. The dog was the bane of her existence. It seemed like that was her lot in life, to live with a houseful of humans and animals that expected her to take care of everything for them and repaid her with trouble and messes. All of whom she loved madly despite it.

"Mo-OM, did you hear me? Ferdie made a bad mess."

"I'm coming." Susanne sighed. After days of getting ready for the holidays and her family, she was beat, and she had so much left to do before she could get herself ready. At least she'd left the vacuum cleaner in the basement.

As she was walking down the stairs with Ferdinand weaving behind her and trying to find a passing lane, the front door opened to Trish's voice. She was giggling as she entered the house. Which meant Brandon had followed her inside. Susanne came around the landing to an eyeful of her blonde-haired daughter pressed up against the wall by her lanky boyfriend, their lips locked.

"Daylight, please."

The two broke apart from each other so fast that Brandon backed into the coat stand, knocking it over. It landed with a crash. Two of the arms snapped off, but not before one of them gouged the wall on its way down. Susanne stopped, holding her breath and counting to ten.

"I'm, like, so sorry, Mrs. F." Brandon crouched to right the stand, his curly, too-long hair flopping across his face. He laid the fallen coats over one arm and held up the broken pieces in the other hand. "Um, what do you want me to do with these?"

Susanne glared at her daughter. Trish's blue eyes snapped defiantly. She looked like an angry, rebellious angel.

Perry appeared, swinging a casted foot out in front of him as he used his crutches to maneuver down the hallway. His dirty blond hair was growing out from a crewcut, and it was spikey. His skin was winter white broken up by a dusting of freckles across his nose. "Mo-om, Ferdie's in the dirt again."

Susanne's patience snapped. "Perry, your ankle may be broken but your arms aren't. Put the dog outside. Trish and Brandon, go out to the shed and find some clamps and wood glue. Glue the stand back together, after you hang those coats in the closet. We have company coming tonight, and from this moment on, everyone is helping, or they're grounded or going home. Got me?"

She got three pitiful 'yes ma'ams' in response. When no one moved, she barked, "Now!"

And that's when the door opened again. Her father—all six foot four inches and two hundred and eighty pounds of him—stuck his white head in the door and hollered, "Yoo hoo, we're here!"

A fresh-faced blonde woman almost as tall as her father peeked around him. "Looks like I stumbled on a party." Susanne's father grinned and let her by. She held out a tray of cinnamon rolls with red and green stick-on bows on the plastic wrap covering it. "How about I just drop these in the kitchen?"

"Ronnie, thank you. You're a lifesaver." Now Susanne knew what she'd serve as breakfast bread, since she'd no longer have time to bake. She pasted on a bright smile while her heart sank. She'd wanted everything to be perfect for her mother and sister. "Daddy . . . welcome to Wyoming . . . seven hours early."

CHAPTER THREE: SCURRY

Patrick

"Congratulations. It's a girl." Patrick held the infant upside down and suctioned her nostrils.

"A girl," Junior said. He beamed at his wife. He'd removed his hooded jacket in the clinic, revealing shoulder-length black hair parted in the middle and a muscular body.

Tears streamed down Eleanor's face. "A girl."

Patrick placed the baby on Eleanor's stomach, clamping the cord in two places and cutting it between them. He handed her to Constance.

Constance cleaned the tiny pink infant then held her close, warming her with her body since the clinic didn't have a heat lamp. "Just a minute while we examine her, then I'll let you hold her, Mother."

Patrick was relieved that the earlier tension between the Mannings and Constance seemed to have evaporated. He administered the APGAR test while Constance weighed the baby.

"She's perfect," he concluded.

"Seven pounds even. And a great set of lungs. Which of you does she get that from?" Constance glanced over her shoulder at them as she swaddled the little girl in a yellow blanket the Mannings had brought with them.

The two pointed at each other, then laughed. It brightened up the little room, bare except for the examination table on which Eleanor reclined, a single straight-backed chair, and a black counter over wooden cabinets. The walls were white and blank, with no windows.

Constance placed the baby in Eleanor's arms. "Do you have a name for her yet?"

Eleanor cooed to her little girl. The infant had thick hair nearly half an inch long. Her eyes blinked open, then screwed shut again.

Junior leaned in close to the baby. "We're naming her after my mother."

"Running Deer?"

"No, she'll discover her Shoshone name later. For now, we'll call her Dora."

"Another Dora Manning. May she be as kind, generous, and beautiful as her namesake."

Junior bowed at her, and Constance backed away. She motioned for Patrick to follow. He exited behind her into the wide hallway that connected the exam rooms. A musty smell met him, stronger than the antiseptic scent underneath it, and probably due to the wet outerwear draped over the hissing radiator in the waiting area. He could hear voices from inside the next room. Wes, talking to a woman and her little boy, who had come in with a high fever. While Wes was an X-ray tech, here on the reservation his general skills and medical knowledge were put to their highest and best use.

Constance stopped Patrick with a touch to his elbow. "The dead guy out in the parking lot. We need to do something about him."

Patrick had told her and Wes about the man before he delivered the Manning baby. He winced. "Didn't Riley bring him in?"

"I didn't get a chance to ask him before he had to run up to Pavilion in my Cherokee. There's an old Arapaho woman without a ride who's having trouble managing her diabetes."

"That's nice of him. Okay, we'll go get the guy as soon as Wes is done with his patient. I could go ahead and call the police."

"Why would we do that?" The look on her face suggested he was soft in the head.

"In case it's foul play?" Belatedly, Patrick made the connection. The police were part of the Bureau of Indian Affairs. Federal government employees. Distrust of the feds ran high on the reservation. Even as an Army veteran and IHS employee, Constance didn't seem to be exempt from the feeling.

"There's only six police on the entire res. We don't involve them unless it's absolutely necessary." She moved closer and slid her hand from his elbow to his bicep.

Patrick took a step back, but she didn't remove her hand. Constance didn't have a lot of respect for his personal space, but this was close talking even for her.

"About the Mannings. They live on the ranch next to ours. And they hate my husband. I think we're about to see a lot more Mannings here in a few minutes, too, to see the baby." She shuddered.

"Uh-oh. Do I need to keep you apart?"

"It would probably be best. They blame Big Mike for the death of some of their cattle dogs."

"Why?"

"We're having problems with coyotes. Big Mike's been killing them with rodent poison, but the Mannings let their dogs roam free. They come onto our place and chase our cows. They get into the poison. They die."

Patrick knew that trained working dogs were highly valued ranch animals. This was the kind of issue that started lifelong family feuds. "Seems like they should control their own dogs."

"That's Big Mike's position. Anyway, I'm sure they'll be too excited about the baby to give me a hard time, but I wanted you to know, just in case. It's a little embarrassing."

"Got it."

She dropped his arm and slumped against the wall. "It's hard to believe Eleanor Manning has a baby and I don't. She's five years younger than me."

"You okay?"

"Just sad. Big Mike and I can't have kids."

"There's a lot that can be done these days for infertility, if it's a medical problem."

"It's not a medical problem. It's a husband problem. Big Mike says he's too old for any more kids."

Patrick racked his brain. Had Constance mentioned that Big Mike was previously married with children? He didn't think so. "So, you're a stepmother."

She snorted. "Hardly."

He shifted uncomfortably from foot to foot. "Sorry. I don't get it."

"I shouldn't have mentioned it." She straightened from the wall. "As soon as the weather permits, we should probably send the Mannings home anyway."

The health center was neither a hospital nor an emergency care clinic, and Patrick agreed with her. If little Dora Manning or her mother needed further medical care, they would need to send them to the hospital in Lander. "Let's keep them here for a few hours, anyway."

"All right. I'll let them know and see what I can do to get them ready." Constance strode back into the small exam room and shut the door behind her.

Patrick decided to use the short break to call Susanne. But before he could get to the phone in the kitchen, the front door to the clinic opened, chiming a bell. Patrick heard murmuring, then stomping feet, a normal sound in the winter as people cleared snow from their footwear on the big mat inside the door. With Wes and Constance otherwise occupied, Patrick went to greet the newcomers. Before he reached the waiting area, Riley appeared around the corner.

He hung his white parka and gloves on a wall hook beside Wes, Constance, and Patrick's gear. "Patient for you in the waiting room."

"Great. I'll go check on her."

"I shoveled out front earlier. The door was getting hard to open."

"Thanks."

"Is Constance here?"

"Yes. She's in with the Mannings."

"Okay. Do you need anything?"

The door opened again. This time along with the bell and the wind, Patrick heard a multitude of voices. Loud, laughing, and talking over each other.

"I'm good, Riley."

"I'll get to work on the kitchen, then."

A glorified break room with a mini-fridge and a sink, but they still called it a kitchen. Walking backwards toward the waiting area, Patrick said, "If there's no coffee, would you mind brewing a fresh pot?"

"Okay."

"Thanks."

Riley went into the kitchen. Patrick turned and entered the waiting room. The hiss of the radiator was louder in there, and it was a packed house, with people in three different parts of the room. Almost in the hall, a lithe, gray-pony-tailed man was congregating with two women who were near Junior and Eleanor's ages. The taller was a Morticia Addams lookalike, smoking a cigarette. Nearer the front door, Constance's brother, Eddie Blackhawk—tall like his sister, but with a pitted face, broken front tooth and a round-brimmed cowboy hat low on his forehead—was standing with a skeletally-thin white woman. A heavy woman with long white hair was seated with her hands folded in her lap.

Patients first, after dealing with the smoker. To Morticia, he said, "You'll need to put that out, please."

She took one last powerful drag, then stepped outside.

Patrick approached the woman in the chair. "May I help you, ma'am?"

She opened her mouth to answer.

Eddie interrupted. "Dr. Flint. Can you tell Constance and Big Mike that I'm waiting for them?"

"Big Mike's not here."

Morticia returned, looking displeased.

Eddie broke out into a smile, then reeled it back in. "Oh. I thought I saw his truck. Must have been mistaken. Just tell Constance then."

"She's with a patient, but after I've helped this woman, I'll—"

Constance's light steps approached from behind him. "Hello, Eddie."

At her entrance, the pony-tailed man turned his back and looked out the window. The women with him stared at their feet.

"It's chillier in here than outside." Eddie grinned. "Sister, may I speak with you alone for a moment?" He whispered in his companion's ear. She shuffled to a plastic chair with metal legs whose feet were stuck in tennis balls. She sat with her legs splayed. The old woman shifted her chair away from her.

Constance's fists balled. "After I see to everyone."

Patrick returned his attention to the old woman. "Would you like to move into an exam room where it's quieter? It might be easier to have a conversation there. And more private." He smiled at her.

She nodded and smiled back, revealing two smooth gums. He put a hand under her elbow and helped her stand.

Constance drew in a deep breath. "Mr. Manning, can I escort you in to see your new granddaughter?"

The pony-tailed man—Mr. Manning—nodded without looking at

her or speaking. Constance caught Patrick's gaze and rolled her eyes. *Those dogs must have been something special for him to treat Constance like this.*

"This way." Constance walked out with the three guests for Junior, Eleanor, and Dora.

Patrick escorted his patient across the waiting area to an empty room. "Right in here. Just make yourself comfortable on the chair and someone will be right with you."

She gave a single nod.

Patrick shut the door, then turned back to deal with Eddie. "Is there something I can do for you?"

Eddie's voice was cutting, his eyes slitted. "It's a family matter."

Patrick tried to like Eddie, out of respect for Constance, but he hadn't succeeded yet. It wasn't just how Eddie treated Patrick, which was with distrust bordering on contempt. The younger Blackhawk was a disruptive force at the center. Constance was the lifeblood of the place, and her brother drained her with every visit.

"All right then."

Wes emerged from an exam room with a chart in his hand. He motioned with his chin for Patrick to join him.

"Excuse me," Patrick said to Eddie. When Patrick reached Wes, he took the chart Wes held out to him. "What's up?"

"Well, Sawbones, we've got a sick little boy in there. Clem, with his mom, Lucy." Whenever life took a more serious turn, Wes stopped calling Patrick "Doc" in favor of "Sawbones."

Patrick tensed. "Any idea what it is?"

"You're the doctor, but I'd say he has pneumonia or spinal meningitis."

Patrick frowned. "If he's got meningitis, we need to get him out of here."

"That's what I thought. The family doesn't have a car. A neighbor dropped them here earlier today. If you agree that's what he has, I can see about getting him to Lander. Or even Denver or Salt Lake City."

Wes ran Patrick through the symptoms. "I hear rhonchi sounds and he has labored breathing. A stiff neck. Fever of one hundred and four. Headache and vomiting. He's listless. And he had a seizure while I was with him. His mother said it was the first one." His face sagged. "He's only three."

"Good catch, Wes. Definitely beyond our capabilities here. Let's get him started on antibiotics, then get him out of here so he can get a spinal tap and IV antibiotics."

Constance slipped out of the Mannings' room and past them toward her brother.

Patrick called out to her. "New patient in room one."

"I'll get to her in a minute."

"Can you give a kid an antibiotic shot first?"

Over her shoulder, she said, "Riley can do it."

Patrick blanched. "Riley is a janitor."

Constance turned and frowned at him. "Keep your voice down. And don't sell him short. We make do with what we have, and there's a lot of things he can do around here. If you don't want Riley's help, could you do it yourself? I'm a little backed up."

"Uh, sure." Patrick wasn't used to nurses pushing work back on him. It wasn't that he couldn't do injections. It's just that the normal division of labor had physicians doing the things only they could do and delegating everything else. He looked down the hall and saw Riley staring at him. Patrick felt his face flush. Had he sounded like an elitist snob?

Constance walked away, again headed toward the lobby and her brother.

"You want me to do it, Doc?" Wes asked.

Patrick would never have asked an X-ray tech to give injections in Buffalo, whether he was capable of them or not. "Are you sure?"

Before Wes could answer, Constance's raised voice rent the air. "I'm not your personal piggy bank, Eddie."

Patrick fast walked to where the hall ran across the back of the waiting room. Wes kept in step with him. Constance was nose-to-nose and eyeball-to-eyeball with her much heavier brother.

"I've got a game tonight. You'd prevent me from making my living?"

"Borrow it from one of your poker club buddies. Better yet, stop hosting these games before you get thrown in jail, or get Big Mike and me in trouble."

"I won't get arrested unless your holier-than-thou husband turns us in."

Patrick and Wes shared an embarrassed look. Riley walked into the waiting room and stopped beside Constance, arms folded across his chest, a stony expression on the unscarred side of his face. The skinny white woman snorted, and Patrick realized she was laughing.

The doorbell chimed for yet another visitor. Patrick doubted the clinic had seen as many visitors at once the whole year. He glanced up. At first, he thought the tall, broad body was a man. The messy hair bun was an odd choice for a man, though.

When she spoke—screamed, rather—he knew he was wrong. "My brother! My brother is dead!"

All heads turned to look at her. She pulled at the neck of her jacket as if fighting for air.

Constance whirled away from her own brother and hurtled toward the newcomer. "What did you say?"

The woman was a good three inches taller than Constance, which was saying something. She also outweighed Constance by at least one hundred pounds.

"My brother, your husband. He's out in the parking lot in his truck. And he's dead."

Constance grabbed the woman's shoulder. "Verna, no!" Then she staggered away from her and out the door.

Verna turned to Eddie. "Like she didn't know."

Eddie looked from Verna to Patrick, then followed his sister. Riley walked to the door and watched through the window.

Patrick had never met Big Mike Teton in life, but remembering the man he'd found in the truck earlier, he realized he'd met him in death. He felt sick at his stomach. He'd left Constance's husband out in the storm. Things had been so busy in the last half hour with the birth of the Manning baby and all the other patients and visitors, that he hadn't had a chance to bring him in. But that didn't make it better. What if it had been Susanne that was left in a parking lot, dead, alone, with him inside?

Sorry, friend, he thought. Then, *Constance.* Pushing past Riley, he bolted out the door after her.

CHAPTER FOUR: BREAKOUT

Buffalo, Wyoming
Sunday, December 19, 1976, Two p.m.

Perry

Perry snuck off toward his dad's backyard tool shed with Ferdinand. It was getting pretty cold outside—cold enough to freeze his nose hairs—and he wished he'd brought his coat. He couldn't even wrap his arms around himself to stay warm because of the stupid crutches. But he wasn't going back inside for his jacket. No way, no how. Because his mom was inside, and she'd lost her mind.

In a funny, squawky voice, she kept saying how excited she was to see all the family early, but he knew she was lying. She'd been a basket case for days getting the house ready, and she wanted everything to be perfect. Now it wasn't. She'd shoved the broken coat rack in the laundry room. She'd left the flowerpots, plants, and dirt on the floor in the basement. Her hair was in a scarf—it was still pretty, but she hated it straight —and she hadn't put on makeup or the outfit she'd laid out on her bed to wear when her family arrived. That wasn't like her at all.

He'd skipped out when she started giving everyone a tour, including their neighbor Ronnie, who he suspected was just hanging around for the laughs. His mom *was* pretty funny when she got like this, but not in the on-purpose way.

Perry opened the door to the shed. Something big moved inside, but he couldn't see what it was. He jumped back, nearly falling on his butt. What if it was a badger? Or a raccoon? Or worse? They could come rushing out and tear his face off.

But it wasn't. His eyes adjusted to the darkness, and he saw two people close together. Really close together.

Then he heard his sister's voice. "Get out of here, squirt. And don't tell Mom."

Perry shook his head. "Uh-uh. You get out of there, or I'll tell."

"Be cool, little man." Brandon moved toward Perry. He had slobber on his chin.

Gross. If that's what kissing is like, I don't want any part of it. "I'm cool. But I need some tools."

Brandon grinned. "Why didn't you say so? Like, what can I get for you?"

"I need to use them in here."

"Come *on*, Perry. We were here first." Trish's voice was a cross between a whine and a bark.

"Fine." He swung his body around like he was headed back to the house. "I'm sure Mom would love to bring Mama Cat and Papa Fred out here on the house tour." Mama Cat and Papa Fred. They were the funniest grandparent names ever.

He hadn't gotten two steps before Trish called after him. "Wait, brat. How long will this take you?"

He looked down at the cast on his ankle. His foot itched so bad, and his ankle didn't hurt anymore at all. When he'd broken it in his first game as a starting cornerback, it had hurt super bad. But it was worth it. His parents almost hadn't let him be on the team, changing their minds at the last second. Then he'd batted away a pass that would have been a touchdown for sure, and his team had won. Mom had been upset, and Dad had talked to himself even more than usual. Something about "knowing better," "too young," and "bad father."

But that had been a long time ago. He'd told them he was healed, and it was time to get it off. No one listened to him, though. It was like he was invisible in this family. How were he and his cousin Matthew supposed to have any fun if they were stuck inside? It was sledding weather outside. Time for ice skating and snow fort building. Not Monopoly and card games.

He needed the cast off *today*. And he was sure he'd find the right tools for the job in the shed. As for how long it would take? No idea. "I don't know. I'll come tell you when I'm done. Not long."

Trish and Brandon looked at each other. Brandon shrugged.

Trish gave her boyfriend a little push in the back, out of the shed and away from the house. "We'll be with the horses. Don't tell Mom."

"Yeah, your mom is on the war path, you know?" Brandon said.

Perry knew. He spit in his hand and held it out toward his sister. "Deal."

She pretended to stick her finger down her throat. "Gag. Don't touch me with that." Then she dashed out to catch up with Brandon.

Ferdinand sprinted after them.

"Traitor," Perry muttered. He would have liked to have the dog with him, in case this hurt.

Crutching his way over to the work bench, he considered his options. A screwdriver? A saw? A mallet and chisel? He decided to try the screwdriver first, because the others looked too scary. He got the others down, too, though, just in case the screwdriver didn't work. Maybe if he stuck the screwdriver down in the cast he could scratch his foot. Then, if he twisted it and got leverage, it might crack the plaster right off.

He lowered himself to the dirt and rock floor, using his crutches for balance. For a moment, he admired the cast. His parents had bought him a box of magic markers—all the colors—to take to school. Everyone had signed it, even some of the kids a year ahead of him. He traced one special signature with his pointer finger. GET WELL SOON, BRUISER! MRS. TAVEJIE. His teacher. She was the most beautiful woman in the world, besides his mom, and he loved her. He prayed every night that she didn't marry someone else before he grew up. Heat flooded his cheeks. Mr. Gagliano had seen him drawing hearts around her name on a piece of paper after lunch one day and teased him about it. Not mean teasing, but Perry had never been so embarrassed in his life. How would he ever get the courage up to ask her to marry him? Well, he'd figure that out when he was old enough. In the meantime, he hoped he wasn't in Mr. Gagliagno's class next year, even if he did sing and dance during lessons and was the most popular teacher in school. He couldn't even look him in the eye anymore.

Perry stuck the screwdriver between the plaster and his ankle. Just thinking about scratching made his ankle itch worse. But the shank was fatter than the pencil he normally used when he had the itchies. He couldn't quite reach the worst spot. He shoved the handle harder, jamming the tip into his calf. "Ouch." He jerked, and it embedded itself in the plaster.

A deep voice boomed from the doorway to the shed. "You're going to bite your tongue off, kid."

Perry pulled his tongue in. He hadn't realized it was sticking out, but Trish made fun of him sometimes for it. It only happened when he was concentrating really hard. He looked up. It was his grandfather. With his mother.

Susanne's eyes scrunched up. "Perry, what are you doing in here? And why do you have out the saw and . . ." She looked from the tools to her son's face. "Perry Alan Flint, are you trying to take your cast off?"

There was a long, heavy silence, then a braying laugh like a donkey from Papa Fred.

"Daddy, this isn't funny."

Papa Fred kept laughing and wiped his eyes. "I'll leave the two of you to work this out on your own." He disappeared in the direction of the house.

Perry tried to wrench the screwdriver out. No luck. Jammed in tight.

His mother stomped in and started putting the tools back on their hooks, making as much noise as she could in the process. "Get that thing out of your cast and go back in the house, right this instant."

Perry pulled again. Still stuck. "I can't."

"Oh, yes, you can. And you'd better not try a stunt like this again. My family is here. I don't need to be dealing with an emergency room visit for you on top of everything else I have to do. You're already on my bad side from that fight in Sunday school this morning. What has gotten into you?"

He wasn't about to tell her what the fight was about. Judd was a bully, and he had it coming. The things he'd said Trish had done with her kidnappers were awful. "Mom, I can't get it out. Really. It's stuck."

Still mumbling, Susanne crouched beside him and wiggled the handle back and forth.

"Ow."

She snorted. "I hope it hurts. Maybe you'll remember this and not do it again."

"I just want to be able to play outside with Matthew."

She wrenched harder on the handle. Perry yelped, but the screwdriver came loose, and she pulled it out. Then she sighed. "I know it's hard. Just a few more weeks and you'll be good as new. Can I trust you not to do this again until then?"

Perry thought about it. The screwdriver hadn't worked. He *for sure* wouldn't try the screwdriver again. She hadn't asked him not to try the saw or mallet though. "Okay, Mom."

"Good. Now, come inside and help me entertain everyone. I need to cook dinner."

"But what about Trish? Doesn't she have to do something, too?"

Susanne stood and hung the screwdriver. "Yes. I need to send her and Brandon to the store. Where are they? Have you seen her?"

Perry smiled. Yes, as a matter of fact, he had. He proceeded to win himself back into his mother's good graces by solemnly describing in exaggerated detail not only where they were, but where they'd *been* and what they'd been doing there.

CHAPTER FIVE: LOSE

Patrick

Constance slumped over Big Mike's body. She kept repeating, "I'm sorry. I'm sorry." The exam room wasn't big enough to contain her emotion, and Patrick backed away to give her more space. From the lobby, the sounds of weeping and voices seemed to grow louder with every passing minute.

"He's so cold," she said, her own voice like ice. "So cold."

And he was. Minus ten degrees, even with the truck door shut, had brought his body temperature down quickly.

"When was the last time you saw him?" Patrick kept his voice low and gentle. He hated asking her questions, but he also knew that he needed to get some idea of the cause of death.

She lifted her pale, tearless face. "This morning, before I came in. I was eating breakfast. It was about six-thirty. He came in the kitchen, and he was normal. He was healthy and fine and . . . and . . . and . . . " Her words trailed off into silence.

Patrick stepped closer. "Did you talk to him after that?"

She shook her head. "No. It wasn't our way. Big Mike didn't like the telephone." She huffed. "We got married before my last tour of duty. He knew I was independent, and he liked that about me. It continued when I came home. He said it made every night a little reunion."

Her words reminded Patrick that he still hadn't managed to call Susanne. Things had been so hectic ever since he got here. There was no way he could make the call now. His heart ached. How could it not, witnessing his friend's loss firsthand? He'd planned to drive back to Buffalo tomorrow night, but he wished he could leave this second. If only he'd brought his own truck.

He cleared his throat. "I've got to . . . examine him, Constance."

She nodded and wiped her eyes. "I know."

"You might want to wait outside."

Her head shake was vehement. "No. I want to be here."

"Okay. Let's start with what he had for breakfast, then."

She rolled her lips in on each other, thinking. "I was running late. I had granola, but he doesn't like it. He was drinking coffee when I left. He said he might make some breakfast tacos."

No clues to what happened to him there. Patrick pressed on. "Did he have any plans?"

"With the weather, he was just going to work in the barn and around the house. In the winter, he lets the hands go. It's mostly just him. The ranch keeps him working. But with the ranch, plus with his responsibilities on the tribal council, he doesn't relax much, even in a blizzard."

"And he wasn't sick?"

She reached for her husband's hand and held it awkwardly. Patrick could see Big Mike was starting to stiffen up. "No."

"No bad test results or medical concerns lately?"

She shook her head. "Nothing. His grandfather lived into his nineties. Neither of us had our parents anymore. It was just us. His father got crushed when he rolled his tractor, and his mother killed herself after her husband died, but they were both in good health when they passed. Big Mike had good genes, and he took care of himself. Didn't smoke. Didn't drink much. Stayed active." She smoothed a hand over his chest.

The man was big, but not fat. He was tall, muscular, and looked fit. He had a few years on Constance, maybe ten or fifteen. But, although death made him look older, he still had to be less than forty. Patrick remembered Constance telling him once that Big Mike could do one hundred push-ups with her on his back. His mind raced through possibilities. A heart attack. A stroke. An aneurysm. An accident on the ranch – something electrical? But no. If he'd had a fatal electrical accident, death would have been instantaneous. Chemical? It was too cold for a snake or insect bite. And he'd driven himself all the way to the health center, only to die in the parking lot. So, it couldn't have been anything that caused an instantaneous death.

Taking care to be gentle and respectful, Patrick examined Big Mike externally from head to toe. He felt self-conscious with Constance standing beside him, although she no longer touched her husband. But, despite being thorough, he found nothing. No marks or rashes. No punctures, infections, or injuries. No weird odors, no oozing. Nothing. No clues as to how or when. The only thing notable were some bruises and scrapes. Not unexpected for someone who worked with big animals for a living, but worth asking about.

"Do you know how he got these?" Patrick gestured at a scratch on his neck and bruise on his chest. "And these?" He pointed at more bruises on his upper arm.

Constance stared at them.

"Constance?"

She shook her head. "No."

"Okay."

Patrick continued examining Big Mike. As far as his insides went, Patrick wouldn't be able to see much except through his mouth. It was tightly closed, so he attempted to open it with a tongue depressor. The jaws resisted, so he increased his pressure.

The jaws opened to a surprise. "Whoa." Big Mike's tongue was mangled. Congealed blood stained his teeth.

Constance gasped and put her hands to her cheeks. "What happened?"

Patrick pried the jaws open further and shined a pen light from his shirt pocket down Big Mike's throat. The damage was solely in the mouth. "Seizures, maybe."

"Seizures?" Constance's eyes were confused. "He didn't have epilepsy."

Patrick ticked through possibilities in his mind. There were so many potential causes of seizures that it would be almost impossible to narrow it down without more information. Vitamin deficiency and malnutrition seemed to be out, as was epilepsy, per Constance. Brain tumor? Drugs or alcohol? He thought about the little boy with meningitis in the next room. Meningitis? Encephalitis? But Constance had said he wasn't showing any signs of illness. Head injury?

Patrick pored over Big Mike's head again, but found nothing. "Did he drink or use drugs?"

"No. No drugs. His older brother died of an overdose when he was a kid. And his mother was an alcoholic."

A knock at the door interrupted them.

Expecting Wes with an update on the little boy with meningitis, Patrick said, "Come in."

Verna Teton entered, followed by a lanky Indian man in a navy Bureau of Indian Affairs police uniform. The BIA was out of Billings, Montana, but from past trips, Patrick knew they had a station in Fort Washakie. His eyes were drawn to a jagged scar at the base of the officer's throat. His mind flashed back to Chester, and he pushed the memory away. Moving with heavy but jerky footsteps, Verna glared at Constance and ignored Patrick. She stationed herself across from her sister-in-law at Big Mike's shoulders. Patrick could see the sibling resemblance in the shapes of their mouths—straight, thin lips— and small, flat ears.

The officer and Constance exchanged a long look.

Then the man stuck out a hand to Patrick. "I'm Officer Justin Dann." His raspy voice combined with the messy scar screamed "emergency tracheotomy," one done outside a medical facility. "Verna called us to report a suspicious death."

Constance made a growling sound deep in her chest. Dann didn't react to it.

Patrick shook Dann's hand. Like a wary trout, he circled around and away from the "suspicious death" bait. "Patrick Flint. Big Mike Teton was found dead in the parking lot here."

"What's the cause of death?"

"I can't say for sure, yet, other than his heart stopped." At its most basic level, all deaths occurred when the heart stopped beating, so this was as good an explanation as any. In fact, Patrick had learned early in his career that physicians generally said a patient's heart had stopped when they couldn't otherwise account for cause of death.

"Heart attack?"

"Possibly."

Verna crossed her arms over her ample bosom. "Isn't it true that he died in his truck, when he came here to see *her*?" She didn't look or gesture at Constance, but from her tone and inflection, it was clear who she was talking about.

"What's that supposed to mean, Verna?" Constance snapped.

"You were alone here. He came to the clinic. I don't know whether you killed him or just left him to die, but it had the same result."

Constance put both hands on the edge of the exam table, leaning at Verna over her dead husband. "How dare you?"

The door burst open. The distinctive metal noise of a spring door stop rattled as Riley stormed into the room. "Are you all right, Constance?"

She took a deep breath then held up a hand in the "stop" gesture. "I'm fine. Thank you."

"Do you need me to stay?"

Dann pointed at the door. "I've got this."

Riley turned toward Dann's voice. His eyebrows rose. "Sorry, Dann. I didn't know you were in here." He backed out, his eyes fixed on Verna until the door shut.

Verna sneered at Constance like they hadn't been interrupted. "Ask her what she gets with my brother dead. Go ahead. Ask her."

Constance didn't wait for the question. "Nothing I didn't have when he was alive."

"What about that life insurance policy? Or did you forget all about how much more he was worth to you dead than alive? Between that and *my* family's ranch, you're set for life."

Constance lunged around the head of the table. Verna held her ground without flinching. Dann intercepted Constance, wrapping her in an immobilizing bear hug. Constance wrenched her shoulders, but Dann held on until she slumped in his arms. "I loved him. I *loved* him."

Patrick stood woodenly, awkwardly. Verna's accusations raised uncomfortable questions. Could Big Mike have been murdered? It would take testing, maybe even an autopsy—or a witness—to make a determination. But his lacerated tongue. The seizures. If none of the other possibilities Patrick had considered were plausible, he knew another that would cause seizures and a fast, unpleasant death. A poison that was sold in every hardware store in the country. Strychnine, a common ingredient in rat poison. He assumed Big Mike had used it to poison the coyotes on his ranch. And the Mannings' dogs, too, unfortunately. If someone had wanted to kill Big Mike, it would have been as easy as lacing something he ate or drank with strychnine.

Dann said, "Verna, could you wait outside, please?"

Verna huffed. "I have every bit as much right to be here as her."

"I have some questions for her and the doctor, and, no, you don't have a right to be present for that."

She tilted her chin up but retreated, shutting the door with a force that rattled instruments in a metal tray on the countertop.

Dann relaxed his hold on Constance but didn't release her. "If I let you go, will you calm down?"

She gazed straight into his eyes, as placid as the surface of a lake on a windless day. "Yes."

He pulled his arms away. "Take me through the day Constance. When you last saw him. Anything going on with him. Anything out of the ordinary."

Constance stepped back from him and repeated most of what she'd already told Patrick. Then she turned back to her husband.

Dann faced Patrick, his face somber. "Dr. Flint, do you have any reason to think Big Mike was murdered?"

Patrick felt like the world was balancing on the axis of his answer. In a way it was. If he spoke against natural causes, it might launch a murder investigation that could have far-reaching consequences. With the opposite, a guilty party could get away with murder and be left free to kill again. "I can't say he was, but I can't say he wasn't."

Dann turned away from Patrick, facing Constance. "Did you kill your husband, Constance?"

She didn't look up. "I did not."

Dann stroked his chin. He had stubble that would have taken Patrick three days to grow. "Doesn't seem there's much to gain by pursuing this."

Patrick tried to keep his chin from dropping. He failed. "You don't want an autopsy, to be sure?"

"We're a poor county, a poor reservation, and a poor people. The price of buying trouble is high. There's no evidence that it's a homicide. But if your opinion changes, let me know."

Patrick didn't say another word. He couldn't. He was dumbfounded. Didn't Big Mike deserve better? Didn't Constance, and even Verna? Hell, the residents of the Wind River Reservation deserved more from their police force. And no matter what Dann thought, Patrick still had to come up with something for the death certificate, which would be required for the life insurance policy Verna had mentioned. The insurance company would likely be skeptical that a healthy forty-year old man died simply because his heart stopped.

Dann walked to the door, put his hand on the knob, then looked over his shoulder at Constance. "May I speak to you outside?"

"In a minute," she said.

He nodded and slipped out.

Constance grabbed Patrick by the forearms as soon as the door had closed behind Dann. "If you think somebody killed my husband, you have to tell me first. Me first, you hear me?"

Patrick swallowed. He shouldn't promise that. He couldn't. But he nodded anyway, and, as Constance hurried after Dann, he immediately regretted it.

CHAPTER SIX: DUMP

Trish

Trish slipped on the snowy doorstep, then stomped up the stairs with the last bag of groceries. Ferdinand passed her, nearly knocking her back down them.

"Ferdie, ugh!" She caught herself on the wall. The dog was out of control with excitement about having company. And about bringing in groceries. It was one of his favorite things to do, although his "favorite things" was a very long list.

Ronnie was standing at the top of the stairs. Trish didn't think she looked like a cop, and she couldn't figure out why she'd wanted to be one in the first place. It was a rough job, and she worked mostly with guys, even though she was married and everything. *You couldn't pay me enough.*

"Bye everyone. Merry Christmas," Ronnie said, waving before descending.

A chorus of voices shouted "Merry Christmas" at her. Trish climbed the last few stairs.

She smiled at Trish. "Your family is the best."

"Thanks." Trish kept going toward the kitchen

"Hot damn." Papa Fred slammed a domino on the table. The sharp noise made Trish jump as she went by. "Domino." Then he laughed like a giant hyena.

Trish loved her family, but right now she wasn't appreciating them very much. It had snowed a couple of inches while she and Brandon were at the store. Everyone knew this, yet no one got up to help them bring the groceries in. They were all gathered around the kitchen table playing dominoes with some hot boozy drinks, staying warm and toasty with a roaring fire, while her mother cooked dinner and Trish lugged in bags. Perry and Matthew were side by side and unmoving on the couch watching Rudolph the Red Nosed Reindeer on TV. She was glad they'd come, she really was, but school was out, and she hoped they didn't expect her to be their servant all week. It wasn't like the Flints were running a vacation resort. It was Christmas. Wasn't everyone supposed to pitch in?

She set the bag on the kitchen counter beside the six others and sniffed. Her mom was making chicken spaghetti. It smelled like boiled gym socks. Cream of mushroom soup, Velveeta "cheese," chicken, spaghetti noodles, and pimentos. Her mom was good at a lot of things, but cooking wasn't one of them.

She heard Brandon shut the front door then pound up the stairs. His wavy blond hair appeared, and he turned toward her. *He's such a fox.* The phone rang, barely audible over the din: the television, her uncle and grandfather arguing over the score of their game, her grandmother and aunt in a cross-room conversation with her mother.

"Is anybody going to get that?" Trish shouted.

No one answered her. No one even looked away from what they were doing. Sighing, she grabbed the phone from the wall on its tenth ring. Her mother couldn't hear her, so she skipped the whole "Flint residence, this is Trish speaking" thing her parents made her do, and instead said, "Hello?"

"Is Brandon Lewis there?"

The voice was female and cranky, but it was old and familiar, so Trish wasn't jealous. Once, Trish's biggest nemesis—Charla Newby— had called and asked for Brandon. Trish had whispered, "Sorry, can't have him, he's mine," and hung up the phone. This time she said, "Let me check." She stuck out the phone to Brandon and whispered, "Your mom."

He shook his head and backed up, making praying hands and mouthing, "no, no."

Trish was still a little irritated that Brandon hadn't taken her by her best friend Marcy Peterson's while they were out. She just needed to pick up a sweater she'd left at a sleepover. But Brandon said they'd promised her mom they'd hurry, and he drove right past the turn to Marcy's house. So, even if he was a fox, Trish decided to get back at him. She lifted the phone to her mouth. "He's standing right here with his hand out for the phone. Just a second." She gave Brandon an extra-sweet smile.

He snatched the phone, glaring at her. "Hello?" He listened for a minute, then his eyes got wide. "But, Mom—" he said, but then grew silent. "That's not fair." Then he swallowed. "I can't." He shook his head and closed his eyes. "Mrs. Flint, my mom would like to speak to you."

"What?" Trish whispered at him.

He didn't look at her. *Are those tears in his eyes?* Ferdinand nuzzled the palm of her hand.

"Okay." Susanne twirled toward Brandon. *Twirled.* What was up with her? She had on a skirted apron that flared like a figure skater's skirt around her new jeans. Her milk chocolate eyes were bright and twinkly, and she'd obviously used hot rollers while Trish was at the store. She'd put on lipstick and mascara. And, Trish noticed for the first time, a homemade Frosty the Snow Man appliqued flannel shirt. *Oh my God. How embarrassing.*

Her mom took the phone. "Hello, Donna." As she listened, her eyes darkened, and her smile reversed on itself. "I understand your wishes." She handed the phone back to Brandon. In a soft voice, she said, "I'm sorry, Brandon."

He nodded. Gritting his teeth, he said, "Happy now, Mom?" Then without waiting for a reply, he walked to the phone's base and slammed the receiver down, making the phone's bell ring once.

"What?" Trish said again.

Brandon shook his head. "I have to go."

Trish's voice rose. She knew it was shrill when all the conversation in the room stopped, and every eye landed on her. "You can't just leave without telling me why."

Her mom laid a hand on Trish's arm. She whispered, "Let him go, Trish. And come with me. I'll explain in my room."

Trish ripped her arm away. "No. I want him to tell me what's going on. Right now."

Brandon was halfway down the stairs. She ran after him. He was leaving in a few days to spend Christmas in Arizona visiting some relatives—luckily on his dad's side, since his mother's side was a bunch of crazy criminals—and she was barely going to see him all week.

He turned back to her, and his voice was a snarl. She stopped in her tracks, mouth open. It wasn't like him to fight with her. "My mother has forbidden me to see you anymore, that's what's going on. She doesn't like you or your family, because my cousin is in juvie because of you. There. Are you happy I told you now?"

Trish felt like she was sinking through the living room floor. Brandon's footsteps receded. The door downstairs opened and slammed shut. The room was so painfully silent that she heard the whine of Brandon's tires spinning on the snow as he sped out of the driveway.

CHAPTER SEVEN: DELIVER

Fort Washakie, Wyoming
Sunday, December 19, 1976, Five p.m.

Patrick

Patrick shivered beside Gussie. "You're a good man, Braten. You got your hose and water in case you overheat again?" He zipped his jacket and popped the collar up.

"Of course, Doc." Wes did a two-finger forehead salute. "Always ready for anything."

Wes and Patrick had loaded three-year old Clem and his mother, Lucy, in the Travelall for the drive to the hospital in Lander, where he could receive the spinal tap and aggressive IV antibiotic treatment Patrick suspected he needed for bacterial meningitis. Riley walked past them toward Constance's Cherokee, his hand in the small of the back of the old diabetic woman he'd brought in earlier. Her treatment complete, he was giving her a ride home to Pavilion. Today, the staff of the Fort Washakie Health Center was a veritable fleet of rescue riders. And the weather was getting even worse. Snow had piled up in the road since the last pass by the snowplow.

Patrick held up a urine sample. He'd drawn it directly from Big Mike's bladder with a syringe, an easy procedure, to test for poison. No matter that Dann had decided it wasn't homicide, Patrick needed to figure out cause of death. While his first duty was to the living, his duty to patients extended beyond last breaths. Big Mike deserved someone to care. For Patrick to care. He was going to do this right.

"The lab is expecting this. It's a sample from Big Mike for testing."

Wes stowed the sample in the back end of the Travelall. "Got it, Sawbones. You sure you don't need me to take his body into Lander?"

"The funeral home is sending transport for him. Should have been here an hour ago, actually, but I don't think folding him in two in your way-back would go over well with your other passengers."

"Probably not. I'll be back in a few hours."

Patrick waved as the big green vehicle lumbered off through the snow. With snowflakes pelting his cheeks, he looked up and mouthed a prayer to the big man, asking for traveling mercies for his friend.

Constance's voice made him jump. "Who you talking to up there?"

"I didn't hear you walk up."

"You know what they say—quiet as an Indian. What was that you sent with Wes?"

"Urine sample."

Her facial muscles tightened. "From Big Mike?"

"Yes."

"Why?"

"Because I'm a doctor, and it's the right thing to do. He may still have to go to Lander for an autopsy."

She shook her head, her mouth in a bullish line. "That's not his way. He wouldn't want it. It's a violation that goes against everything we hold sacred. I don't want it."

"I'm sorry. I hope it doesn't come to that."

She gazed northward, where the sky was darkest. Just when Patrick was growing too uncomfortable to let the silence continue, she spoke.

"There's a Shoshone legend about the origin of death. Wolf—he's like the creator, a hero who often appears as a man—has a younger brother, Coyote, who's a trickster. Wolf said, 'When people die, they must die twice.' Coyote said, 'That isn't right. I don't want people to die twice. They must die only once and be buried.' So, Wolf bewitched Coyote's boy, his own nephew, and wished that he would die. Coyote knew that he had done this. The boy died. Coyote went to Wolf crying. He said, 'Oh, brother, you said when people die they should get up and die again. When will my boy get up?' Wolf said, 'Don't you remember saying they should die only once?'"

Patrick inclined his head, not sure what Constance was getting at.

She continued. "Big Mike has died, and it's time for him to be buried, Patrick. Not to put him through a bunch of tests."

"It's just a urine sample. Nothing more."

She sucked in her cheeks. "Are you going to tell Dann?"

"Not unless he needs to know."

"What do you expect to find?"

He decided to tell her a half-truth, mindful that until he knew how Big Mike had died, it could have been at anyone's hands, even a friend. "Nothing in particular. I'm just looking for anything toxic."

"You think it was poison?"

"Could have been. Lotta things out there that can hurt you, things most people have in their homes."

She stared at him, looking unconvinced.

He gestured toward the building. "Let's go back inside. It's getting colder."

Before they reached the building, Eleanor and Junior exited with their new baby, patriarch Joshua, Morticia, and the woman Patrick hadn't met.

Junior walked straight to Patrick and threw his arms around him. "Thank you, Dr. Flint. For stopping on the road, and for everything."

Eleanor rocked the tiny infant in her arms, her eyes soft, her smile tired. "Yes. Thank you very much, Doctor."

Patrick smoothed the blanket wrapped around the baby's head. "I wish we could offer you accommodations, but you'll be more comfortable at home anyway."

Eleanor smiled. "Yeah, it's cold in there. I'm going to put my feet up by the fire and let my man take care of Dora and me."

Junior put his arm around her shoulders.

"Sounds like a great idea."

Joshua and the two women got into a white late model Ford Bronco that blended into the storm and landscape. Junior drove his Dodge truck up for Eleanor and the baby. She handed Dora in to her husband, then turned back to Constance.

"I'm sorry about your man."

Constance nodded, a stiff gesture with her shoulders tight and high.

"Junior doesn't hold grudges like his father. In case you ever need help or anything."

Constance's rigid posture softened. "Thank you."

Eleanor climbed into the vehicle as nimbly as if she hadn't given birth only a few hours before. As the truck drove away, Patrick heard a strangled noise beside him. Constance's composure had cracked, and she was sobbing.

He turned to her. "Are you okay?"

Constance threw herself at his chest, wailing and clutching his shoulders. He hesitated for a second, uncertain what to do, then put his arms loosely around her and patted her back. Her grief was so loud that Patrick couldn't hear anything but her cries. A flash lit up the sky in his peripheral vision, reflecting off the snowflakes. Lightning in a snow storm? Patrick, still supporting Constance's weight, swiveled his head toward the source. An Indian man stood behind them with a camera pointed their way. He was wearing so much winter gear, it was hard to tell whether he was young or old, big or small, dark-haired or gray. *Why did he take a picture of us?* Patrick looked past the man and saw a pickup idling in the parking lot. It had a snow scraper on its front bumper.

The man dropped the camera, revealing an unlined face. He looked barely twenty. "Constance, is it true that Big Mike Teton passed away here today?"

Constance pushed back from Patrick, rubbing her eyes. "Yes, Big Mike died." She hiccupped. "Are you writing this up for the newspaper?" To Patrick, she said, "Jimmy's a reporter for the *Riverton Ranger*. And I used to babysit him. He was nosy even then, going through my purse and coat pockets when he didn't think I could see him."

Jimmy's cheeks flushed. "Sorry. I wasn't taking anything. I just had a little crush on you." He smiled at Patrick. "She was the star of the Lady Chiefs basketball team and the school production of *Romeo and Juliet*. So beautiful, then and now."

Constance waved off the apology and the compliment.

Jimmy cleared his throat. "Has a cause of death been determined?"

Patrick put his arm in front of Constance, like he was protecting her. "We don't have any information on that at this time."

"And you are?"

Constance pushed Patrick's arm down, following it with her body until she was leaning against him. "Sorry. I should have introduced him.

This is Doctor Patrick Flint, from Buffalo. He volunteers once a month at the clinic."

"Did you examine him, Dr. Flint?"

Before Patrick could give another non-answer, Constance said, "Listen, Jimmy, it's been a really, really hard day. We need to get back inside."

Jimmy nodded. "I understand. Listen, you know that Big Mike was important to a lot of people. The paper will be running a story tomorrow."

"I understand."

"Not everyone liked him, Constance."

A strange energy pulsed through Constance. This close to her, Patrick could feel it, and he would swear the very hairs on her head bristled.

"What does that have to do with anything?" she demanded.

"There's a lot of information about him coming in, all the time. Not necessarily stuff that we run."

Constance stepped toward him, agitated and pushing her hair off her face. "You leave them out of this."

Patrick's brow furrowed. *Leave who out of this?*

Jimmy didn't clarify. "People want to know more. Especially if he was murdered."

"Who said anything about murder?"

"Was it natural causes, then?"

This was Patrick's bailiwick. He jumped back in. "We aren't sure what killed him."

Jimmy fiddled with his camera. "I know you're grieving, but I thought you'd want to talk to me, so I could ask you about these things. Then they won't be a surprise when they're in the paper."

"I can't. Maybe tomorrow." She turned and walked back toward the clinic without another word.

Patrick hesitated. "Nice to meet you."

"You, too, Dr. Flint."

Patrick ran to the clinic in time to slip in the door before it closed behind Constance. Eleanor had been right. It was cold. The air inside didn't feel much warmer than outside. Patrick rubbed his arms, then blew on his hands. Constance was frozen in place on the snow mat with her face in her hands.

He put a hand on her shoulder. "What did he mean out there, about people not liking Big Mike?"

She dropped her hands. "Oh, nothing."

"You asked him to leave 'them' out of it. Is there something going on you need help with?"

She pasted on a sincere expression that somehow still seemed artificial. "You've already helped. Taking care of Big Mike and looking out for me. Thank you."

"Do you have someone you can call to be with you tonight? Friends? Family?"

She snorted. "Verna and my brother are my only family. With them as my choices, I'd rather be alone."

"I understand."

She took a deep breath. "I'm just going to clean up and shut things down."

The dark smudges under her eyes tugged at his conscience. "You go on home. I've got it."

"Are you sure?"

"Positive. And Wes and I can handle the clinic tomorrow."

"I guess I'll shut it down for a while after you guys go back to Buffalo."

"Or call IHS. Maybe they can send someone in to cover." He walked to the desk and reached for the phone. "But before I do anything else, I've got to call my wife. There hasn't been a quiet moment to check in with her since I got here."

Constance frowned as she grabbed her coat and purse from the wall hooks.

He put the receiver to his ear. It was silent. He depressed the tab to reset the connection. Nothing. He did it again several times to no avail. "The phone's dead."

"Must be the storm."

He set the phone back down in its cradle. "So much for that. She's never going to believe the day I've had."

She shrugged on her coat. "When is the funeral home coming for Big Mike?"

"They should have already been here."

She bit her lip. "Maybe I'll just stay with him until they come to get him."

"Whatever you want."

She disappeared into the exam room with Big Mike. Patrick gathered up the trash and put it in a bag in the kitchen, straightened chairs, and swept the floors everywhere except in the closed exam room. As he worked, his hands started getting stiff, and his nose and toes grew icy. It felt colder by the minute. He went to the waiting room to check the radiator. It wasn't giving off any heat. Tentatively, he put his hand to it, jerking back fast when his fingers first touched it, then holding them to it longer. It wasn't even warm. He pressed his whole palm against it. It was stone cold, as a matter of fact.

Maybe the boiler had run out of wood. The boiler room was beside the kitchen. When he opened its door, he got a good whiff of sawdust, ash, and pine resin. But the boiler wasn't lit, and there was no cut wood in the room.

He knocked on the door where Constance was with Big Mike.

"Come in," she said in a muffled voice.

He stuck his head and shoulders in. She had her head cradled in her arms on the counter. She lifted her face. Her arm had made a red mark across her cheek.

"Sorry to bother you."

"Are they here?"

"Not yet. But the radiator isn't heating. I checked the boiler, and it's unlit. There's no firewood inside. Where would I find more?"

"Shit. Riley was supposed to refill the bins today. He must have forgotten. I'll call him."

"The phones are dead."

"Right." She shook her head. He saw fresh tears in the corners of her eyes, unshed. "Well, we've got to get the boiler lit to keep things from freezing. We can gather up wood outside from our trees and bushes. But you and Wes can't stay here. It's going to get too cold."

He and Wes normally stayed on two cots set up in the exam rooms on their visits, to save money. "No problem. I'll get a hotel in Lander."

"Nonsense. You guys will stay with me. I have plenty of room."

"I don't want to impose."

"You're not. I could use the company." She snorted. "But we need to get word to Wes somehow."

"I can wait for him here."

She shook her head. "It's too cold for that Patrick. It's supposed to get down to twenty below tonight."

Patrick glanced at his watch. "And the transport for Big Mike was supposed to be here an hour and a half ago."

Constance closed her eyes and leaned her head against the wall. "I'm so tired."

"Then let's just leave notes for Wes and for the transport guy that we had to go. It's dark, the snow is high, and I don't think the transport is coming, anyway."

She agreed and gave him the address. "Tell him it says T-Ton Ranch on the gate."

"Got it. And don't worry. Big Mike will stay as cool here as he'd be in Lander."

She bit her bottom lip, then said, "Big Mike would be the first one to tell us to get out of here and get him a ride tomorrow. How about you follow me to the ranch in his truck? I'll be taking Riley's snowmobile."

"All right. Unless you'd rather me drive that?"

"No. The cold wind will help clear my head. Just let me say good-night to him, then I'll meet you out front to gather wood."

Patrick left the room. He collected his holster and revolver from a cabinet in the break room where he'd stashed them with his medical bag earlier and fished a book from the bag, as well. Unfortunately, his duffel was still in the Travelall. He strapped the weapon on, then scribbled a note to the driver. HAD TO LEAVE. PLEASE COME BACK TOMORROW FOR MR. TETON. Then one to Wes. HEATER BROKE. COME SPEND THE NIGHT AT THE RANCH. He added directions and taped them both to the outside of the front door. His outerwear had dried on the radiator, and he put on the coat, hat, and gloves. Then he lifted the phone off the receiver one last time, just in case.

No luck. No dial tone. No good.

CHAPTER EIGHT: MOTHER

Susanne

Susanne stroked a loose strand of her daughter's hair back from her forehead. Trish was lying on her side across her bed. Susanne usually avoided coming in here so Trish's dirty laundry all over the floor could stay out of sight, out of mind. But tonight it wasn't bad, because she'd ever-so-grudgingly cleaned it for the visit from Susanne's family. It was a pretty room, with blue flowered wallpaper, a coordinating blue bedspread, a hanging basket chair, and a giant burlap-covered bulletin board, painted with toadstools and plastered with pictures of Trish, her friends, and her animals, as well as prize ribbons and certificates. A Holly Hobby rag doll dressed in a green floral calico jumper, lovingly hand-made by Susanne, lay propped against Trish's pillow.

Susanne gently tucked it under her daughter's arm. "Everything will be okay, Trish. You'll see. Just give it some time."

What she didn't say, because it wouldn't do either of them any good, was what a witch she thought Donna Lewis was. The woman could have just told Brandon to come home. She didn't have to orchestrate a scene or involve Susanne. But while she ached for her daughter and felt a sting of personal humiliation in front of her parents and sister, she couldn't say she was unhappy that Brandon and Trish wouldn't be seeing each other. It wasn't just his awful, criminal family. For God's sakes, his uncle had held Susanne hostage, kidnapped Trish, and killed three men. The cousin in juvie she had a little sympathy for, as he'd been forced into going along with older men's plan.

No, it wasn't just them. It was also Brandon's sexual maturity. Trish could hold her own with him in most things—in fact, she more than held her own. She ran Brandon like she was a sheep dog and he was her lamb. But her daughter wasn't mature enough to fully appreciate the consequences of an eighteen-year-old boy's sex drive. Trish sure hadn't been rebuffing his advances from what Susanne could see, either. She seemed to *welcome* them. Patrick and Susanne were living in terror that Trish would get pregnant and end up married to this boy who—to be honest—wasn't her intellectual equal, didn't have the ambition Trish did, and didn't bring out the nicest side of her, either. Not that Brandon was a slouch. He was bright. It was just that Trish was as smart as her father. They had high hopes for her future, and her happiness, with someone she didn't criticize and control. The girl had a lot of growing up to do before that could happen, even if she didn't think so.

Trish moaned into her arm. "It won't be okay. I love him. He's my soulmate, Mom."

Whether Susanne approved of the relationship with Brandon or not, she could relate to being fifteen and in love. Oh, how she'd loved Patrick then, and how much more she loved him now. Had her parents disapproved of their relationship as much as she did Trish and Brandon's? Probably. Had she ever been as melodramatic as her daughter? Maybe. So, she held her tongue now and kept stroking Trish's hair.

"And it's not my fault Ben's in juvie. I tried to explain he didn't want to kidnap me. That his dad made him do it. How he helped me. It just didn't do any good. Why is Brandon's mom blaming me?"

Yes, against her parents' wishes, Trish had pleaded Ben Jones' case, but luckily her pleas had fallen on deaf ears with the judge. Patrick had caught Ben burying a man up in the mountains, for God's sake, and even Trish had admitted Ben had tied her up and hauled her into Cloud Peak Wilderness, then refused her pleas for him to escape with her. The boy was in the right place.

She rubbed circles on Trish's back. "I know, honey."

"Brandon's going to find someone else."

"So will you, someday. So will you."

"Gee, thanks, Mom." Trish jumped up, then pounded her fist on the bed. "Way to make me feel better. I don't want anyone else! I'll never love anyone else."

Susanne's mother, Catherine—Mama Cat to the grandkids—poked her head in the door. If Elizabeth Taylor had a doppelganger, Catherine was it, even in drawstring red sweat pants and a matching sweatshirt, without any makeup. "Everything all right in here, ladies?"

Trish flopped back on her stomach.

Susanne put her hand back on Trish's hair. She felt a soft, pitiful moan escape her, but ignored it. "We're fine, Mama."

Catherine lowered herself onto the opposite side of the bed from Susanne, and they faced each other over Trish. Despite Catherine's traditional Mississippi raising, she'd gone to Mississippi University for Women long before most other young women of her age were pursuing higher education. Then, while raising three children with Fred—who didn't go to any college—she'd worked as a teacher and continued on to earn her master's in education from Texas A&M, at a time when women were only allowed to enroll in graduate programs. As a largely military school, it was considered improper to have undergraduate women among the cadets. After Susanne married Patrick and left home, her mother had become a high school guidance counselor. She had a knack for helping teenagers, talking to them like adults yet guiding them with a light touch and deft hand toward good decisions. How Susanne would love to turn Trish over to her now and let Catherine sort this out. But that wasn't how the world worked. Susanne was Trish's mom. She had to bear up through this with Trish—and she had a feeling the issue wasn't going to resolve itself any time soon. Besides, as good as her mama was with teenagers, hadn't Susanne secretly eloped with Patrick before she'd graduated from high school? *Ah, motherhood. When does it get easier?*

"Let me give you a hug, Trish." Catherine held out her arms, and Trish sat up and put her head on her grandmother's shoulder. To Susanne, Catherine said, "Your father is worried we haven't heard from Patrick."

"I am, too."

Susanne hated not knowing if he was okay, and she hated that she couldn't talk to him about the pending counter-offer on the Clear Creek house. There was another buyer with an offer pending as well, according to her realtor. For just a brief moment, she pictured the house in her mind. The sumptuous master bedroom with plush shag carpeting and a clawfoot bathtub. The enormous butcher block breakfast bar in the kitchen. The sewing room with a south-facing window seat that she wanted to use as a reading nook. And the view off the bluff down to the creek bed and the giant cottonwoods on either bank. With all the houses they'd looked at in the last few months, this was the one she was excited about. This was the house she wanted, the one that would make staying in Wyoming tolerable. Because living here was hard. This was Patrick's dream, not hers. It was cold, the women were nothing like Susanne, and her family was over a thousand miles away.

And if they lost this house because Patrick had to make this trip, he was going to owe her, big-time.

"He got on his CB and raised some truckers through a relay, near where you said Patrick would be. The Fort Something-Or-Other clinic on the Wind River Indian Reservation, right?"

Other than her father was obsessed with them, Susanne didn't know diddly squat about CBs, so she wasn't sure what a relay was. It sounded good, though. "Right. What did he hear?"

"They're having a blizzard, and electricity and phone lines are down."

Susanne didn't know whether to feel relieved or even more worried. If phones were out, that meant Patrick hadn't been ignoring her or the house negotiations. Or at least that he *might* not have been. He could have been trying to call all day. On the other hand, with bad weather, bad roads, and bad communication, she still had no way of knowing whether he was safe or not. "I wish he'd just stayed home."

Trish looked out the window over her grandmother's shoulder. Susanne's eyes followed her daughter's gaze. Dusk was giving way to dark, early this time of year, and made more dramatic because of the clouds and snow.

Trish said, "It's barely snowing here."

Susanne sighed. "We've got two mountain ranges between us and him."

"When's he coming home?"

"He was supposed to come back tomorrow night. I guess that will depend on the weather."

Catherine slid her fingers through Susanne's. She squeezed.

Trish seemed to be distracted from her Brandon troubles. "Should we go get him?"

Susanne took Trish's fingers with her free hand, turning the three of them into a support chain. "I don't know. First, we have to figure out how to get in touch with him. Mama, do you think Daddy could try to convince some trucker to stop by the clinic?"

Catherine smiled. "He'd like nothing better."

Fred Brown would have been a long-haul trucker in another life. As it was, he'd run a wrecker and repair service Susanne's entire childhood. She'd survived, just barely, the mortification of his tow truck driving past her school with DON'T CUSS, CALL US painted on one side and DON'T FROWN, CALL BROWN emblazoned on the other. He spoke the lingo of the truckers and had a CB in every one of his vehicles, and a long-range ham radio in his office.

"Good." Susanne squeezed Trish's hand. "I'm having flashbacks to September when I couldn't find you guys up in the mountains and you were missing. Kidnapped." No one had thought anything was wrong then, and Susanne was the only one who really did. And she'd been right. She knew, now, that anything can and does happen. She couldn't assume everything was all right ever again when there were so many horrible possibilities.

"I'm sure there's nothing wrong." Catherine stood up, breaking the chain. "Patrick's tough."

Trish wiped the last of the tears from her eyes. "It's just snow, Mom. He'll be fine.

Susanne shook her head. "I'd feel a lot better if I could talk to him."

CHAPTER NINE: GUEST

KINNEAR, WYOMING
SUNDAY, DECEMBER 19, 1976, SEVEN P.M.

Patrick

"Sorry the kitchen is such a mess." Constance sank into a spindly wooden chair that didn't match the heavy pine kitchen table. A candle flickered in its center, casting a meager glow that illuminated a white refrigerator and laminated cabinet fronts. The flame and another like it on the counter were the only light in the house. Not only were the phones down, but the electrical power was, too.

Patrick worried his sweater sleeves down to his wrists inside his puffy coat. Now that he was here, he was uncomfortable alone in the house with Constance. Susanne probably wouldn't be thrilled about the arrangements. He hoped Wes would arrive soon. The house was as cold as a meat locker, too. And, yes, a mess, at least what he could see of the kitchen. The remains of a fry-up of taco meat were on the stove, and the scent of beef grease, onions, cumin, and chili powder lingered in the air. The stovetop was covered in a solidified oily sheen broken up only by thicker splatters, some embedded with meaty chunks. A dirty plate, a half-full cup of milk with a nasty film on top, and several utensils with caked on food residue were piled in the sink. A bottle of salsa sat opened on the counter, shredded lettuce and grated cheese leavings around it.

"Don't worry about it. Please." He put his hands on a chair back, then stuck them in his pockets, then pulled them out again.

On both sides of her face, Constance pushed back hair that had come loose from her fat French braid, the kind Trish wore in her hair. "I don't even know what I have to offer you to eat."

"If you don't mind me looking around, I could try to put us something together."

"You're welcome to look around, but don't make anything for me. I'm not hungry. I just want a bath and my bed."

"Well, then, I'll start by building a fire. Warm things up."

"Thank you. That would be good. We can't let the pipes freeze." She rose. "There are two guest rooms down the hall, with a bathroom between them, for you and Wes. Towels in the bathroom closet. Clean sheets on the bed, I hope. The hot water is gas heated, so feel free to use the shower."

He waved her away. "We'll be fine. Take care of yourself. And let me know if there's anything I can do for you."

"I will. Oh, there's a kerosene lantern under the sink." She opened the cabinet doors to double check, then, satisfied, closed them. "Thank you." She took the candle from the counter with her and wandered down the hall, turning before she entered a room at the far end. "Good night, Patrick. I'm glad you're here."

"Good night, Constance."

The door closed behind her.

Alone, the quiet in the house beat at his ears. The snow had stopped falling, but the air still felt portentous, like the eye of a hurricane. It felt spooky, being here where Big Mike had been alive earlier in the day. Patrick thought about the urine sample he'd sent to Lander. If Big Mike had died from strychnine, had he been poisoned here? His mind raced through the possibilities. Inhaling, swallowing, injection, or absorption through his eyes or mouth.

Swallowing. The hair on his arms rose, feeling like the legs of a legion of spiders.

Reaching into the cabinet under the sink, he grabbed the lantern and shook it. From the sloshing sound, it felt like it had plenty of fuel. He set it on the counter, adjusted the wick upward a quarter of an inch, and lifted the globe. Constance had left matches on the table after lighting the candles. He got one out, then he struck it against the box and held the flame to the wick, gradually adding some kerosene to it.

When the lamp was lit, he lowered the globe and turned his attention to the food in the kitchen. If Big Mike had swallowed strychnine, it could be in the food he'd left behind. Or the drink. Patrick had seen powdered strychnine many times. It was popular as a pest poison because it was simple to stir into food, like hamburger meat. He looked around the kitchen for traces of powder. There was none on the floor, countertops, or table. The food and milk were probably a dead end, as far as visual inspection went. Any powder would have absorbed into invisibility hours ago.

He ran his hand along the edge of the stove, thinking. Symptoms from strychnine typically onset within fifteen minutes of ingestion, and death can occur in two to three hours. So, it was possible he was looking at Big Mike's last meal. Dann seemed ready to write the whole thing off as natural causes, so Patrick assumed no police had visited the house or talked to Constance about preserving evidence. Yet if the sample tested positive, this food could be an important piece of the puzzle. Patrick scooped up a spoonful of the taco filling and held it over the remaining candle, turning it to catch the light from all angles. If there were poison in it or anything else in this kitchen, then the killer was brazen. And indiscriminate.

Constance. Himself. Wes, when he got here. They could all be at risk.

That sealed the deal for Patrick. He couldn't just clean the kitchen. He had to preserve possible evidence first.

Opening and closing drawers and cabinets, he searched for containers for the leftovers. He found a cabinet of Tupperware bowls and selected the smallest ones. He spooned the sautéed meat mixture into one bowl and scraped the cheese and lettuce scraps into another. He found a paper grocery bag. He placed the containers inside it, then used a rag to move the skillet and salsa jars into the bag, too. Thinking one step ahead, he used the rag to open the refrigerator as well, in case of fingerprints.

If someone poisoned Big Mike, what else might they have touched? He studied the contents of the refrigerator. An aluminum foil packet of homemade tortillas. A mason jar of sliced jalapenos. A tub of sour cream. The milk jug. All of them went in the bag. When he was satisfied that he'd done all he could, he labeled, dated, and signed the bag.

Finally, he created a clear spot on a shelf in the refrigerator and forced the bag in it. It wouldn't do to let things spoil further.

His stomach growled. His bowl of Life cereal was a long time ago at five a.m. back in Buffalo, with nothing but coffee since then. Could he trust the food in this house, though? He decided he could risk food Big Mike hadn't eaten, if it was unopened and untampered with. Rooting in the refrigerator, he discovered a jar of chokecherry jam with the canning lid still sealed. In the pantry, in front of a variety of half-full whiskey bottles, a brand-new jar of Jif crunchy peanut butter. In the freezer, a loaf of Wonder Bread. A few hard blows to the counter's edge and he was able to break apart the bread. He slathered jam and peanut butter onto two frozen slices. Spotting a bunch of extra ripe bananas, he mashed one in a bowl, then scooped the mush onto the bread. He scarfed the over-full sandwich, standing over the sink. Globs of jelly plopped into it. The frozen bread hurt his teeth, but it wasn't bad. *What hunger can do to a man's taste.* He made another and wolfed it down, too.

All done, he surveyed the kitchen. It looked a little better. He wanted to clean it, but he didn't want to risk messing up anything else the police might want. It probably wouldn't meet Constance's standards. It certainly wouldn't have met Susanne's.

Worrying about strychnine, he'd quit noticing the cold. He needed to get the place warmed up. In the living room, Patrick went to work at the stone fireplace. Once he had a fire lit, he stood with his back to it, waiting for it to generate warmth. Shadows danced around the room on mustard yellow walls covered with memorabilia and photographs. A picture of Constance in an Army medical unit in Vietnam riveted his attention. When the fire had taken the chill off, he stepped closer to the photo. Was that Riley in it with her, his face swathed in bandages? Had to be. He kept scanning the walls. A wedding picture of Big Mike and Constance, her short-sleeved dress suggesting summertime. Portraits of people he assumed were family members. Constance in long basketball shorts, surrounded by smiling girls, holding a giant trophy. Big Mike with livestock at shows and auctions, and with his own share of prizes. Shoshone art and artifacts—a fringed woven rug, beaded moccasins in a shadow box frame, and a painting of a buffalo hunt.

There was a rolltop desk in one corner of the room, and he wandered over to it. The top was up. The items on the desk looked to relate to the running of the ranch. A receipt from a feed store. Registration papers on a bull. A bill of sale of a truckload of steers. Absently, he picked up a page that seemed out of place. It was a note in black magic marker, all caps. YOU'LL GET WHAT'S COMING TO YOU. He dropped it like a hot potato. In light of Big Mike's death, the note seemed ominous. Threatening. Patrick rifled through the rest of the papers on the desk, looking for anything else like the note, but he found nothing. He studied the note again, not touching it, considering the possibilities. The words had both positive and negative connotations. Maybe someone owed him money. Or was encouraging him that he'd get a reward for work well done. Big Mike could even have written it to send to someone else. He leaned against the desk, closed his eyes.

He was so tired, but he was determined to wait up for Wes. He left the note behind and settled into the couch, reached down and stroked it. Velour. Burnt orange in the fire light. Then he pulled his copy of DANCE HALL OF THE DEAD from the inside pocket of his coat, the one he'd retrieved from his doctor's bag. He regretted that he'd left the bag at the clinic—hated being without it. But he was in a nurse's home. If he had a sudden need for the tools and tricks of his trade, he was sure he could find what he needed here.

He turned his attention to the book. He'd recently discovered the author, Tony Hillerman, when someone gave him a copy of the author's first novel, *The Blessing Way*. He tried to immerse himself into the adventures of Navajo tribal police offer Joe Leaphorn, but it was hard to focus, and his eyes were tired. He put on a few more logs.

Headlights in front of the house caught his attention. He walked to the window, expecting to see Gussie and Wes. The snow hadn't restarted, and the howl of the wind had eased. His breath condensed into an icy cloud on the glass. Through it, he saw a shadowy figure, low to the ground, slinking toward the window. With a start, Patrick recognized it as a coyote. They didn't usually come so close to people. Maybe it was hungry. He rubbed his eyes. When he refocused on the animal, it stood up on its hind legs and kept walking, turning into a man. Patrick drew in a sharp breath. A large Indian man. He looked familiar, like the man he'd seen today in the truck, down to the gray felt cowboy hat and eagle feather. Big Mike? He was imposing, more so than he'd seemed in death. Tall, thick in the shoulder and thigh, trim in his waist, dressed like the rancher he was in life. Muddy boots, even though the ground was covered in snow. Heavy jeans. A collared shirt under a dirty oilcloth jacket. He looked younger, too. His face unlined and his hair jet black. Something was different though. It was his chest. It . . . glowed. Like there was a light shining straight through him where his heart should be. But that couldn't be real. *He* couldn't be real. Patrick was hallucinating.

Big Mike's lips moved, and Patrick read them. *Help me. Find the trickster.*

Patrick fell back a step. Then Big Mike crumpled to the ground. "What in the world?" He ran to the door and wrenched it open.

There was no Big Mike on the ground, no coyote. Patrick's brain felt foggy and muddled. He *had* been hallucinating. Frigid air gusted in his face, and he shut the door. *How embarrassing if someone had seen me.* He returned to the window for one more look, just in case. For the first time, he realized that there was another, smaller house beyond the barn and stable. There was a vehicle—something like a Bronco—parked beside a truck in front of it. The headlights he had seen? Two figures exited the Bronco and walked to the front door. It opened, spilling out a thin stream of light. Two more big vehicles, one a truck with a camper shell, the other a snowmobile, arrived. Three more men entered the house.

Who lives there?

He leaned his hands on the windowsill and noticed a pair of binoculars. He held them up to his eyes. A dark Suburban parked. Two men walked to the house. When the door opened this time, Patrick had a clear view of the host greeting them. Eddie Blackhawk, Constance's brother.

Patrick thought back on the conflict between brother and sister that afternoon. Eddie had wanted money for a game. Constance had turned him down. It had sounded like he was running for-profit poker games, given that she had warned him about going to jail. In Wyoming, most gambling was illegal. Social poker games, even high stakes ones, were allowed as long as the participants had a bona-fide relationship and nobody was raking the pot or making a profit from hosting the game. Come to think of it, Constance had been worried that Eddie would get her and Big Mike in trouble, too, which made sense if Eddie was engaging in illegal activity on their ranch.

He lived onsite, in the little house, Patrick realized. It wasn't unusual for multiple families to share properties on the reservation. Even for multiple generations or arms of a family to share one roof. Private land ownership had arrived on the reservation with the Dawes Act in the

1880s. But at heart, the Indians were still a tribal community. All for one and one for all.

Or, down with one, down with all, in this case?

The voice at his elbow startled him. "Eddie's not lazy. If he'd just turn his efforts into making money legally, he'd do well. But his scheming is always on the wrong side of the law."

He glanced at Constance, who was standing so close to him that their arms where only a whisper apart. He was glad she had on a heavy robe and he was wearing his coat. "That has to be hard for a sister, especially when he lives here."

"It was harder on Big Mike." She pushed back her long, wavy hair, which was hanging loose and unbraided, then crossed her arms low over her gut. "After everything Big Mike did for him—bailing him out of jail more than once, letting him live here, giving him work—this is how Eddie repaid him. Big Mike is—was—a community leader. He kept warning Eddie to shut it down before he had to turn him in. But Eddie didn't listen. It's my problem now, I guess."

"I'm sorry."

The CRACK of a gunshot reverberated. It was like a cattle prod to Patrick's psyche. Without a glance at Constance, he sprang for the door before the second shot, aware and glad he hadn't taken off his jacket or the revolver and holster underneath it.

"Wait for me. They don't know you." Constance stuffed her feet into a pair of boots that had been sitting inside the door, tripped, and righted herself.

Standing outside waiting for her, Patrick's nerves jangled. With the power out, it was dark as pitch, except for the light from Eddie's windows. Patrick heard a loud, steady engine. He cocked his head. Eddie was running a generator. Constance shut the door, and the two of them ran across the parking lot, hunching over as if by tacit agreement. Cold air seared Patrick's lungs and stung his nose. He slipped. The traction from his running shoes was terrible, and he reached out a hand to steady himself on Constance's Cherokee as he passed it, realizing as he did that Riley must have dropped it off and picked up his snowmobile earlier. In the distance, the sound of a vehicle engine approached. For a moment, he was relieved. *Wes.* But it was higher pitched than a car, he realized. More like the snowmobile, and coming fast, but not from the driveway. From behind the house and barn. From the depths of the ranch.

"Is that Riley? What's he doing here?" Between running, the cold, and the mile-high altitude, he half-whispered, half-panted, pointing toward the sound.

Constance answered without breaking stride or losing her breath. "He lives in a trailer out there in exchange for helping out around the place."

Patrick remembered the Vietnam hospital picture hanging in the living room. Between Constance's brother and her war buddy both living onsite, he was beginning to think Big Mike was a saint.

They reached Eddie's house as the snowmobile raced into view and pulled to a stop beside them. Curled over the handlebars, Riley looked like a half moon in his white snowsuit.

"I heard gunshots." Riley jumped off his sled toting a shotgun. "Are you okay?"

"I don't know if I'll ever be okay again. We were just going to check it out." Constance jerked her head toward the cluster of vehicles. "Eddie has a game tonight."

Riley nodded. "Yeah. I'd heard about it."

Glass busted outward from a window on the front of Eddie's house. A body followed and landed in the snow with a thud and a breathless OOMPH. Riley brought his shotgun up to his shoulder, aimed at the window. Patrick drew his revolver and ran to cover the figure on the ground. It groaned, then rolled over onto its back. A man. When he saw Patrick and the gun, he lifted both hands and lay still, like a beefy snow angel.

Constance yelled, "Eddie, get your ass out here."

Her brother's grinning face peered out the window framed by a few remaining glass shards. "We had a cheating rat in our midst, but he's decided to donate his money to the pot and move along. It's all under control, Sister."

"It's not under control when you're firing shots and breaking windows on my property."

A face appeared beside Eddie's. The man was older than Eddie, his skin paler, his hair salt and pepper. "Big Mike's body isn't even cold, and you're already calling it yours? Maybe Verna's right about you."

"What's that, Elvin Cross?" Constance shrieked and charged toward Eddie's door. "Dastard."

Patrick abandoned his post and dove after her, grabbing her by the sleeve of her robe. Constance was fierce, but, unarmed, she was no match for a half dozen or more gun-toting men inside. With all that had happened today, she also wasn't her normal, rational self. Or at least the rational self he was used to at work. Maybe outside of it, she was always this feisty. She shot him a dirty look, then turned her attention back to the man taunting her.

His voice was mocking. "Verna says you had a lot to gain by Big Mike dying."

Patrick winced. Exactly what Verna had told Dann earlier.

"You've got a lot of nerve saying that on my property." Constance balled her fists on her hips. "Eddie, I want everyone off the ranch. Now."

"Game's not over, Sister. Too much money on the table."

"I mean it," she screamed. "I'm calling the cops."

Patrick tensed, expecting her to charge the house again and ready to tackle her if he had to. But instead of going on the attack, she started stomping back toward her own house. Riley and Patrick fell in behind her.

"That's a real unfriendly idea, Mrs. Teton." Patrick turned back and saw Elvin raise a whiskey glass to her. "Do unto others as you would have them do unto you, isn't that how the saying goes? You call the cops on us, we call them on you, maybe tell them about how Eddie here was paying Big Mike and you a cut of the games."

She whirled. "That's not true. You're the one getting a cut, at our expense."

"Prove it."

"Whatever. You won't implicate yourself."

"Maybe I'll tell them I know you killed your husband."

Patrick's blood boiled. "Maybe I'll be the one who reports you instead."

Elvin scowled. "Who's this pantywaist, Eddie?"

Eddie kicked out a dagger of glass from the window. It plopped into the snow. "Do-gooder doc from Buffalo. Patrick Flint. Don't worry about him. He'll be gone tomorrow."

Constance over-enunciated. "Get off my ranch, now, Elvin. I mean it."

Patrick heard the distinctive, chilling sound of the action on a shotgun. He glanced over at Riley. The barrel pointed at Elvin. *Oh shit.* He wished he could have called Susanne. He put his finger over the trigger of the .357 Magnum but kept it trained on the ground.

Eddie laughed. "Relax and have another drink, everyone. My sister didn't kill anyone, even in Vietnam. She's a healer, not a murderer." He clapped a hand on Elvin's shoulder. "Come on. It's brass monkey cold. Help me nail some plywood over this window so we can finish up the game. You'll all be long gone before the cops get through on these roads, if they even come at all."

Constance shot birds from both hands at her brother and his guests as she stalked into her house and slammed the door without looking back.

Riley and Patrick looked at each other.

Patrick shrugged. "I'm not sure whether she really needed our help."

Riley stopped at the doorsteps. "She needs a lot more help than she thinks she does. Wolves at every gate."

"Wolves at the door, you mean?"

"No." Riley ejected the shell from the gun, then leaned over like a stork to fish it out of the snow. "Acts 20: 24-32. Paul says that there will be a time that savage wolves will try to come in and distort the truth."

"Oh." *Should have paid more attention in Sunday school.*

Riley's lips started moving, but no sound came out.

Patrick almost laughed. A kindred spirit. "What's that you're saying?"

"Huh?"

"Your lips were moving."

He smiled. "Oh. Sorry. I was wondering what you're doing here anyway?"

"No heat at the clinic. Constance is putting me up for the night."

Riley frowned. "That's not good for her reputation."

Patrick flinched like he'd been slapped. "It's not like that. Besides, Wes is staying here, too."

"Where is he?"

"On his way. He ran into Lander, should be here any time."

"Why Lander?"

"To take in a boy with meningitis. And he was dropping off a urine sample for me."

"Are you sick?"

"Not mine. Big Mike's."

"Why?"

Patrick opened the door to the house. "Just trying to pin down cause of death."

Riley stepped up onto the porch. "Wasn't it a heart attack?"

"Can't be sure."

The two men toed the snow off their feet and entered the house. Riley stood like a sentry inside the door.

Riley turned to him. "Dr. Flint, be careful of Eddie."

"Yeah, he'll be pretty angry after my involvement with this incident tonight."

"He's got a history."

"Of?"

"Violence. He did a few years in state prison for assaulting Constance's former fiancé."

"Holy cow." And then he thought *Constance had a former fiancé?*

"You've got your gun. That's good."

Patrick swallowed, trying to process the new information about the man drinking and gambling in the next house over. He took a deep breath. "Constance?" he called.

She didn't answer. Patrick walked further into the living room.

To fill the silence, he pointed at the photo of Constance and Riley in Vietnam. "You met Constance in Vietnam."

Riley stared at his feet. "Yes. Were you there?"

"No. I was in medical school."

Riley looked up and drilled him with his eyes. "Must have been nice. I was drafted because I couldn't afford to pay for college until I worked for a few years. I'd planned to go to medical school."

Patrick remembered the things he'd said earlier in the clinic, that Riley had overheard, and he felt horrible. "You could still go."

Riley shook his head. "Things changed for me."

Patrick had no idea what to say. He walked to the fireplace and put on another log. When he was done, he straightened and cleared his throat. "Earlier, at the clinic. What you heard me say. I'm sorry."

Riley saluted. "I'm a good soldier. I do what I'm told. Nothing more."

"I—"

Constance walked through the kitchen doorway into the living room. "Riley, what are you doing here?"

Riley nodded. "You need anything else?"

She pulled the belt of her robe tighter around her narrow waist. "I'm good. Thanks for your help out there. Good night."

Riley backed out the door. He looked from Constance to Patrick, then turned and disappeared, white on white, into the night.

CHAPTER TEN: BROADCAST

Perry

"You've gotta saw harder than that." Perry twisted his leg to give Matthew better access to the lip of his cast. "You're not even making a mark on it."

"It's not easy." Matthew's eyes flitted from the cast to the door and back. "I can't do this."

"Yes, you can. Come on. We've got to hurry."

"If you want it done so bad, do it yourself. I don't want to get in trouble. My dad will whup my ass."

"You won't get in trouble. You'll be saving my mom a visit to the hospital to get my cast off. She's really freaking out with my dad gone and all of you here because she has so much to do."

"If that's true, then why are you in such a big hurry?"

Perry was the one glancing at the door now. Nevermind Uncle Will. His mom would whup their ass if she caught them. "I don't want to miss breakfast."

Matthew shivered. "I'm cold, too."

"You won't be if you saw harder."

Sighing, Matthew took the saw up again. He gritted his teeth and the skin on his forehead bunched. His sawing was tentative again at first, then he leaned down on the blade. A tiny spray of plaster dust poofed from under it.

"You're getting it!" Perry shouted.

Matthew put more weight into it, and the saw bucked off its line, turning sideways with a TWANG. He slipped, and his hand came down on the teeth. "Ow!" He jerked back.

"Are you okay?" Perry rotated his upper body to get a look at Matthew's hand.

"I don't know," he wheezed.

"Let me see it."

Matthew cradled it, his eyes closed. "It hurts."

Perry grabbed his cousin's hand. The palm had a row of shallow holes and some torn skin. There wasn't any blood, unless you counted the little bit seeping to the surface in a few of the punctures, which Perry didn't. No gushers, no problem. Or, like his dad always said, no pain, no gain. Which he'd follow up by saying what doesn't kill you makes you stronger. That's about when his mom usually rolled her eyes and walked away. "You're fine. Just a scratch."

Matthew stared at his hand, his face chalk white. "I want to go inside."

"But you've just gotten the hang of it. You can't quit now!"

Matthew shook his head, looking like he was going to throw up. Then he jumped to his feet and ran out. Perry heard the door to the house slam. While his cousin was one of his best friends, in Perry's opinion Matthew needed to toughen up. Perry grabbed the saw and attempted to cut the cast himself, but he couldn't get the right angle on it. Disgusted, he put it away and went back in the house.

When he opened the door, warmth and the sweet smell of Belgian waffles met him. His mouth watered. They were his favorite. Every birthday his mom let him pick anything he wanted for breakfast, and this was always his choice. There was a tall stack of them on the table with bowls of homemade whipped cream and strawberries. Trish was sitting in her usual seat, her eyes dark and puffy. His mom was supposed to sleep with Trish since Mama Cat and Papa Fred had the master bedroom, but Trish had cried so hard all night that his mom dragged in a pillow and blanket and slept on the floor in the game room with Matthew and him. Mama Cat was rocking baby Leslie. Uncle Will was already done eating and getting up from the table. The only person unaccounted for was Papa Fred.

He took Uncle Will's chair. "I thought we were having the cinnamon rolls Ronnie brought?"

His mother arched her eyebrows at him. "Are you complaining?"

"No, ma'am!" He grinned.

"We'll have those tomorrow."

Perry stabbed two waffles with his fork and slung them onto his plate. He scooped big mounds of whipped cream on them then poured the goopy strawberries straight from the bowl. His mom had used the extra sugary frozen kind that he loved, instead of fresh ones.

"Perry Flint, no sir," his mother said. "Use a spoon."

Too late. He dug in, loading his fork and mouth up so much that his cheeks bulged. After he'd managed to swallow a huge bite, he poured himself a tall glass of milk from a pitcher. He could get used to having company.

A loud noise squawked from the living room, followed by a grunt. Papa Fred was sitting on the couch in front of his CB radio, the microphone in one hand, the other twisting knobs. "Almost had it."

"What are you doing, Papa Fred?" Perry asked.

Papa Fred didn't look up from his work. "Breaker 1/9. This is Papa Fred in Buffalo, Wyoming, looking for a relay. I need a 20 on a buddy on the Wind River Reservation. Anybody near me got their ears on?"

Perry was transfixed. He took another big bite then wandered over to sit by Papa Fred, resting his plate on his knees. His grandfather knew everything about trucks and CBs. Everything. "I thought you kept this in the car."

"I've got it set up so I can run it in the house, too."

"Oh."

Papa Fred handed the mic to Perry. "I'm trying to find someone to check on your dad. You want to give it a go?"

A big lump formed in Perry's throat. Talk on the radio? Talking to people made him nervous. That's why he liked sports. You didn't have to say anything. Your play did the talking for you. But he kinda wanted to try talking on a CB. He wasn't sure why. It just seemed cool. He gulped. "Um, okay."

"Just repeat what I said."

"Uh . . . "

Papa Fred wheezed a laugh. "Breaker 1/9. This is Papa Fred in Buffalo, Wyoming."

Perry depressed the TALK button. His voice squeaked. "Breaker 1/9. This is Papa Fred in Buffalo, Wyoming."

"Looking for a relay. I need a 20 on a buddy on the Wind River Reservation."

"Uh, looking for a relay. I need a 20 on a buddy on the Wind River *Indian* Reservation."

Papa Fred grinned. "Free style. I like it. Now say, 'Anybody near me got their ears on?'"

Perry giggled. "Anybody near me got their ears on?"

"Good."

The speakers burst to life. "Copy that Papa Fred. I'm west of you, and I'll start your relay now."

Papa Fred took the receiver back from Perry. "What's your handle friend?"

"You can call me Chuckles."

"Thanks, Chuckles. Can you hear me okay?"

"Wall to wall and treetop tall."

"Great. I'm looking for the 20 on a doctor out of Buffalo who was working at the Fort Washakie Health Clinic yesterday."

"Hang on. Let me start passing the word along."

"Thanks, good buddy."

Papa Fred put the mic down.

Perry frowned. "Now what?"

"We wait. Eat your waffles while they're hot. This could take a little while."

"Why does it take so long?"

Papa Fred grunted as he stood up. "A CB has a range of twenty to twenty-five miles, depending on the weather and geography. Not like law enforcement radios, which can transmit a lot longer distances. Think of it like the game where you get in a line and whisper a message from one friend to another, then the last person answers, and the line passes the answer back to you."

"Oh. But what if people are farther apart than that on the road to where dad is?"

"Then the relay fails. Which it might."

"Wyoming doesn't have a ton of people."

"And there are storms. And the roads between here and Wind River aren't busy, especially this time of year. We may or may not get lucky."

Perry tucked in another whopper of a bite while Papa Fred loaded up his own plate. By the time Papa Fred sat back down, Perry had cleaned his plate. He patted his stomach, considering whether he could fit another in. He was one of the smallest guys on the football team, and the coach had told him he needed to think about putting on some weight for next year.

The radio squelched, then Chuckle's voice came on. "Papa Fred, you read me?"

Papa Fred nodded at Perry.

Perry made a face, but he keyed the mic. "Uh, right here Chuckles."

"Your voice keeps changing."

Perry widened his eyes and Papa Fred laughed. He rolled his hand at Perry.

"Um, this is Papa Fred's grandson. Papa Fred is eating waffles."

Chuckles laughed. "Tell him he's in luck, Papa Fred's grandson. The relay located a guy who gave your doctor friend a ride to Lander in a meat wagon."

Papa Fred's eyebrows shot up. He grabbed the mic.

Perry whispered, "What's a meat wagon?"

"An ambulance." To Chuckles, Papa Fred said, "Really? Patrick Flint?"

"No, this fellow said his name was Wes. He was hauling a woman and a sick little boy to the hospital when our buddy found them stuck on the side of the road."

Behind him, Perry's mother said, "Wes and Patrick rode to Fort Washakie together."

Papa Fred keyed his mic. "That's his traveling companion."

Susanne sat in a rocker across from Perry and Papa Fred. "They were in an old green International Harvester Travelall."

Papa Fred repeated the information for Chuckles.

"Yeah, that's the vehicle described to me. Near as I can figure, the driver was headed to Fort Washakie to pick up a load, but had to turn back because of the roads. Found your guy on the flip-flop."

"10-4. Any idea how the roads are there now?"

"Give me a moment and I'll see what else we can find out for you."

"Chuckles, you're the best."

While they waited on Chuckles, Perry stuck his plate and fork in hot, sudsy dishwater.

Aunt Shelley smiled at him from the table where she was eating her waffles in tiny, slow mouthfuls with a lot of talking between bites. "You keep eating like that and you'll be as big as your Papa Fred someday."

Perry stood up a few inches taller. He hated being short. Papa Fred was so tall he had to duck to go through doors sometimes. Being that tall would be the best. He wouldn't want a big belly like his though.

Chuckles' voice came through on the CB. "Got your weather report, Papa Fred."

Papa Fred said, "Excellent. Fire when ready."

"The plows have been through, so the roads and the weather are clear. The meat wagon is leaving in ten to fetch that load in Washakie. He said he'll give you a shout through the relay if he runs into your guy."

"Thanks. I'll be 10-10 on the side."

Perry had followed most of the conversation, but he didn't know what that one meant.

Chuckles clicked on again. "One more thing the meat wagon driver passed along. There's a picture of your guy in the *Riverton Ranger* this morning."

Susanne put her hand on Perry's shoulder. "What is he talking about?"

"10-9, Chuckles. We're not following."

"The *Ranger* is a newspaper. There's a picture on the front page with a caption that said something like—and don't quote me on this, although I pulled over and wrote it down—"Doctor Patrick Flint of Buffalo, Wyoming, with Constance Teton at the Fort Washakie Health Center on December 19, 1976, after the death of "Big Mike" Teton, of the Eastern Shoshone Tribal Council." He snorted. "And they said she didn't look too sad about her husband, the way she was snuggling up to your buddy. Apparently, the girl's a looker."

Susanne's fingers dug into Perry's neck.

"Ow, Mom."

She eased up. "Sorry."

Papa Fred looked at his daughter. "What do you want me to ask him?"

"Ask him if the article mentions Patrick."

Papa Fred nodded. "Does the article mention him?"

"If it does, they didn't pass that information along."

Susanne nodded.

"10-4, Chuckles. We appreciate your help," Papa Fred said.

"No problem. I'll transmit if I hear anything else. Over and out."

"Over and out."

Perry looked at his mom. Her lower lip was trembling. What was the matter with her?

Papa Fred said, "That's promising. I'm sure we'll hear something soon."

Susanne nodded. In a too bright voice, she said, "Last call on breakfast. Leftovers to Ferdie. Perry and Trish, you're on dishes."

Perry and Trish groaned in unison.

CHAPTER ELEVEN: GAPE

Patrick

P atrick woke to the smell of coffee and the sensation of drool on his cheek. He stretched and fought for his bearings. A couch. By a stone fireplace with a smoldering heap of ash in the grate. Frost on the inside of the windows. He exhaled and saw his breath. The condensation reminded him of his breath on the window the night before. An image of the walking coyote and Big Mike's words came back to him. *Help me. Find the trickster.* Finally, his brain kicked into gear. He had been hallucinating. There was no walking coyote. No vision of Big Mike. There'd been a power and phone outage. A wild poker game and gunshots at Eddie's next door. He was at Constance Teton's house, and he'd fallen asleep on the couch while he waited up for Wes.

Who had never shown up.

Wiping sleep out of his eyes, Patrick sat and swung his still-shod feet to the ground and stood. Where was Wes? He walked into the kitchen. Constance was there, in jeans and a wool sweater. She was pouring a mug of coffee from a percolator on the gas range and looking like she hadn't slept at all.

"Good morning," he said.

"Morning. Power's still out. Can I pour you one?" She held up the percolator.

"Yes, thanks. Have you seen Wes?"

"I haven't. Is he here?"

"I don't remember him coming in. I don't think so."

"Did you check the bedroom?"

Patrick walked down the hall. More Shoshone artwork hung on the walls, but it was too dark to see it well. He checked both guest rooms. Both beds were made, and there was no Wes.

He returned to the kitchen. "He's not here."

Constance handed him a mug of black coffee. "Maybe he stayed at the clinic. No way to know, with the phones not working."

The phones were still out. That meant he couldn't call Susanne. He hated not being able to check in with her. Especially when he'd accidentally put her through something similar only a few months before and sworn never to do it again. Susanne had tried to bring dinner up to him and the kids when they were up in the mountains, but he'd changed campsites without telling her. For days she'd been worried sick about them, until she'd taken matters into her own hands and come after them. Good thing she had, too, as it was a bullet she fired that took down the murderer and kidnapper Billy Kemecke before he could get to Trish—who was bound, hands and feet or Patrick, who'd been helplessly unconscious.

The situation now wasn't as dire, at least on his end. On hers? Well, her family had been due in last night, right in the middle of negotiations on the house on Clear Creek that she wanted. That they wanted. It was his ticket to keeping the family in Wyoming. So, he wanted that house even more than she did.

Patrick sipped the coffee. It scalded his lips. He set it down. "I'm a little worried about him. I hate to ask this, but could I maybe borrow Big Mike's truck to go look for him? I'd find a way to get it back here for you, I promise."

"I have to go to the funeral home in Lander anyway. And I forgot my purse in the clinic, too. Why don't I just give you a ride?"

"That would work. Thanks."

With the hallucination and walking coyote fresh on his mind, he decided to ask Constance for her take on it. She'd probably just tell him he was losing it, but it was worth a try. "So, I had a crazy dream last night about a coyote."

She shook her head. "Oh, he's the trickster. You can't trust anything he tells you."

Trickster. *Find the trickster. Was Big Mike the trickster?* He nodded. "Well, good, that makes me feel better, since it was a crazy dream."

She laughed. "Glad to help. I was going to make breakfast, but the larder is pretty bare."

Patrick thought about the possibly contaminated food in her kitchen. "Any restaurants on the way?"

"We're not exactly like the Vegas Strip, but there's a diner. Well, more of a café out of someone's parlor, but Lawanda keeps it open 24/7. Give me five minutes, if you can be ready that fast."

"Wes has all my stuff, so I'm as ready as I'm going to get."

She winked at him. "Toothpaste and new toothbrushes in the bathroom. Deodorant too, I think."

"Sounds good."

She disappeared to her bedroom, and Patrick went to the guest bathroom. He found everything she promised in a drawer, then splashed water on his face and used a little more to smooth his hair over the thinnest spots on his scalp. Male pattern baldness. Why couldn't he take after his father, who was thirty years older than him and had kept his full head of hair? Sniffing his armpits, he decided he didn't smell so offensive that a shower was required. He swiped on deodorant, brushed his teeth, and called it good.

Back in the living room, he stood at the window and waited for Constance. The parking area had been plowed, and the snow was piled high around the perimeter and up against the barn. *Eddie?* He couldn't imagine Eddie getting up early to plow after a night of drinking, fighting, and poker. Plus, on closer inspection, the snow perimeter ended before Eddie's place. His pickup was barricaded behind a snow mountain. Patrick smiled. *Riley.* It made Patrick feel guilty he was cutting out this early in the morning without doing something himself to help the new widow.

"You ready?" Constance jingled keys from a ring of dangling bear teeth. She was wearing a mid-thigh-length fur coat in tawny colors.

"Ready. That's a heck of a coat."

"Coyote. Big Mike may have not wanted them on the ranch killing our calves, but he didn't let anything he killed go to waste if he could help it."

In her Cherokee, the going on the road out was easy, since Riley's plowing extended all the way to the highway, which had also been plowed. The difficult travel of the day before was becoming nothing more than a memory.

"Did Riley do this?"

"It sure wasn't Eddie. Mike used to get up and do it. Most of the plowing in the area is done by the community. Even the bigger roads. All property owners pitch in."

"Better than waiting on someone to come do it for you."

"We'd still be waiting this morning. Like we'll be waiting on the phones and electricity."

"Riley seems like a nice guy. I saw a picture of you two in the living room."

"He is. I took care of him after he was injured in Vietnam. He adopted me." She put on her blinker. "A lifetime ago."

"Like you saved his life and now he owes you his?"

"Not that dramatic, but something like it. We have each other's backs."

A startled coyote ran across the road in front of them, its back end tucking up and under its body so far that he moved like a rabbit. Patrick wouldn't have expected to see one in broad daylight.

"I guess the coyotes are a problem out here."

"A bad problem. They go after the calves and lambs. Less of an issue for us since Big Mike started dealing with them, although as you found out yesterday that created other problems."

Constance pulled into a gate. A small, hand-lettered sign hung from the top strand of barbed wire, inches above the snowline. It read LAWANDA'S LUNCHES AND MORE. This drive, too, had been plowed. Constance parked facing a rock house alongside four other vehicles. One was covered in snow. The other three were not, including an eye-catching green camo truck.

Constance and Patrick walked inside a cozy wood-floored dining space halved by pony walls. An old parlor and dining room configuration, by the looks of it. A fire crackled and popped on one end, the stone fireplace blackened with soot. Patrick breathed in the thick, rich scents of bacon and coffee. His stomach rumbled. A small sign read, "SEAT YOURSELFS".

Constance pointed at an empty table for two near the fire. Patrick nodded.

"I'll join you in a minute. Too much coffee already." She walked through a door on the far side of the dining room. Over the door hung a sign. BATHSROOM.

Heads turned to watch her go. Patrick took a seat. He picked up a typewritten, laminated menu from the table. FRY BREAD, BREAKFAST TACO, BISCUIT AND GRAVY, EGG AND BACON were the choices. Lawanda, or whoever, didn't really care much for grammar.

A woman with frizzy long, gray hair appeared at his elbow. She was as skinny as the pencil tucked behind her ear and wore a dirty white apron with LAWANDA embroidered across the chest. "Coffee, juice, milk, and water are self-serve. Are you ready to order?"

"My friend is in the restroom. Could we have a minute?"

"Take your time."

She walked to the next table with a very conspicuous limp. From the other end of the fireplace, Patrick noticed two men barely out of their teens. They were loud and angry in a way that suggested they wanted to be overheard by as many people as possible.

"If Big Mike's hunting regulations had passed, I wouldn't have enough meat to feed my family," one of them said.

The other man answered in a gruff voice. "It's a good thing he croaked. There was a line of people who would have been happy to help the Coyote Hunter on his way. Trying to take away the food from our tables—that's not the Shoshone way."

"Damn straight. Dead is what you get when you steal from your own people."

Constance dropped into the seat across from Patrick. "The fry bread is good, but don't be fooled into thinking it's really a native food. It's just what our people learned to cook when flour and water were the only food the government sent us. I served my country, and I'm proud of it, but the things the U.S. government has done to Indians are appalling. There's no treaty or agreement they won't break. Don't even get me started on their promises about health care." She gestured at her knee. "If my family had private insurance, my knee would have been repaired and I would have gone to college on a basketball scholarship. Because I'm an Indian, the U.S. government is responsible for my health care under treaty, so I ended up in Vietnam instead with the cycle of poverty ensured to continue. But at least it didn't cripple me, disfigure me, or cost me my life. I got lucky." She winked. "I guess I got started after all, huh?"

Patrick had written an undergrad term paper on the Apache. His research had appalled him. The duplicity, double-dealing, and genocide of the US government toward the Indians across the nation were horrific. "I'm sorry."

"I know. And it isn't you I'm mad at. I appreciate you coming here to help."

"It's the least I can do. The very least."

"It all worked out for me anyway. I got my medical training on the Army's dime, and the bonus of combat training. Most people don't think of women so near the front line but where else would we have been to care for the wounded? In the same conditions, facing the same dangers as the men most of the time, all 7500 of us women. I learned to take care of myself and not be scared of much of anything."

That certainly described the woman that had wanted to rush into Eddie's house and fight armed men with her bare hands. "It's good for the Wind River Health Center, that's for sure."

"I think so. Have you decided what you're ordering?"

He put down his menu. "I'm going with the eggs and bacon."

"Me, too."

The two men who'd been badmouthing Big Mike earlier dropped money on their table and left, but not before shooting dirty looks at the back of Constance's head. One of them winked at Patrick from the door. It closed after them. From Patrick's perspective, the atmosphere improved immediately.

Lawanda took their order.

When she left, Patrick leaned across the table, lowering his voice. "Was Big Mike working on hunting regulations?"

Constance frowned. "He was. Why do you ask?"

"Some guys that just left were talking about it while you were in the bathroom."

"Let me guess. They weren't fans."

"You could say that."

Her voice was fiery. "Subsistence hunting has decimated our game population. It worked for us years ago when people populations were lower, the buffalo hadn't been slaughtered, and the tribes moved around. It doesn't work anymore. Mike was working with a wildlife biologist out of Billings on regulations that would help feed our families at the same time as strengthen and build the herds back up. People that say otherwise are just ignorant troublemakers."

"Sounds like he had a good plan."

"Unfortunately, his opponents included a majority of the tribal councils for the Shoshone and the Arapaho. It was going to be an uphill battle."

"Your husband wasn't afraid to make enemies."

She smiled, but it didn't reach her eyes. "No, he certainly wasn't."

"They called him the Coyote Hunter. Is that because he was poisoning them on your ranch?"

"No, that was his Shoshone name. He's had it since he was a young man." She snorted. "It certainly fit him."

"Because Big Mike hunted tricksters?" he said, remembering earlier that she'd called coyotes tricksters.

She looked at her placemat menu. "Maybe that, too."

Patrick was confused, but when she didn't meet his eyes, he let it go.

After their breakfast, the two traveled on to the health center, driving past mile after mile of barren fence line until they started coming upon isolated mobile homes with tires on the roofs and furry dogs in the yard. When they reached Fort Washakie and the clinic, there was no green Travelall in the parking lot. Patrick felt a sense of disquietude. Where the hell was Wes? Had he stayed in Lander? The roads were clear. He could have been back to the clinic by now. Patrick was getting close to reporting him missing. Hopping out of the vehicle, he was hit by a wave of warmth. The temperature had climbed rapidly. It felt twenty degrees hotter than it had at Lawanda's.

With Patrick standing beside her at the building, Constance reached for the knob to insert her key. The door swung open on its own. "Did you do this?"

The doorknob and latch weren't working. The clinic had been broken into. He lifted empty hands. "Didn't touch it. Let me go first."

She swept her hand ahead of them. "Be my guest."

He stepped in front of her, doing a quick pat-check confirming he still had his revolver and pocketknife. Frigid air hit his cheeks, colder than outside. "Hello? Wes?"

There was no answer.

"Is anyone in there?" Then, a few seconds later, "Come out, come out whoever you are." He raised his eyebrows. "Is there a back door?"

"Yes."

"Well, let's hope whoever broke in is either long gone or making a quick exit now. I don't feel like running into anyone desperate."

Constance brushed past him, cursing under her breath. Her voice was like a saw-tooth knife. "My purse. I left it on top of the front desk. It's gone, dammit."

After seeing her temper the night before, he knew better than to try to slow her down. "Maybe Wes didn't see our note, and he had to break in to stay here."

"He has a key."

"Right." A thought struck him. If her purse was stolen, would his doctor's bag be gone, too? He should never have left it here. It was as essential to him as his wallet, wristwatch, and Sawbones pocketknife.

Constance was rifling the desk. "Not in here either." She made a disgusted noise. "And even if he lost his key and it was him, then where is he now?"

Patrick didn't have an answer.

She threw up her hands. "I should just start leaving the door open, so people don't break windows or locks."

"It happens a lot?"

"Oh, sure. People think they're going to find a stash of good drugs in here. Surprise, surprise. We barely have aspirin."

Patrick went back to the door and checked the knob and lock. "I think it's salvageable."

He couldn't see her anymore, but he heard her answer. "I'll ask Riley to work on it later." Then he heard, "Shit. My wallet. My checkbook. My ID. My money."

Patrick had little hope for his doctor bag then. But when he went to the break room cabinet, it was there. He grabbed it, then stood for a moment, thinking. The clinic had stayed above freezing, but he should light the boiler again. He went into the little room and used the last of the wood they'd gathered the night before for the fire.

In the hallway, he checked the phones and flipped a light switch off and on to no avail. "Still no dial tone." Then he went to the waiting room and turned on the radiator.

Constance stalked in. "Well, I looked everywhere. My purse is definitely not here. And getting replacements will be next to impossible. Nothing is going to be open around here over Christmas." She sank into one of the lobby chairs and dropped her head into her hands.

"Do you have another checkbook?"

"At home. And I need to go by the funeral home and leave a deposit today. It's going to take another hour or more back tracking to get the checks."

"I can write a check, and you can pay me back."

"I can't do that."

"Of course you can."

Constance looked up with wet eyes. "Are you sure?"

"I'm sure."

For a moment, she looked relieved, then her face changed to utter panic, and she leapt to her feet. "Big Mike. Big Mike was here and someone broke in."

Their eyes met. How could Patrick have forgotten about Big Mike? For that matter, how could he have slipped Constance's mind for so long? She took off like a sprinter out of the blocks. Patrick ran after her, bracing with one arm on the wall as he rounded a corner. His worn running shoes squeaked and slipped, but he stayed upright, wishing for the aggressive tread of his hiking shoes, which were probably dry now in the backseat of the Travelall. At the doorway to the exam room, his momentum carried him into Constance, who had stopped suddenly.

Over her head, he could see into the tiny room. Big Mike was still there, *Thank God*. Patrick moved around Constance for a better look.

A word had been scrawled in black block letters on Big Mike's forehead: BETRAYOR.

CHAPTER TWELVE: DUCK

Patrick

Constance hovered over Big Mike's face with a bowl of sudsy water and a sponge. She'd regained her composure. It was funny, but she'd seemed more emotional about the writing on Big Mike's forehead than she had about his death, muttering to herself, her voice ranging from angry to sad to almost scared. Patrick hadn't been able to make out the words completely, but he could swear it was a woman's name and death threats against her. Alice or Felicia or Bernice or something. In the mood Constance was in, he didn't dare ask.

But he did need to stop her from destroying evidence, however well-intentioned. "Before you do that, we need to call Dann." Patrick eyed Constance.

She scowled at him, then dropped the sponge into the bowl. "It'll be a waste of time. They'll never catch whoever did this."

"It's more than just a simple break-in and theft, though. The person who broke in might have come specifically to do this."

"Maybe. But maybe not."

"Either way, someone did this to your husband. It's desecration of a corpse."

"But that's not illegal is it?"

Patrick muddled it over. Morally, he'd always known it to be wrong. In his profession, he'd been trained to treat the dead with the utmost respect and care. Once, in medical school, a fellow student had been caught with his pants down, so to speak, posing with a spread-eagled nude female corpse. The student had been expelled. But, as he thought back on it, he realized it hadn't been a police matter.

"It could be related to his death."

"Or it could be completely unrelated and cause nothing but headache and delay."

"As the attending physician today, please humor me. I want to make that call." The words on the paper on Big Mike's desk flashed back through his mind. Black marker, all caps. YOU'LL GET WHAT'S COMING TO YOU. The marking now most definitely could be related, as could the note. Then he remembered their logistical problem. "Only we don't have a phone."

"We don't need one. I have a CB in the Cherokee."

Patrick hadn't joined the CB revolution, even though his father-in-law lived on his. He thought they were kind of hokey. A toy for truckers. It had never occurred to him to get a message out that way. Maybe he could ask Constance to put him in touch with Susanne, on their way into Lander. His mood lifted. "Perfect."

Constance went to make the transmission. She returned quickly, and Dann showed up on her heels, carrying a Canon 35mm camera case over his shoulder. *Was he parked outside?*

He looked somber and tired and put his arms around himself, mock shivering. "No need to take off my jacket in here."

"Thanks for getting here so fast." Patrick shook Dann's hand.

"I was driving by when dispatch called. Show me."

They led him in. Dann leaned close over Big Mike's face. When he stood up, he got out his camera, attached the bulky flash, and adjusted the lens. The flash warmed up with a clack and an escalating high-pitched sound. Moving around the room, he took pictures from multiple angles.

"I'm sorry, brother." Dann gently rubbed the letters with his first two fingers. They didn't smudge. He touched his finger to his tongue, tasting, his face impassive. Then he leaned over and sniffed Big Mike's forehead.

"Smells like black magic marker to me," Patrick said. "There was a note on his desk at home like this, too."

"Where?" Constance said, at the same time as Dann said, "It said BETRAYOR?"

"Sorry, Constance. It just caught my eye on his desk in the living room. It said YOU'LL GET WHAT'S COMING TO YOU."

Dann frowned. "That's not the same thing."

"I know, but it was similar."

"Hmm." Dann asked Constance, "Do you have any idea who might have done this?"

She shook her head. But Patrick remembered her muttering. Then his mind turned to all of Big Mike's enemies. The Mannings, Eddie and his poker club, the hunters badmouthing him at Lawanda's. They all at least had a reason to wish Big Mike ill, although whether they'd stoop to corpse desecration—or murder—he didn't know.

Something about Constance's face made him stay mum.

Dann asked, "You lose anything?"

"My purse. Some meds."

"Was it a break-in, or do you think someone had a key?"

Patrick said, "The lock was forced. There wasn't a lot of damage, but it won't latch or lock now."

Dann kept his eyes on Constance. "You know the drill. I'll need statements. We'll keep an eye out for your missing items. And, if you want, I can dust for fingerprints."

"No need."

Dann slow nodded in agreement.

Patrick sputtered. "No. I mean, yes, we want fingerprints."

Constance shot him a death-ray glare.

He held his ground. "It could be related to his death."

Dann bristled. "Have you got new information for me about how he died, doctor? Because to me it seems pretty clear these are two separate events."

"Not yet, but I'll know more when I get the results from the test of his urine sample."

Dann puffed before Patrick's eyes. "His what?" He sounded resistant. Territorial.

"Urine sample. To help determine cause of death, if possible."

Constance crossed her arms. She slitted her eyes at Patrick. "I didn't know he'd done it until afterward, Justin."

It was the first time Patrick had heard her call the officer by his name.

Dann jerked his head toward the door. "I need to talk to Constance alone. Can you give us a moment?"

Patrick stared at Dann then Constance, in turn. Their faces were impassive.

"Fine."

Dann closed the door behind him with a sharp click. The hallway was empty. So was the reception area. His pulse had escalated and his emotions made him feel overheated. Stifled. He decided to get some fresh air. Outside, he leaned against the stucco exterior of the clinic. *What the hell was that about?* Patrick's lips started moving.

Lost in thought, he almost didn't notice the green camo-painted truck cruising past until it stopped and someone rolled down the passenger-side window. A man shouted, "Hey doc." Patrick raised a hand to wave just as a loud blast ripped into the silence. Stucco exploded to his right.

He dove for the ground, rolling and catching a glimpse of a black shotgun barrel being pulled back through the window. *They're shooting at me.* The driver gunned it, and the tires peeled out. Patrick squinted after the truck, trying to read the license plate. The sun was too bright in his eyes, though, and he couldn't make out any of it, not even the state. But it sure looked like the one he'd seen at Lawanda's earlier. He just wished he knew who'd been driving it.

He scrambled to his feet and rushed into the clinic. Constance and Dann had moved from the exam room to the hall. They didn't see him. Constance was jabbing Dann in the chest with her pointer finger. Dann caught her wrist, holding it in the air. They locked eyes until Dann opened his fingers. Constance dropped her arm. Then the man's eyes strayed to the door of the clinic, meeting Patrick's. The two played chicken for a moment, and Dann balked. He leaned in and said something to Constance, his mouth blocked by her hair.

Constance gave Patrick a half smile. What had he interrupted? But it didn't matter. He had to tell Dann what had happened.

A little out of breath, Patrick said, "Excuse me. But someone just shot at me out there."

Dann squinted. "What?"

Patrick raised his voice, almost shouting. "Someone took a shot at me. With a shotgun. Outside the clinic."

The officer walked toward him, pulling at his chin. "Do you think it was an accident?"

Patrick's ire was rising. "Not given that they yelled 'hey doc' before they fired."

"Do you know who it was?"

"Someone in a camo truck that I'm pretty certain I saw at Lawanda's this morning. Other than that, I have no idea."

"License plate?"

"Couldn't say."

"Hmm. Well, a lot more of those camo trucks on the road than you'd think. Maybe just someone passing through."

Patrick felt heat rush to his face. There were *not* a lot of them on the road. "Were you listening to me? They yelled 'hey doc' before they took the shot."

"Good guess, since you're standing outside a clinic. They didn't hit you?"

Patrick clenched and unclenched his fists. Hey patient, hey nurse, hey you, all had a higher likelihood of being a correct guess. Why was Dann so determined not to do his job? "No, they didn't hit me."

"A harmless prank then. I'm glad you weren't hurt." He turned to Constance. "Write up everything that happened, then sign it and date it. You can bring it to me out in my truck, where there's a heater."

"What about me?" Patrick said to Dann's retreating back.

But the door closed behind him without an answer.

When he was gone, Patrick wheeled on Constance. "What's going on here?"

"Nothing." She didn't meet his eyes. "But we need to write our statements. I have paper in the desk." Opening a drawer, she pulled out a yellow pad and tore off a sheet for him.

Fighting down his ire, Patrick wrote his statement without another word, including the part about him being shot at. Constance finished up first and took hers outside. By the time Patrick got to the parking lot, Dann was pulling away.

"Wait," Patrick shouted, waving his paper. "You left without mine."

Dann didn't look back or slow down. Patrick dropped his hand.

Constance took him by the elbow. "I'm sorry. My fault. I think he assumed I brought both of them to him. He'll pick it up later."

"I'm sure."

"What?"

"Nothing. You could radio him to come back."

"I can only get through to dispatch."

Patrick shook his head and gritted his teeth, trying to suppress his urge to vent his frustration on the nearest person available. Constance.

She bumped his hip with hers. "Come on. It was just prankster kids. The usual vandals. They were probably drunk. Or high."

"The ones that desecrated Big Mike, or the ones that shot at me?"

"Both."

He wished he was as sure as she was. "Do we need to leave Big Mike here while Dann investigates?"

Her eyebrows shot up like a high jumper over the bar. "No. No more delay."

"Can you use your CB to try to get him transported then? It just feels wrong to leave him here."

"Let me see what I can do. Would you mind leaving a few more notes on the door? One saying we're closed for repairs. Another for Riley, asking him for firewood and to fix the door knob?"

"Sure. Can't you get hold of Riley on the CB?"

"He doesn't have one."

Wes either, Patrick knew. How dependent his world had become on telephones. What had people done before them? Especially in places like Wyoming. Like Wind River. Communities and ranches were far flung. Communication had been dependent on feet—human or horse— and sometimes waited months at a time. Now he was worried about being out of touch with his wife for a day and a half. With Wes for less than that. He needed to keep things in perspective, although he was still going to see if Constance could get through to Papa Fred on the CB.

Patrick went back in the clinic for his bag and to write two more notes. The adrenaline surge from almost getting killed was wearing off, but his heart still pounded like a jackhammer on a city street. He taped the notes next to the one for Wes that was still where they'd left it the night before. When he got to Constance's car, she was tapping her fingers on the steering wheel and singing along to "Play That Funky Music" on the radio, over static from the CB.

He stopped, staring for a moment. He'd known Constance for more than a year. Her behavior had never seemed inappropriate or erratic before. Grief did strange things to people. It could be unique from one person to the next. But was this grief he was seeing in her or something else—drugs, alcohol? There'd been no evidence of substance abuse.

Could it be relief or even happiness? And what had that altercation with Dann been about?

It was all very strange.

He opened the Cherokee door and set his bag in the floorboard. His holster and revolver were uncomfortable, so he took them off and stuffed them and his book in the bag. "Did you get transport arranged?"

"Yep. Someone's on the way." She turned off the CB.

He sank back into the seat. "Great. Hey, do you think we could try to call someone on that thing?"

"Who?"

"My wife's father in Buffalo. Susanne is probably ready to scalp me." He made a funny face, stretching his mouth wide. "Sorry. I mean, ready to roast me alive."

"I knew what you meant." She studied him for a moment, then put the car in reverse. "Sorry. They're too far away for me to reach them. Range is only about twenty miles."

Patrick deflated. He hadn't realized how much he'd been counting on the CB idea to work. "All right."

"Next stop, Lander. After we finish with the hospital and funeral home, I can take you to lunch at Dairy Land."

"But you don't have a wallet."

"We have an account there. Big Mike always settled up at the end of the month."

Patrick tried to imagine how he would feel if Susanne was sharing every meal with an attractive man in a faraway town. Not good, he decided. "That's not necessary."

"As a thank you for writing the check for me. I insist."

On the other hand, Patrick did have to eat. His brush with death had left him ravenous. And since it was completely innocent, Susanne would never need to know.

CHAPTER THIRTEEN: SCHEME

Trish

From her position belly flopped on her bed, Trish counted the days on the calendar again. She didn't know why she bothered. Her birthday was still fifty days away, just like she'd known, since yesterday she'd counted fifty-one days. She absolutely couldn't wait another minute to get her driver's license. Not one more minute. If she had a license, she could run the errands her mom was yammering on about. And if she could do that, she was free anytime to go anywhere she wanted to.

Like to Brandon's to beg his mom to change her mind. But anywhere away from here would be good.

She'd asked, repeatedly, for a lift to town, until her mom wasn't even bothering to say "no" anymore. Her house had too many people in it. They had gone from giving her pitying looks to avoiding her altogether. Her mom had cornered her in the bathroom after breakfast and told her to buck up. To stop being so hangdog. That she wasn't the first girl in the history of the world with a broken heart. *Easy for her to say.* Her parents had been sweethearts since they were fourteen—nearly two years younger than Trish—and were still together. How could her mom possibly understand when she'd never been through losing the love of her life? It wasn't like her mom was helping, either. She'd forbidden Trish to call Brandon, claiming she'd promised Donna Lewis to support her decision as a parent. And she was watching Trish like a hawk, too, every time she went near the phone.

If her dad was here, he'd understand. Everyone said they were just alike. He *got* her. He'd take her to her best friend Marcy's house, or drop her downtown at the library or at the movie theater for a double feature. He wouldn't hold her captive here like her mom was doing.

A knock sounded on her door.

"Who is it?" she grumbled.

The door wasn't locked, and someone pushed it. It swung open, revealing her six-and-a-half foot tall grandfather, with his rooster comb of white hair and his jolly belly. She hadn't inherited any of his height, although she was taller than her mother, and she was a heckuva lot taller for her gender than Perry ever would be for his. If she had been tall like Papa Fred, she could have tried to be a model. Except if she'd gotten his belly, too. Maybe she was better off like she was.

"Hey." She listlessly alternated kicking her feet up and down, hinging at the knee.

Papa Fred's deep voice rumbled. It reminded her of Brandon's motorbike engine. That made her miss him even more. "You up for riding into town with me? Your mother handed me a grocery list. She said you could help."

Trish jumped up, dropping her calendar. Twelve Months of Ranch Horses flopped onto the carpet, open to December and a team of Belgians pulling a hay sled. "Yes. Sure. Now?"

"Now. She needs something that she forgot for our lunch. Everyone will be waiting on us."

Even if he was in a hurry to get back, maybe he could still give her a lift to the library on the way home. And if he returned without her, her mom would be serving lunch and have no choice but to let Trish stay an hour or two before coming to get her. Worst case scenario, Trish could walk home. She'd done it before, carrying the maximum-allowed checkout of seven books the whole two miles. And Trish could make the most of the time at the library. There was a pay phone outside. She could call Brandon. Maybe he would meet her there. They hadn't even talked since he had to leave the day before. Were they broken up or what? Just because they couldn't see each other except at school didn't mean he wouldn't still love her, would it?

It had snowed another few inches the night before, so she hopped into a pair of red, white, and blue moonboots. Her corduroy bell bottoms flared around them. Maybe not the best choice with the footwear, but she was in a hurry, and Brandon liked these pants. And the Gunne Sax top she had on with them had buttons up the back, pleats down the front, and a lace inset on the chest and collar. It was fab.

She grabbed a quarter from her dresser and stuck it in her pocket. "Ready."

Papa Fred grunted and walked out. Pulling a coat out of her closet, she dashed behind Papa Fred to the front door. Grandfather and grand-daughter climbed into his Cadillac DeVille. It was big, but she couldn't believe the whole family had squished into it for the two-day drive from Texas to Wyoming. Trish laid her coat in her lap. It really wasn't that cold outside. The snow would probably be gone by the end of the day.

"You're going to help me dig out if we get stuck?"

"You won't get stuck. The snowplows have been out."

"Except in this driveway."

"Want me to drive it out of here?"

"You can drive through snow?"

"My dad has made me learn to drive in everything. I'm sooo ready for my driver's test."

"All right then, let's switch seats."

They did. Trish threw the car into gear and powered around the circle drive. The snow was melting, so it was easier than it looked.

"Impressive. Now show me what you've got, kid."

Trish turned downhill. The trick was to keep up speed and bust through the place with the perpetual drift, right before the driveway ended. She gave the Cadillac some gas. The back end lost traction for a second and fishtailed, but she hung on, and the wheels slipped back into line. Then, WUMP. The car hit the drift and shied sideways, but she kept the momentum going, just like her dad had taught her. Snow flew onto the hood and windshield. Then the tires found the plowed gravel road.

Papa Fred's laugh vibrated like her favorite recliner in his house back in Dallas. "Outta sight."

"You want to drive now?"

"Why don't you take us there since you know the way?"

She nodded, trying to hide her smile. Driving on the empty roads was awesome. If only Brandon was with her. He'd be proud of how good she was driving. Sadness blew through her, like wind snuffing out a candle. But then the CB radio between Papa Fred and her crackled with a burst of static. The static morphed into words.

"Breaker 1/9, this is Chuckles for Papa Fred. Come in Papa Fred."

"Huh." Papa Fred snatched up the receiver. "This is Papa Fred for Chuckles."

"I just got a message through the relay that our meat wagon friend went to the Fort Washakie Health Center to pick up his load."

"Did he find Dr. Flint?"

"No, sir. He did not. But he said the medic who radioed him to make the pickup was with Dr. Flint at the time. And that the heater was on the fritz at the clinic. He said it was colder than a witch's tit."

Papa Fred winked at Trish. "Huh. We're trying to figure out whether he needs a ride back to Buffalo. Any idea whether he had wheels??"

"None. Sorry."

"Well, we know now he's alive and well this morning. That's something. Thanks."

"Yep, better than the guy the meat wagon was picking up."

"Oh?"

"That guy was a stiff. And after a night in those conditions, I can imagine he's really, really stiff."

Papa Fred clicked on his mic. "Thanks again, Chuckles."

"You bet. Over and out."

"Over and out."

Trish shuddered. "A stiff like a dead body?"

Papa Fred nodded. "Yup."

"I don't want to be a doctor." Her mom was dying for Trish to go to med school. But her dad was encouraging her to follow her heart. She wanted to be a wildlife biologist, like he'd dreamed of. After Trish was born, though, he had to make money, so he'd become a doctor instead. The moral of that story was don't have kids. At least not as teenagers like her parents. "I don't like dead things."

"You and me both, kid."

Trish parked at the grocery store, thinking about Brandon's uncle, who had killed his own cousin right before Trish's eyes. Witnessing the murder and being stuck there with the dead body was awful. Brandon's uncle was awful. She hoped he ended up in jail the rest of his life. She knew his mom was really upset about the trial, and about Ben being in juvie. Now that Trish had time to think about it, she figured juvie probably wasn't the worst thing for Ben. He had helped kidnap her, after all. Luckily Brandon was nothing like the rest of his family. He was the nicest guy she'd ever known, except for maybe her dad.

"Do you think my dad is really stranded on the reservation?"

"Maybe so."

"With no way to get hold of him?"

"Not right now there isn't."

The two of them hustled around the grocery store and soon had her mom's emergency items in their cart. Papa Fred was pretty much just along for the ride and to pay, but Trish didn't mind if it got her to the library.

As they were checking out, Trish said, "Hey, Papa Fred, would you mind dropping me off at the library? I have a school project to work on." She crossed her fingers behind her back.

"Isn't school out?"

"Yes. It's make-up work."

"Is it okay with your mother?"

"Oh, yes. She encourages me to be a straight A student."

"I guess that will be all right, then." He handed a twenty-dollar bill to the cashier.

Trish smiled to herself. If she was lucky, she and Brandon would be together in fifteen minutes. Half an hour, tops.

CHAPTER FOURTEEN: SLIDE

Patrick

Constance steered into the hospital parking lot too fast. The tires hit a patch of packed snow and their back end slid to the left.

Patrick automatically mashed a brake pedal that wasn't there on the passenger side. "Watch out."

Her voice was strained. "Something's wrong with the brakes."

A car half the size of her Cherokee veered in front of them. Constance spun the steering wheel hard to the right. The other driver honked. The parking lot wasn't large, and it was relatively full. All around them were rows of parked cars, including in front of them. There was no way for Constance to maneuver her way around this. She either stopped the Cherokee or they crashed.

"Downshift," Patrick shouted.

Constance shifted into first, and the engine whined in protest. The Cherokee slowed, but not enough.

"Emergency brake."

She grabbed the brake and yanked it upwards. The wheels on the

Cherokee locked up, sliding again, but the vehicle stopped nose-to-nose and inches from a delivery van parked backside in.

"That was close." She turned to Patrick, leaning in. "Thank you. My brain went blank. If it's a medical emergency, I'm steady as a rock. Mechanics and cars have never been my thing."

Patrick inched his upper body toward the door. The interior suddenly felt way too close. "You're welcome. Where's a runaway truck ramp when you need one, huh?" He was referring to the sandy, gated lanes cut uphill for trucks to steer into if their brakes failed descending the steep grades that were common to the mountainous parts of Wyoming.

"If my brakes were ever going to fail, this was the best possible spot." She pointed past a parked van they'd narrowly missed, to an automobile repair shop.

"Convenient. And safer than a downhill curve at seventy miles per hour."

The two of them got out. Constance walked around to meet him behind the rear of the Cherokee.

She put her hand on his arm. "I'll see if they can fix it, then walk over to the funeral home when it's squared away."

Through the thick sleeve of his coat, he felt a thumb stroking him. What was wrong with her? She'd never come on to him in the past, but he was almost certain she was now. Grief, it had to be the grief. He cleared his throat. "No taxis?"

"No. But around here, you can always get a ride if you ask nice."

He backed away from her vised hand like it was the jaws of a crocodile. "I'll check at the auto shop when I'm done here, and if you're not still there, I'll meet you at the funeral home."

She gave him directions, a slight smile on her face, and they parted ways. He was glad for the break from her. Pushing open the glass doors to the Lander Hospital, the smell of vomit permeated surprisingly hot and humid air. The hospital was half the size of the one in Buffalo, but twice as busy. A baby squalled. A toddler screamed. An old woman moaned and rocked in her chair. Patrick almost felt like he should grab his doctor's bag and pitch in. After a moment, he noticed he was the only Caucasian in the room. The faces staring back at him weren't bathed in welcoming smiles, either. He was getting a distinctly bad vibe from the place. He hoped it wasn't a sign.

He walked up to the receptionist. The woman's hair was a gray frizz ball in front with a braided tail down the back. She was wearing a tank top with sweat around the armpits and had a ball point pen clamped in her teeth.

"Excuse me, ma'am? My name is Dr. Flint. I'm here to check on a sample that I had sent over for testing."

She looked up at him with her eyes while keeping the pen and chin pointed down.

After a long, awkward silence, Patrick said, "If you could just direct me where to go, I won't bother you anymore."

The pen clattered to the desk. "Oh, you're in the right place. You're just going to have to wait, like everyone else. Half our staff didn't show up today."

"I'm sorry to hear that. Do you need any more information from me to check on those results?"

She scratched her neck. "I won't be checking on your results until I deal with the thirty other critical items on my list ahead of you. Have a seat, sir."

He winced. "One more thing. My Buffalo Hospital colleague brought in a little boy last night with suspected meningitis after I saw him in Fort Washakie yesterday."

"I'm not checking on him right now for you either."

"I *would* like an update on him, but that's not what I was going to ask." He smiled at her, tamping down his irritation. "My colleague is missing. I haven't heard from him since yesterday, and I'm worried about him. His name is Wes. Tall, thin white guy with a walrus mustache. Did you happen to see him?"

"Sounds like a question for the police, not me."

"So, you didn't see him?"

"I saw him yesterday. But he wasn't missing then."

Patrick almost argued with her. *Yes, he was missing to me then, thank you very much.* "Great. That's comforting at least. Thank you."

Settling into an uncomfortable plastic seat, Patrick's thoughts turned to Big Mike. His concern about the word BETRAYOR on the man's forehead had only intensified since he'd first seen it, compounded by Dann's cavalier attitude and the shooter in the camo truck. Patrick wondered who was behind the desecration. Had it been directed at Big Mike, or at Constance, and why? And what or whom had Constance been muttering about afterwards? Her reactions might be a cultural thing Patrick lacked context for. She could have even been praying. But it was concerning. All of it was concerning. He really wanted these test results to prove him wrong. To prove that Big Mike had died of nothing more than natural causes.

He passed another ten minutes reading a three-year old copy of *Highlights* before the receptionist waved him over.

"Your name?"

"Doctor Patrick Flint."

"And the problem?"

"I had a urine sample delivered yesterday to be sent off for testing. It was from a death we had in Fort Washakie. I'm coming by to check on it."

She glared at him. "Why didn't you just call?"

"Because our phones are out at the clinic."

"Can I see your identification please?"

Patrick showed her his driver's license.

She gave it a cursory glance. "And what was the name on the sample?" She grabbed a pencil and stared down at a scrap of paper, showing him a lot of scalp in the thick part in her hair.

"Big Mike Teton."

Her eyes popped up. In a loud voice, she demanded, "Eastern Shoshone Tribal Council Member Big Mike Teton?"

Heads whipped around at her words. Suspicious, accusatory eyes bored into him from all directions.

Patrick shifted from foot to foot. "Yes."

She dialed back her decibels. "I read about him in the paper this morning. He died yesterday?"

"Yes."

"And this urine test was going to tell you how he died?"

"Possibly."

She nodded. "I'll be right back. Have a seat again."

"Wait. Could you also check on a patient of mine? His name is Clem, his mom is Lucy. I can't remember their last name off the top of my head, but he came over from Fort Washakie with suspected bacterial meningitis."

The receptionist didn't write it down, but she grunted. Maybe it was the same thing? He shuffled back to the waiting area. He didn't think he could bear any more *Highlights*. Luckily, a back issue of *Ranger Rick* had just become available. The plastic seat in the chair creaked as he sat. He wondered if he had time to find a pay phone and call Susanne, since the phones were obviously working here. But before he had a chance to look for one, the receptionist was back.

"Nelson," she shouted. "You're next."

Patrick dashed up to her. "Did you find the results?"

"Someone will be out to talk to you about that shortly."

"I'll take that as a no."

She leaned to the side to see around him. "Nelson, front and center."

A female voice with a hint of New York City said, "Patrick Flint?"

He turned toward it. A heavily freckled red-haired woman half his body weight was staring at him—and drowning in a too-big pair of blue scrubs.

"That's me." He walked over to her.

"I'm Canis Latrans. I'm with the lab. I'm sorry, but we don't have a sample by the name you provided."

Her name niggled something in his brain, but he ignored it, too focused on her declaration. "It could be under another name. Big Mike Teton. Dropped by Wes Braten on behalf of Doctor Patrick Flint, taken at Fort Washakie Health Center, to send off for testing. It could be under any of those names."

"It could be, but it's not."

"I don't understand."

"There's nothing to understand. We don't have your sample, so there was nothing to send out. No test, no results. Sorry." She turned to go.

"Wait. Do you have a record of *any* samples sent over from us yesterday?"

"None."

"Did you meet my colleague Wes Braten?"

"No. Now, I have to go. We're really busy today." She manhandled a door open and disappeared behind it.

Patrick was stunned. He walked out slowly, heading toward the BRONCO'S AUTO REPAIR sign next door and thinking about what could have possibly happened to the sample. When he reached the entrance to the auto shop, a thought struck him.

The receptionist had seen Wes yesterday. The hospital *had* received the sample. So, where had it gone? Something had happened to it. Or someone was lying.

The bad vibe Patrick had felt in the hospital just got a whole lot worse.

CHAPTER FIFTEEN: IMPROVISE

Susanne

"What do you mean you left her at the library, Daddy?" Susanne fought to keep her voice from sounding shrew-like. Girls shouldn't talk like that to their fathers. Even grown up women-girls.

Papa Fred stepped over Ferdinand, who had arranged himself like a living rug in the center of the room. He set the bag of groceries on the kitchen counter. "She told me you gave her permission."

"I didn't."

"Sounds like an issue for you to discuss with her when you pick her up. Now, I'm on vacation, and it's cold outside." He raised his voice. "Mama Cat, how about some hot toddies?"

Her mama stood up from the chair she was sitting in beside the black cast iron stove. "Who else wants one?"

Michael Jackson rocked "Santa Claus is Coming to Town" as loudly as if the Jackson 5 were performing in the living room. Perry and Matthew were playing Battleship and manning the record player at the same time. They couldn't just let a record play but were lifting the needle—scratching all her holiday albums and setting her nerve endings on fire with the high-pitched scritchy needle sounds halfway into each song. Her sister Shelley shifted Leslie to her other knee and raised her hand for a hot toddy, as did her husband Will. Susanne did not. She liked the occasional glass of white zinfandel, but she didn't drink hard alcohol, and she didn't like having it in the house. All she'd stocked for their visit was wine and beer. Her father and Will had known to BYOB, and they had: a fifth of Crown Royal and a fifth of Jack Daniels.

"Any for you, sweetie?" her mama said as she swayed and weaved into the kitchen, catching herself on chairbacks as she went by. The house still smelled like nutmeg, cinnamon, and vanilla from the batch of eggnog she'd whipped up for the revelers while Trish and Papa Fred were at the store.

"No, thanks, Mama." Susanne's nails dug into her palms. "I have to go get Trish. Back in fifteen minutes. Lunch is ready except for the chile con queso." Papa Fred had brought Velveeta, Ro-Tel tomatoes, and tortilla chips. She'd already made tacos and guacamole.

Shelley, a taller version of Mama Cat, stood. "Got it. We can eat the moment you're back."

"And can someone keep an eye on Perry?"

Will tilted one of her prized dining room chairs back on two legs. He sat with his hands behind his head and his knees apart. He hadn't shaved since they'd left Texas, so whiskers the same dark brown as his hair framed his face. His blue eyes twinkled. "Relax, Susanne. The boys will be fine." His second empty eggnog glass had been heavy on the nog and light on the egg. Susanne was afraid that if someone struck a match near the Bourbon fumes coming from his mouth, he'd go up like a tinder box.

Susanne slung her bag over her shoulder. If she said left, Will would always say right. He loved to get her goat. She wasn't going to let him. "If the house is burned down when I get back, I reserve the right to say I told you so."

Papa Fred took a seat across from Will. Her father and the chair groaned simultaneously. "Someone throw the doors open on that stove and let the heat out."

Susanne smiled at him, but her teeth were gritted. "It stays warmer in here with them closed, Daddy. I promise." She'd told every single one of her family members this at least three times already.

"Huh. Well, I like to look at a fire when it burns."

"Suit yourself."

The phone rang. Susanne lunged toward it. *Patrick. Please God, let it be Patrick and let him be calling from the gas station in Buffalo, five minutes from home.* Susanne needed help. Normally—with or without her glass of wine—she was the life of the party. Smiling. Vivacious. Dancing to every song that came on the radio. She wanted to relax and have fun now, but she couldn't. This was not the carefree holiday she'd planned. The carpet was covered in melted, dirty snow, dog hair, and piles of discarded shoes and socks, and it smelled like it. She had two boxes of Christmas decorations that still hadn't been put up. None of the baking had been done. Trish was morose and rebellious. Perry kept sneaking off and coming back bruised and bleeding. And her family was getting unhelpfully sloshed all around her.

She snatched the phone off the wall. "Hello?"

"May I speak to Patrick Flint, please?"

"This is Susanne Flint, his wife. May I ask who's calling?"

"Oh, hi, Susanne. This is Steve down at Buffalo Real Estate." Steve was a partner at the firm, but not the agent they were working with.

Susanne sucked in a deep breath. The sellers were waiting to see how the Flints responded to their counter-offer, and she was waiting on Patrick. "Hi, Steve. What's up?"

"Barbara is out, and she asked me to contact you if I heard from the sellers on the Clear Creek house you're interested in." His voice sounded nasally, like he was holding his nose.

Susanne crossed her fingers. "Yes?"

"One of my clients has made the sellers a higher offer on the house than the counter they made to you." He sneezed. The sound was explosive, like he hadn't covered the mouthpiece, and Susanne winced. "The sellers still want to give you a chance to beat the other offer."

"How much higher is it?"

"They wouldn't say. But they did withdraw their counter, since you hadn't responded yet."

This felt like a serious conflict of interest. Anger flared inside her, and she raised her voice. Ferdinand cocked his head and whined. "But your clients made the offer, so you know the amount."

"I can't disclose confidential client information."

"I need to talk to Barbara."

"As I said, she's out. Unreachable until tomorrow. So sorry."

Susanne's heart plummeted, leaving a searing path of sadness on its way down. Her house. Because that's how she'd started to think about it. As *her* house. Never mind that it was in Wyoming, and she was a Texas girl. As clear as day, she could see their lives there. Wine and candles and a romantic dinner with Patrick in the majestic dining room. *More* wine and candles and the two of them in the clawfoot tub. Trish in a lacy, pink prom gown standing with a date—not Brandon Lewis—by the living room fireplace. Perry holding a Bison's football helmet in one hand as he walked past golden aspen trees to leave for a high school game.

And now all of it was slipping out of her grasp.

"Patrick—my husband—has been volunteering on the Wind River Reservation this week, at the Indian Health Services Clinic. There's been a blizzard, and their phones are down. I haven't heard from him. That's the only reason we hadn't responded to the counter."

"Well, regardless of your reason, you have until five p.m. today to make your best offer. After that time, they'll accept the other one."

Steve didn't seem sympathetic to their plight. And why should he be? His firm got the commission either way. Her rage at him ebbed, replaced by something equally firey. Anger at Patrick. Maybe it was irrational to be mad at him. The blizzard wasn't his fault. But he did insist on making this late December trip across two mountain ranges when they had family in town and were trying to buy this house. And then there was that picture in the paper of him hugging another woman. Not that she'd seen it, but it was bad enough hearing about it. So, yeah, she was mad. She was furious. And just a little bit jealous, if she was being completely honest.

"I need to call my bank and see about the money, and they're in Texas. They close at two," she lied. "Maybe if you told the sellers the problem, they could work with us? We're very serious about this house. Twelve more hours should do it."

"I can ask."

"Thank you. Please call me as soon as you know anything." Susanne hung the phone back on its wall base, then turned to her father. "Have you heard from your CB friend about Patrick?"

Papa Fred took a long draught of his hot toddy. "Huh. Did I forget to tell you I talked to him?"

"When?"

"On the way to the store."

"Then, yes, you forgot."

He grunted. "The short story is that Patrick is fine."

A cool wave of relief washed over Susanne, but it wasn't enough to douse her anger at her husband. "I need to talk to him."

"We-ell, I suggest you get on the road then, because the phones are still down on the reservation, according to Chuckles."

Her daddy was kidding, but it was an idea worth considering. If she went to Fort Washakie, Susanne could get an answer from Patrick about the house. And she could see for herself what was up with this overly friendly widow while she was there. But did she really want to uproot herself and make a winter trek across the state to find her husband when she had a houseful of guests to entertain in Buffalo?

She hesitated for a split second, then put both fingers in her mouth and whistled. Heads swiveled her way. "Listen-up, everyone. When I get back from the library, I'm loading up the Suburban to go get Patrick, leaving in one hour. Who's up for a scenic road trip to one of the largest Indian reservations in the world?"

Perry groaned. Leslie babbled, and Matthew didn't look up from sinking Perry's battleship. But Ferdinand stood and woofed, bass and booming.

"Not you, hound. You're going to visit your Aunt Ronnie next door."

The dog ran to the back door and whined, then put his feet up high on the glass half-light.

Despite herself, Susanne laughed. Her friend Ronnie outdid her in everything fun and outdoorsy. Even Ferdinand thought so. Susanne had resented it at first, even been intimidated by it, but she'd gotten over it, mostly. "Down, hound. I didn't mean literally this second."

Papa Fred was already on his feet. "Let's get moving, then."

No surprise there. He was happiest doing something—anything—and Susanne had actually worried their visit would be too sedentary for him.

Catherine said, "I'll make hot toddies for the road. Non-drivers only, of course."

Shelley and Will looked at each other, shrugged, and grinned.

Shelley said, "Sounds like an adventure. Count us in."

Susanne warned, "Be sure anyone who's coming packs an overnight bag. This trip comes with no guarantees."

"Where will we stay?" Mama Cat asked.

"There's bound to be hotels available in Lander. Daddy, can you book us some rooms?"

"Sure thing, Tootie." He goosed her on the bottom, which she hated, then grabbed the phone book.

Just like that, the whole group was going along for the ride. Susanne nodded in satisfaction. This felt right. It was what she needed to do. She hustled to the door to go pick up her errant daughter.

CHAPTER SIXTEEN: SURPRISE

Patrick

Someone had burned the coffee at Bronco's Auto Repair, from the smell of the shop. It was even stronger than the odors of rubber, exhaust, cigarettes, and petroleum products. A tool company calendar, three years out of date, hung on the wall beside a clock that promised it was 10:17. A stack of fly-fishing magazines on the counter looked positively antique. Patrick lifted the top one. 1963. He set it back down.

He didn't see Constance anywhere, but he decided to stick around and check on the status of the Cherokee before following her to the funeral home. No one was at the counter, however. A sign taped to it said: RING THE BELL, HAVE A SEAT. He did the first, electing to stand at the counter and wait instead of the second.

Five minutes later, he was in the midst of learning how to tie "the most productive nymph pattern ever" when a man walked in. He limped badly on the left and was wiping his hands on a greasy rag, a cigarette with a red tip hanging from the corner of his mouth and threatening to drop a load of ash on the floor. He tucked the rag into a back pocket. "Can I help you?" His left eye blinked repeatedly and never quite opened the whole way.

"My friend has a Cherokee in for brake work. I'm swinging by to check on it before I join her."

The man adjusted his glasses with his left hand. The fingers were bent stiffly at an odd angle. "Should have that finished up in an hour or two."

"Were you able to tell what happened?"

"Oh, sure. That was easy enough. The brake line had been cut."

In a day of bad surprises, the man's words were another sucker punch to Patrick's gut. "Cut? Are you sure?"

"One hundred percent. I did the brake pads on the Jeep myself last year. The lines were in great shape. Them brake pads should've lasted another forty-thousand miles, and the hoses were good for life."

Cut. When had it happened? The Cherokee had been left alone at the ranch, the café, and the clinic. But surely it couldn't have made it all the way from the ranch before failing in Lander? "How far could she have driven it after they were cut?"

"Hard to say. Depends on how fast the fluid leaked out. The line was only cut at one wheel. As cold as it's been, and with the way the line was crimped where it was cut, it wouldn't have leaked too fast."

"So, it could have happened as far away as their ranch."

"The T-ton in Kinnear? That's a long way, but maybe. The brakes would get a little soft before they went out. When did you notice that?"

"I wasn't driving, and Constance didn't mention anything."

The man's eye twitched and batted open and closed. "Wherever it happened, I'd say somebody isn't feeling very friendly toward Mrs. Teton."

Patrick pulled at his chin. Clearly. An image of the word BETRAYOR on Big Mike's forehead flashed through his mind, followed by faces. Her brother. His poker buddies. Verna. The hunters in the café. Officer Dann, with Constance's finger in his face.

Whoever it was, hanging out with Constance Teton was beginning to feel like high risk behavior.

CHAPTER SEVENTEEN: CONFRONT

Lander, Wyoming
Monday, December 20, 1976, One forty-five p.m.

Patrick

Patrick walked up the shoveled front walkway to a dilapidated two-story wooden home with a Blackhawk Brothers Funeral Home sign nailed to a column. An under-nourished German shepherd was sitting on its haunches on the porch. Patrick ascended the steps, then did a double take. It was no dog. It was a coyote. He jumped back, startled. The animal dashed past him down the steps, disappearing around a snow-covered hedge.

Not normal coyote behavior. But the sight of the animal did more than startle him. At the hospital, the lab tech. Her name. Canis Latrans. He shook his head. If he was recalling things correctly from wildlife biology at the University of Texas, canis latrans was Latin for barking dog. It was also the binomial name for a coyote. His skin tingled like someone was watching him, and he turned in a circle on the porch. He didn't see anyone. His mind returned to the lab tech. It was a decidedly odd name. He must have misheard her.

Patrick entered the lobby. "Hello?"

No one answered. He was alone in a room that was masquerading as a 1950s parlor, and doing it pretty successfully. It smelled like the perfume Susanne's grandmother used to wear. A Southern garden, complete with Spanish moss and magnolia trees. What had been the name of it? He concentrated for a moment, and it came back to him. White Shoulders. He smiled, but it was rueful. Thinking of it made him miss Susanne, and her Chanel Number Five scent. He'd first bought it for her as an anniversary gift, years ago, and it had become a tradition. An image of the soft skin of her neck, a memory of the unique smell of the perfume on her skin, and he drooped. Susanne. He didn't travel much, and when he did, he never went a day without calling in. Had it only been thirty-six hours since he'd left home? It seemed like a week.

He paced the small room, wondering what the family had done for their first night together. He could almost hear his father-in-law's wheezing laugh escalating to a rumble, then a boom. No one could resist laughing when Fred was in the room. And his mother-in-law, Catherine. Prettier than a movie star, soft spoken, but with a wicked sense of humor. She made every grandchild her "Little Precious." How many times had she let Trish stand on a chair at the counter in the kitchen of the Brown's Dallas home making "salad," a concoction of all the odds and ends in the kitchen? Vegetables. Condiments. Bread. Cheese. Left-over meats. Flour. Sugar. Dressings. Trish would stir it up and serve it proudly, and they'd all pretend to take bites. Then Catherine would bustle in with a big bowl of sugared strawberries to divert Trish's attention while she hid the nasty salad concoction.

The memories tugged at his heart. He wished he was there. He hated that he'd left the hospital without calling Susanne. Or demanding an update on Clem. He'd just been so thrown off stride by the lab tech insisting Wes had never dropped the urine sample with them. There was no way there'd be a pay phone at a funeral home either. Maybe they'd let him make a collect call? If anyone ever came out to greet him, that was.

"Hello?" he called again. "Constance?"

The mechanic at Bronco's Auto Repair said Constance left the shop half an hour before him. Unless someone had spirited her away from the funeral home or she'd made an unexpected stop, she had to be here, and nearly done.

A woman in a head-to-toe traditional beaded Indian dress emerged from behind a door. He would have expected pearls and heels in this "Leave it to Beaver" parlor.

"May I help you?" She had a voice like a gentle wind. Never mind the attire, her soothing tone was definitely a match for a funeral home.

"I hope so. I'm meeting Constance Teton here. I've, um, brought the checkbook."

The woman raised an eyebrow. The gentle wind turned gusty. "I taught Constance in high school. She was always a fast—"

The door opened again. Constance stuck her head out and waggled her fingers. "I'm back here, Patrick."

Pulling at the collar of his coat, he looked at the woman who had greeted him, and he saw the expression on her face. It mirrored his own feelings about the finger waggle. *Inappropriate.* Had the time come to say something to Constance? He wasn't sure what to say though. For now, in front of this woman, he could only ignore it.

He nodded at the woman, hoping she didn't think there was something going on between Constance and him. "Um, thank you."

Constance beckoned him again, and he walked through the door and into a carpeted hallway with her, careful to stay an arm's length away. As soon as the door shut behind them, the lights dimmed. He swiped the wall by the door frame, looking for a light switch but didn't find one.

She put her hand on his bicep as they walked. "We're in the back office going over the invoice. If we give them a check, we can be on our way."

Patrick weighed whether to tell her about the cut brake line. But anything that slowed down their departure from the intimate hallway was a bad thing. He moved out of her reach. He'd tell her later. "Why don't I just sign one and let you give it to him?"

"No, come on, you're almost there." She pushed through a swinging door.

Patrick moved gratefully toward the bright light beyond it into an office that was more like a little display room. Open, silk-lined caskets crowded in on the room from a sturdy display rack on one wall. Photographs of past services hung on another. The smell of White Shoulders was gone, replaced with Pinesol and mothballs. It wasn't a good combination.

A man stood beside a desk. He was dressed more in line with Patrick's expectations. Wyoming formal. A brown three-piece suit and striped necktie. A dressy Western shirt and cowboy boots. His hair looked wet, long and slicked back into a low ponytail. He pinched at a slim, straight mustache as he motioned them in.

Constance put a hand on Patrick's back, bringing him forward with her. He was unnervingly aware of how close their bodies were, but he couldn't get any distance from her without jerking his arm away.

"Joe Blackhawk, this is Doctor Patrick Flint. Patrick, this is Joe Blackhawk. He's my uncle. And he's giving me a good deal."

Patrick shook the older man's hand. "Nice to meet you, Mr. Blackhawk. Was that your aunt out front, then, Constance?"

She dropped her arm from his back. "It was. Her name is Jo, too. Funny, I know."

Joe smiled. "It was meant to be. Written in the stars. Sometimes you just know. Like with Constance and Big Mike. We're so, so sorry, niece."

"Thank you." Constance paused but didn't elaborate about her relationship with Big Mike. She lifted a sheet of paper from the desk and handed it to Patrick. "Here's the total. Make it out to Blackhawk Brothers Funeral Home."

He took the chair in front of the desk and wrote the check carefully. Susanne was always teasing him about his doctor's scrawl. He'd had checks returned more than once because the name and amount weren't readable. As he pushed it across the desk to Blackhawk, he stood. "I'll just be out front. Nice to meet you."

"You don't have to go," Constance said.

"I need to, uh, make a phone call."

Joe nodded. "Just ask my wife to borrow one. She can show you where it is."

"Thanks." Patrick nearly sprinted out of the close confines of the office. In the dark hallway, he bumped into someone and backed up quickly. "Pardon me. Is that you, Jo?"

But even as the words left his mouth, he realized the figure was too substantial to be the woman he'd seen in the lobby. As his eyes adjusted, he thought he recognized the person. A man with dark sunglasses and a round brimmed hat.

"No," the man said.

The voice was one he definitely recognized. "Eddie?"

"And you are?"

"Dr. Flint, from the health clinic."

Eddie's face took shape. He tipped the sunglasses down his nose. "You mean Patrick, the guy that helped my sister try to ruin my livelihood, then spent the night with her on the day her husband died?" His tone was terse and hostile.

Patrick was nearly speechless. "Uh . . ."

"When you stick your nose in other people's business, it might get bitten off. Something for you to remember."

If his first comment had been hostile, the second was threatening. Patrick decided the best way to defuse the situation was to refuse to engage. "Listen, about last night and your game. We heard gunfire, and Constance was worried you might have been shot." It was only stretching the truth a little.

"I'm not talking about last night. I'm talking about those medical tests you did on Big Mike. It wasn't your place. You're disrespecting our ways. Go home to your own people and leave us alone."

Patrick found it rich that a man who'd disrespected Big Mike on his own property, taking for granted all the help Big Mike gave him, would lecture Patrick on the subject. But he kept his lip zipped. "It's my duty as a physician to determine a cause of death."

"It was a violation of his body that went against his wishes and those of my sister."

He wasn't going to win this debate. Lifting his hands, he said, "All right. I don't want any trouble with you."

"You've already got trouble with me."

"Defuse" and "refuse to engage" went out the window. This guy was a jerk. Patrick stepped closer to him. "Yeah? So where were you this morning? In a camo truck taking pot shots at me by any chance?" As soon as he'd said it, he remembered the camo truck at Lawanda's. Just because it had been there for breakfast didn't mean Eddie hadn't been in it at the time the shot was fired.

"What are you talking about?"

Gritting his teeth, Patrick spat, "Just let me by, and I'll be on my way."

Eddie stepped partway aside, but Patrick still had to bump him to get past. It felt like two big horn rams butting heads, save for the pawing of hooves. As he entered the parlor-lobby, he felt the heat of Eddie's glare on his back until the door shut behind him.

Exhaling, Patrick searched the front area of the house, but he couldn't find Aunt Jo. There was a phone on the reception desk, though. He picked it up. Dial tone. He put thoughts of Eddie aside. He could finally call his wife.

"Hello, Mrs. Blackhawk?" He waited a moment, then, when he didn't get a response, he dialed zero. He rolled his shoulders, trying to get his hackles down before he talked to Susanne.

"Operator, may I help you?" a woman's voice said.

"I'd like to make a collect call." He gave her his home phone number.

A few seconds later, he heard a busy signal. Disappointment knocked the wind out of him.

"I'm sorry, sir, but your party's line is busy."

"Thank you."

Patrick walked to an ornately draped window. He hated not talking to his wife. Besides just wanting to check on her, he wanted to tell her about his encounter with Eddie. It was beyond uncalled for, and on a day where someone had shot at Patrick, a little frightening. What was it to Eddie whether Big Mike's urine was tested? He hadn't acted like he cared much about anything except his sister's wallet until now.

But then Patrick had a disturbing thought. Maybe Eddie didn't want Patrick to identify the cause of death, because he knew how Big Mike had died. Possibly even had a hand in it. Eddie stood to gain as much as anyone by Big Mike's death. To hear Constance speak of it, Big Mike was a slim whisker away from kicking Eddie off the T-ton ranch and reporting his illegal poker club to the authorities. Eddie seemed the self-interested type. Was he the murdering type as well? A chill rattled through him. Or was he the kind instead to cover up for his sister? It amounted to the same thing—he kept his standing on the ranch, even bettered it if Constance's pockets were fatter. Hell, they could have plotted and carried out Big Mike's death together.

But if that were the case, who wrote BETRAYOR on Big Mike's forehead? And who cut Constance's brake line?

"You ready to go?"

Constance's voice startled him, and he jumped. He turned to her, keeping his gaze on his feet. It felt silly to think it, but he was afraid Constance would see his thoughts in his eyes. "Um, yeah. I guess." Remembering Eddie, he asked, "What's your brother doing here?"

Constance seemed not to notice his hesitation. "Eddie's here?"

"Yeah. I just ran into him."

"He does odd jobs for my aunt and uncle sometimes." When Patrick nodded, she added, "How did it go at the hospital? Did you find Wes?"

Patrick was grateful for the safe topic. "No. I found someone who saw him there yesterday, but they didn't know where he went."

"I'm sorry. I guess you're stuck with me." She smiled. "I'm starving. Let's get lunch."

He fell in step beside her and kept his tone casual. "The lab said they never got the sample Wes was supposed to drop off."

She frowned, then shrugged. "I don't trust anybody at that hospital. If I'm ever really sick, ship me off to Salt Lake City or Denver."

Patrick pushed open the door. The mid-day sun was bright, and the snow sparkled like a blanket of diamonds. "I'm thinking we should contact Dann again."

"Why?"

"Don't you think it's weird that the sample just disappeared?"

"Honestly, no. And maybe it's for the best—a sign from Big Mike."

Patrick didn't think so. "Does it change your mind at all that someone cut the brake line on your Cherokee?"

She whirled to face him. "What did you just say?"

CHAPTER EIGHTEEN: WITNESS

LANDER, WYOMING
MONDAY, DECEMBER 20, 1976, TWO P.M.

Patrick

The Dairy Land Drive-In was neither solely dairy nor solely a drive-in, but it did seem to pattern itself after Dairy Queen. Being from Texas, Patrick had come of age on Dilly Bars and Hunger Busters. Every small town in the state had a Dairy Queen, and that was a lot of small towns when you lived in a state roughly the size of France. Dairy Land served a packed house of customers under a four-sided red roof. Enlarged photographs of food from their menu hung from the walls, along with old vinyl records. The smell of cigarette smoke and frying beef and potatoes filled the air.

Constance had insisted on him claiming a table while she placed their orders, but first Patrick had tried the pay phone. It was out of order. So, he grabbed a table and watched the traffic roll by on Main Street, letting his mind wander. His previous trips to volunteer at the Fort Washakie clinic had been so normal that he'd considered bringing Susanne and the kids with him sometime for a minivacation. They could use it as a jumping off point to the wonders of the western side of the state. They'd been to Yellowstone before, but there was so much more to see. The Tetons. The Jim Bridger Mountains. The hot springs in Thermopolis. The Snake River on the Idaho border. Taking the long way home on the Beartooth Highway. After this visit, though, he wasn't so sure he wanted his family here. All of Wyoming was rugged. Don't tread on me was the state motto, after all. But he was seeing a side of the reservation that was a little more lawless and a lot more unwelcoming than he liked.

The door opened, and two men joined the line. He recognized them both. The first was long-haired Joshua Manning, he of the ranch next door to T-Ton and the chip on his shoulder toward Big Mike. The other was Elvin, whose last name he couldn't recall—the light-skinned poker player who had been so confrontational with Constance. The men were deep in conversation and didn't see him.

Constance approached with a red tray that barely contained all the food she'd ordered. She put it between them. "Thanks again for writing the check. I'll pay you back as fast as I can get a check to you."

Patrick claimed a double cheeseburger, large fries, and chocolate milkshake. "No problem." After Constance removed her food from the tray, he added it to a stack on top of a trashcan lid.

When he returned, Constance held a hand in front of her mouth, talking while she chewed. "I want to hear all about the brake line."

"The mechanic said someone cut one of them in two." Patrick popped some French fries in his mouth. They were hot, salty, and tasty. He followed them up with a few more.

She shook her head. "But where? When?"

He repeated what he'd learned from the mechanic, that with the cold weather and the crimped edges of the cut line, the Cherokee could have driven a considerable distance before all the fluid ran out. "So, it's hard to say. The health center. The café. Maybe even your house. What's easy to say is that someone tried to cause you big problems. They didn't care if you were hurt or killed, which you could have been."

There was a snort from a table next to them. Glancing up, Patrick discovered Joshua and Elvin had chosen to sit there. He looked around the restaurant. It had been the only empty table in the place, of all the luck. The two men had spotted Constance and were listening intently and blatantly to their conversation.

Elvin stabbed a steak finger at her. "It's almost like you'd caused someone problems and they were trying to pay you back, Constance."

Joshua nodded. "Maybe your husband killed more dogs somewhere."

Constance dropped her burger, then started wrapping it in the paper it was served in. She lowered her voice. "Let's eat on the road."

Without comment, Patrick wrapped his food, too.

As they stood, Elvin threw an arm out. "Ah, and the atmosphere improves, just like that."

Patrick had had enough. "Stop harassing her. She has every right to determine who comes on her property and what they do there."

Elvin narrowed his eyes. "What business of yours is it, doctor? Sounds like you're taking a personal interest in the widow. Spending the night alone with her will do that to a man. Or so I've heard."

Patrick was stunned. First Eddie, now this guy, wanting to smear his and Constance's reputation. He'd done nothing wrong. To say otherwise was insulting and potentially damaging.

Before he could fire back, Constance slammed her hand down on the table between the two men. The sound was like a gunshot. "Listen, you sleazy bastard. What I do is none of your business. But what you do on my land is, whether it's an illegal poker club, or tampering with my brakes. You're a bully, but that doesn't scare me. I meant what I said last night. Don't make me prove it."

Joshua laughed.

Elvin clapped. "Bravo, Connie. Reminds me of your thespian days. But rumor has it that you've already proven what you'll do to people who mess with you."

Constance growled as she stood, then blew like a norther out the door of the restaurant. Patrick gathered trash from the table and threw it away. He stole one more look at the two men before he left the building. Joshua was reaching across the table. Elvin stuck his hand out, and the men shook, like they'd struck some sort of agreement. They wore satisfied smiles, and, when their eyes lifted, Patrick followed their gaze to Constance, who was pacing back and forth along the front sidewalk.

Someone had sabotaged her car. Desecrated Big Mike's body. Killed him. It had to be tough, even if his doubts and discomfort warred with his empathy for her. Frowning, he joined her. Tears had dried on her cheeks.

"Assholes." She wove her arm through his. "Let's go get the Cherokee."

Just like that, she made him uncomfortable again. With their food cradled in his arms, he couldn't get away from her without dropping it all on the ground. He let her lead him back toward Bronco's Auto Repair, feeling like every eye in town was watching and judging them. Elvin's words rang through his head again. "Spending the night alone with her will do that to a man. Or so I've heard." He clenched his jaw.

Then he had a thought. Elvin hadn't just insinuated Patrick slept with Constance. He'd been saying she slept around with other men, too. Before or after she was married to Big Mike? She already had the means and opportunity to kill her husband, and an incentive to cover it up and block any testing or autopsy. Verna was claiming Big Mike's ranch and life insurance was motive. A lover would only strengthen it.

The Constance he knew just wouldn't. Couldn't. But did he know the *real* Constance Teton?

"Constance?" A woman with the voice of a little girl stopped in front of them.

A head shorter than Constance, she wore her hair shoulder length, straight, and down. She was holding the hand of a red-cheeked little boy who looked to be two or three years old. His steps were slow and wobbly in snow boots and a puffy yellow snow suit. The woman and Constance seemed about the same age—mid-twenties—but, while Constance was lean and athletic, the other woman was curvy-headed-toward-plump.

"What is it?" Constance was expressionless.

"I'm sorry about Big Mike."

"Thank you."

The little boy leaned over, pulling his mother's hand and whining. She was firm as a rock against his efforts. "He owed us money. Do you know if he left anything aside to cover it?"

Constance fixed her eyes in the distance over the woman's head. "I have no idea."

"He promised us." She scooped the boy into her arms, facedown with his legs dangling.

"That was between you and him. I had no part in it. Ever."

"It's just hard to believe a man like him would betray his responsibilities."

Constance stepped around the woman and child, tugging Patrick with her. "Sorry."

Patrick's ears pricked. Betray? He swiveled his head back toward the woman. The sweet mask on her face had slipped, leaving an expression of pure hatred in its place.

CHAPTER NINETEEN: CRASH

Buffalo, Wyoming
Monday, December 20, 1976, Two p.m.

Perry

Perry's mom was standing in the middle of the living room with her hands on her hips and bags at her feet. Her voice was irritated. "Hurry up, Perry! I don't want to be driving after dark on strange roads."

He ignored her. He was sitting in the dining room chair closest to the back door, waiting for his chance to make a break for the shed. His mom wasn't really talking to him anyway. He was packed and ready with his bag by the door downstairs. She was just using him to send a message to get everyone else moving. His mom always said that Mama Cat and Aunt Shelley were born a day late and a dollar short. He wasn't entirely sure what that meant, except for the late part, which was pretty obvious every time he was around them. They were S-L-O-W. Aunt Shelley was cooing to baby Leslie and feeding her a bottle. Mama Cat had decided to go change clothes. Uncle Will and Papa Fred were having some kind of drinking contest while Papa Fred was working the CB again, this time for a road and weather report.

"No new snow between us and Lander since last night. The roads have been plowed. The low today was a brisk five degrees. But there's a storm blowing in this evening." He held up a coffee mug. "Top me off, Kitty Cat?"

Mama Cat turned around from her clothes-changing mission and went back to the kitchen. She picked up one of two thermoses and poured Papa Fred a steamy refill. Uncle Will tipped his mug back and drained it, so she refilled his, too.

"Mama," Susanne pleaded, now standing at the top of the stairs, an overnight bag on one shoulder and her purse on the other. "Please. We have to get moving."

"Just a minute, Tootie."

The childhood nickname for his mom made him giggle. She claimed it was because her sister couldn't say Susanne when they were little. She'd tried to say Susie instead and it had come out as Tootie. Papa Fred swore it was because Susanne had been a tooty little girl, as in butt toots. Perry giggled again.

"Daddy, do we have a hotel reservation?"

"All set."

Mama Cat disappeared down the hall again. She and Papa Fred were staying in his parents' room. Aunt Shelley and Uncle Will had his room, with baby Leslie. His mom was sleeping with Trish for now, but when his dad came home, Trish would be out in the basement playroom with him and Matthew. Trish had been a real turd ever since Brandon dumped her, and he was dreading her sleeping in the same room as him. But it would give him a chance to pay her back for how mean she'd been to him. In the middle of the night there would be no parents around for her to tattle to, either. But revenge was on hold for this crazy trip to the reservation. What was up with his mom, anyway, that she was dragging them across the state? Dad was working. No big deal. He'd be home soon. But being stuck in the Suburban with his cast on was going to suck for Perry. If their hotel had a hot tub, he wouldn't even be able to get in it.

He had to get this cast off. *Had to.* Since his grandmother wasn't going to be ready in the next five minutes, he had a chance. His last chance.

He snuck a glance at his mother. She wasn't paying any attention to him.

"Trish, where are you? Are you packed?" she shouted.

Trish came pounding up the stairs. "No, I'm not packed. I just got home."

"We're leaving in five minutes."

"Fine. Go."

His mom pasted on a fake smile. "We would have had more time if you'd been at the library, and I hadn't had to go looking for you."

"Uh-oh, Trish is in trouble," Perry said. He hated drawing attention to himself before his covert mission to the shed, but this was too good to resist.

She shot him the bird behind her back.

"Mom, she's flipping me off."

"Trish, stop . . . gesturing rudely at your brother. Stop antagonizing her, Perry. And, Trish, next time, don't go sneaking off, because I know exactly where to find you."

"I wasn't sneaking off. I was on the phone."

"You were waiting on a street corner for a certain boy you're not supposed to be seeing, and we both know it. Now you're just wasting time. And I still need you to check on the horses—you remember Goldie, the one you've been neglecting since you started going with Brandon?"

"I have not been neglecting her. It's winter."

"Meet me at the Suburban. You'd better hustle." His mom disappeared down the stairs.

Trish growled.

Perry hid a smile with his hand, then bolted. Ferdinand met him outside the door, shoving his cold nose into Perry's hand. "Hey, boy. Come with me."

The dog flopped down in the dirt floor of the shed, pretty much taking up the entire space. Perry stepped over him and considered his tool options. The screwdriver had been a bust, as was the saw. That left the mallet and chisel. They looked wicked, big, and scary. But he'd been thinking about how to do this. Most kids would probably put the chisel on the outside of the cast. If the mallet missed the chisel, it would bash into the side of his leg. Or if he hit the chisel too hard, it could go right through the plaster and stab him. So, he had decided to put the chisel inside the cast and angle it sideways, then use the mallet to drive the chisel from the inside of the plaster to the outside.

He felt pretty smart, if he did say so himself.

He sat down and pushed his butt against Ferdinand. "Scoot over, Ferdie."

The dog didn't give an inch. Leaning against him for support instead, Perry inserted the chisel and levered it back and forth until the tip was embedded in the plaster.

"Ready, boy?"

Ferdinand thumped his tail against the ground, stirring up a dust cloud. Perry coughed and waved one hand. When it cleared, he raised the mallet high, ready to strike the chisel. Picturing it slipping and impaling him in the leg, he lost his nerve. He pulled up mid-strike and barely tapped it. Nothing happened, good or bad, and he laughed.

"Okay, that wasn't awful."

Using one hand, he reared back again and gave the handle of the chisel a good thump. The chisel's spikey end slid against the inside of the plaster cast. It didn't gouge him, but it didn't feel great either.

"I've gotta be braver, Ferdie."

Perry thought about his football games earlier that fall. The other boys had been playing longer than him, and he rode the bench at first. When the coach had finally called his number to put him in the game, he'd been terrified. His dad had warned him there was a big difference between thinking about football, practicing football, and playing in a game. The other team was bigger, faster, and stronger than you'd imagined. The ground was harder. The hits more bone-crushing. Perry hadn't believed him until he'd stepped on the field. Seeing his opponents lined up on the other side of the ball, Perry had never been more scared in his life. But he'd pictured his favorite animal, the wolverine. The wolverine might be small, but it was always the toughest animal in a fight.

In Perry's heart, he knew he was the wolverine, and all his fear had fallen away. Or most of it. The hits had hurt, but he'd given it all he had, and a few games later, he was starting. Everything had worked out fine until he'd broken his ankle. But even that hadn't been as bad as he would have expected.

He was the wolverine, and he was tough. The mallet and chisel weren't going to be as bad as his fears either.

He growled like a wolverine at Ferdinand. "Grrr."

The dog lifted his head and cocked it, then whimpered.

Perry laughed, took a deep breath and then another, and swung the mallet. CLANK. The point seemed to dig into the plaster a little bit. He pushed the handle. It was wedged in solid.

"Okay!"

He gripped the mallet in both hands and swung it like a baseball bat. CLANK. The mallet caught the head of the chisel a little off center. The chisel slipped sideways. The tip gouged his ankle, and he smashed one of his fingers between the mallet and the chisel.

"Ouch!"

For a moment, Perry held perfectly still, trying to decide if he'd broken anything. Definitely not the plaster. But the throbbing pain in his ankle and his bleeding finger probably weren't good. He took a few more deep breaths. The pain started going away. He was fine.

He re-evaluated his process. Judging by how his first few strikes had gone, one-handed was the way to go, but with more arm strength. The chisel tip had slid out of the groove he'd made with his one good strike. He repositioned it.

"Ready, aim . . ." As he said, "fire," he swung.

"Perry! What the hell are you doing?" his mom said from the door of the shed.

His mother never cursed. Her voice and words startled him, and his muscles jerked harder than he'd planned. Ferdinand leapt to his feet and howled. WAM. The mallet connected with the chisel head, and the point busted out the other side of his cast. Perry dropped the mallet. The chisel was jammed tight against his leg inside his cast.

It didn't feel good, but he wasn't about to show it.

"Uh, hi, Mom."

CHAPTER TWENTY: REUNITE

Patrick

Constance didn't speak the whole way to Bronco's and back to the clinic, where they were stopping to check the doorknob and feed logs to the boiler. They'd camped in the dingy waiting area at Bronco's for two hours, until the Cherokee was finally ready. She'd barely said a word the whole time. From her black mood, Patrick decided it was best to leave her to her silence, despite how badly he wanted to ask her about the woman and child they'd seen.

Patrick was in a dark mood of his own. He'd tried to call Susanne collect from Bronco's shop, but no one had answered. She'd been his best friend and closest confidante since the day she'd invited him to their high school Sadie Hawkins dance. With all that was going on here, he needed her. If he were able to vocalize all his thoughts about Big Mike and Constance to her, she'd help them make sense. But he was foiled at every turn when he tried to reach her.

He mouthed a prayer. *Dear God, please help me catch a break. I miss my wife and kids.*

He felt Constance's eyes watching him when she should have had them on the road, but she didn't say anything about his lips moving, at least. When they reached the clinic, she parked at the front door but didn't turn off the Cherokee.

"Are you coming?" he asked.

"Give me a minute."

"Suit yourself."

He hefted the bundle of firewood they'd brought from Lander out of the back. He walked to the building and grasped the doorknob. The door swung open. He looked at the notes taped to it. Where before there were four, now there were only two. The note to Wes was gone, with nothing in its place, as was the note to the transport driver. Riley's note and the one to the public at large were still there. Over his shoulder, Patrick looked back at Constance. She had the CB mic to her face. He pushed the rest of the way into the building. It was much colder inside than outside, and there was no hiss from the radiator. He picked up the phone. No dial tone. He flicked a light switch. No electricity. He checked the boiler room. No wood. Nothing was fixed.

First things first. He fired up the boiler and radiator. Then he checked the exam room where Big Mike had been earlier. The man's body was gone. Well, that was something, at least.

He returned to the doorknob just as Constance reached it.

"Someone's been here." Patrick scraped leftover tape off the glass.

Constance frowned, examining the door. "Must not have been Riley. He would have fixed the doorknob."

"And lit the boiler. If you've got a toolbox, I can try to fix the knob." He eyeballed the handle, squinting and turning his head.

Constance rummaged in the trunk of her Cherokee. She set a big, well-stocked kit on the ground.

Gray clouds were amassing on the northern horizon. "Looks like we're going to be getting more weather." Patrick crouched and dug through the tools. He selected a screwdriver.

"Just what we need. Let's see if we can get the weather report." Her words were friendly, but the atmosphere between the two of them had soured. She opened the driver's door and turned on the engine and the radio. A country song crackled from the speakers. "At least this works, even if nothing else in Fremont County does."

Willie Nelson crooned "Stay All Night." Patrick twisted the cover plate off the door, then loosened the bolts. When the song ended, the weather report came on. After he re-centered the knob in the door hole, he tightened the bolts with the screwdriver and replaced the cover plate.

"Looks like it's going to be a really white Christmas as part two of that big storm we just dug out from under hits tonight. Stay off the roads after the dinner hour, everyone."

"Great," Patrick muttered. He straightened. "Got it, I think." He tested the knob. It worked.

The sound of approaching vehicles pulled his eyes to the north. A Toyota Corolla with a deer carcass strapped to its roof sped down the road. Behind it was Gussie. He squinted, trying to see the driver of the Travelall. As the big green beast pulled closer, he spotted the walrus mustache. Wes. He waved, and his relief made him feel loose and light-headed. Wes was a grown man and could take care of himself, but Patrick had his doubts about their ongoing reception on the reservation. Wes followed the Corolla into the parking area.

The Corolla pulled to a stop next to the Cherokee with the Travelall one space further down. A thin, knobby young man jumped out of the Corolla. He strode quickly toward them, eyes on Constance. Wes followed at a slower pace.

The man addressed Constance. "My kid's got the chicken pox. Are you open?"

Wes waved to Patrick but hung back, giving the other man a chance to address his medical concerns.

Constance seemed to notice the deer for the first time and scowled. "You know hunting out of season hurts us all, Tall Horse."

He stepped into a wide-legged, pugilistic stance and crossed his arms. "We're not going to have the same problem with you we had with your husband, are we?"

Constance locked eyes with him. "I think wildlife management is in the best interests of our people. If that's a problem to you, then, yes, you're going to have the same problem with me you had with Big Mike."

"Well, you know what happened to him."

"Is that a threat or an admission, Tall Horse?"

Patrick stepped between them. "You said your child has chicken pox. May I help you?"

Constance didn't look away from Tall Horse. "We're not open. You'll need to take him into Lander or Riverton."

"You look open to me."

"You need to get your eyes checked. We've got no power, no heat, no nothing." Constance turned away from him and fiddled with the door-knob, not seeming to notice it had been fixed.

Patrick cleared his throat. He could understand why Constance was upset. But a child shouldn't be punished because of it. "Sir, you don't really need medical care unless he's got an infection. Why don't I come take a look at him? I can give you some suggestions on how to make him more comfortable."

Tall Horse sneered. "Mrs. Teton already made it clear she doesn't want to help us. We'll go where people care about the children of the Eastern Shoshone." The man glowered at Constance, then turned and stalked back to his car.

"But, sir." Patrick called after him. "Sir." He gave up and put his hands on his hips. That had been intense and unfortunate. Big Mike had certainly made some unpleasant enemies, and Constance had inherited them along with the ranch and the life insurance, it seemed.

"That was . . . something," Wes said.

"Man, have I been worried about you." Patrick clapped him on the shoulder.

"And vice versa. I got stranded in Lander last night. Long story. But I got your note earlier. I tried the ranch, and you weren't there, so I was heading back into Lander to call Susanne, and here you are."

"Hi, to you, too, Wes." Constance cocked a hip and tossed her hair over her shoulder, her onyx eyes snapping.

He hugged her. To Patrick, she seemed stiff and resistant. "Hello, Constance."

Patrick said, "How's Clem?"

"He's a sick little boy. They confirmed bacterial meningitis, but they got him started on the antibiotics. The doctor there expected he would be fine"

"That's good to hear. I went by the hospital earlier to check on the urine sample."

"Did they get it sent off to Denver?"

"The hospital lost it."

Wes put his hands on his hips. "You're shitting me?"

"Nope. They claimed they never received it."

"I dropped it off personally. With explicit instructions."

"I believe you. And the receptionist remembered seeing you. It was pretty weird."

Wes frowned, pulling his bushy mustache down with his lips. "They told me they liked to send their samples out for testing to the lab at Saint Joseph Hospital in Denver. I okayed it, and they said it would be on the road first thing this morning."

Patrick shrugged. "I don't know what to tell you, except that we're dead in the water."

"Dammit. Do we need to go get another sample?"

Constance's eyes were hooded. He decided it wasn't a good idea to talk about Big Mike's cause of death in front of her.

He said, "We can talk about it later. Meanwhile, there's still no power or phones here. We were about to leave anyway."

Wes held a palm up, catching a handful of the snowflakes that had just started falling. "The radio guy made it sound like we're in for another big dump of snow."

"I heard. As badly as I want to get home, I don't think driving out right now is a brilliant plan." The thought of his warm bed and hot wife was crushing. He hated missing Christmas vacation with the kids and Susanne's family. And he really wanted an update on the house they were trying to buy.

"Can't argue with that, Doc."

"You guys should just stay out at the ranch with me." Constance's offer lacked the warmth it had the day before.

Patrick was *not* about to stay with her. He shook his head. "I can't impose on you again. You've had a major tragedy, plus with all that's happened today, we need to give you some space. Wes, I'll spring for a motel room for us. I have a lot to catch you up on." Patrick saw a peculiar look cross Wes' face, but he kept his own eyes on Constance.

"Okay." Her voice was listless. She used the toe of her boot to crush a clump of snow into the concrete. "I've got to figure out what to eat. There's no food or power at my house. Not that I have the energy to cook anyway."

Wes patted her shoulder. "Why don't you follow us to Lander, and we can all eat together? If that's okay with you, Patrick?"

Patrick pursed his lips. He had a feeling his friend would regret making this offer, but he didn't blame him. It's what he would have done himself—had done—before today. "Fine by me."

A smile returned to Constance's face, if not yet her eyes. "Okay. That sounds good."

"It's settled then." Wes smiled back at her.

Patrick fetched his doctor's bag from the Cherokee while Constance got behind the wheel. He put it in the back seat of the Travelall.

Wes was in the driver's seat, spinning his keys on one finger. "Got your bag of snake oil, I see. Now you're ready for anything."

"You know it." Patrick settled into the familiar passenger seat. As they pulled away from the health center, he noticed a brand-new CB on Wes's dash. "Nice. This wasn't here before was it?"

Wes checked his rearview mirror. "There she is. For a second I thought Constance wasn't behind us." He returned his focus to the road in front of them. "I got the CB this morning. After spending an hour on the side of the road with Clem and Lucy yesterday, I'm not going to be stranded in the wilds again. I'm part of the CB generation now."

To the west, white-topped mountains pushed up against the encroaching gray clouds from the north. The bright sun from earlier was gone, replaced by a gloom appropriate to Patrick's mood. They were already out of the town of Fort Washakie, and barbed wire fence ran along both sides of the road. Cattle huddled together in the southeast corner of a pasture, their butts toward the clouds and their heads low.

Patrick dropped his voice and added a twang. "10-4, good buddy." His forehead bunched. "Hey, I don't suppose you'd help me try to contact Susanne on that thing, would you? Constance said it's too far from here to Buffalo, but I thought I'd ask you."

"We could try a relay."

"What's a relay?"

"Come on, Doc. Didn't you run track in high school? You pass the baton from one runner to another?"

"I know what that kind of relay is. What does it mean in CB terms?"

"Same thing, but the CB users are the runners, and the message is the baton, of course. They pass it off one to another until it's in range of the recipient."

Patrick rolled his eyes. "Of course."

"Does she have a CB?"

"No, but her father is visiting, and he does. I haven't been able to check in since I left, and I imagine she's worried." He left out the part about him missing her so bad it was burning a hole in his chest, but he figured that Wes knew him well enough by now that it was a given.

"You're tough as old shoe leather, but you are a flatlander. I can see why she'd be concerned." Wes picked up the receiver. "What's his handle?"

"I don't know. But his name is Fred. Everybody calls him Papa Fred."

"That's as good a place to start as any." He keyed the mic and cleared his throat, then he released the button. "I don't have a handle."

Patrick thought for a moment, then grinned. "How about Captain X-ray?"

"That's not too bad. Except I'd feel like a dumbass saying it."

"Got something better?"

Wes tilted his head and chewed on the inside of his lip. He keyed the mic again. "Um, this is Captain X-ray near Lander, Wyoming, looking for a relay to reach Papa Fred, out east in Buffalo. Anybody out there with their ears on?

Patrick leaned toward the base unit, willing someone to respond. After a minute, he said, "Try again."

Wes repeated it. "Anybody out there can help us with a relay?"

The speakers on the unit crackled to life. "Captain X-ray, this is Bar None. I talked to a relay earlier today about Papa Fred."

Patrick whispered, "Tell him his son-in-law Patrick Flint is trying to reach him."

Wes whispered back, "You don't have to whisper. The mic isn't on until I press the button." Then he punched it in. "I'm with Papa Fred's son-in-law, Patrick Flint. He's trying to reach him."

The response was immediate. "Yeah, that's what I was talking to Papa Fred about. He was trying to get hold of Patrick."

Wes held up a hand as Patrick started to speak. "Patrick wants to let his wife know he's okay."

"Oh, I told him Dr. Flint was good, since I read about him in the paper."

Patrick shifted and turned. "What paper?"

Wes put the mic against his chest. "I've got one in the backseat. The Riverton newspaper. They quoted you this morning talking about Big Mike." He put the mic to his mouth. "Great. Thanks, Bar None. Well, if you hear from him again, Dr. Flint is still fine, but it looks like we'll be stuck in Lander with this new storm."

"I'll see if I can pass it along. No promises."

"Roger. I mean, 10-4."

Satisfied with the direction of the conversation, Patrick reached into the backseat and felt around. Nothing. He got on his knees and leaned over. The newspaper was on the floorboard. He brought it into the front seat and put it in his lap.

"I gotcha. Be safe out there, Captain X-ray."

"You, too, Bar None."

"Over and out."

"Over and out."

Wes put the mic back on the base unit. "How did I sound?"

"Like a dumbass."

Wes tweaked his mustache. "Sounds like your jealousy talking."

The radio crackled back to life with a woman's voice. "This is dispatch with the police in Fort Washakie, looking for anyone with the Fort Washakie Health Center. Come in Fort Washakie Health Center."

Wes picked up the mic. "This is, uh, Captain X-ray with Fort Washakie Health Center. Wes Braten, I mean. With Doctor Patrick Flint."

"We heard you guys are shut down. Samson Gray Bear from up on the north end of res needs to come in."

"Yes, the clinic is closed. What's the matter with Mr. Gray Bear?"

"He needs a tetanus shot. Tangled with some rusty old nails in his barn this afternoon."

"Stitches?"

"Nah. He said he washed it good and glued it closed."

Patrick winced. Whatever he'd said before about self-reliance in Wyoming, it was that times ten on the reservation. He nodded at Wes. "We can do it in the morning. Anytime within twenty-four hours is good."

Wes keyed the mic. "Can he meet us in the morning. Say about nine o'clock?"

"We'll let him know and make sure he has a ride. Thanks, Captain X-ray. Over and out."

"Over and out." Wes switched off the CB.

Patrick looked down and saw a picture on the front page of the paper. It was him, consoling Constance. "What the heck?" It looked disturbingly intimate. That reporter Jimmy had printed *this* as the picture of the grieving widow who used to babysit him? She must not have been a very nice babysitter.

Wes glanced over and saw the object of Patrick's ire. "Oh, yeah. Some picture, Doc."

"It's not what it looks like. God, I hope Susanne doesn't see this."

"I noticed you couldn't wait to ditch Constance back there. It's not like a cheapskate to turn down free room and board."

"She's acting a little . . . "

Wes tapped the paper. "Like that?"

"Yeah. Like that. And more. That urine sample you took in?"

"What about it?"

"I told Constance the hospital denied ever having it and that we should contact the police, thinking she'd agree."

"She didn't?"

"Not only did she not agree, but she was adamantly opposed to me contacting them. She said it was a sign from Big Mike to let well enough alone."

Wes frowned. "I understand she might not want an autopsy done. But a simple urine test?"

"I know. It definitely got me thinking. Especially after everything that's happened today."

"What else did I miss?"

Patrick filled him in on the marking of Big Mike's face, Dann's confrontation with Constance and reluctance to investigate, the pot shot someone had taken at him, Elvin's pointed comments at Dairy Land, Constance's funk after talking to the woman who claimed Big Mike owed her money, both altercations with Eddie—at the ranch and at the funeral home—and the comments the men had made about Big Mike at Lawanda's cafe. "And the kitchen at the ranch was a mess from Big Mike's last meal. I bagged it all up and labeled it. In case he was poisoned."

"Jesus, man. You've got to go to the cops."

"The cop doesn't like me much. He's already blown me off twice. But I think you're right. I just haven't been able to do it, since I was stuck with Constance." Patrick looked at his wristwatch. "It's too late now. Maybe I can call in the morning after we get in to see Mr. Gray Bear."

"I also think you need to read that article." His tone said Patrick wasn't going to like what he read.

"Why?"

"Just read."

Patrick's mouth dropped as he scanned the article. He was so shocked that he went back and read it again, more slowly, a second time. When he was done, he shook it. "Her sister-in-law has formally asked the police to investigate Constance for murder?"

"That's not the biggest shocker in there."

"You're right about that." Patrick lifted the paper and read aloud from the article. "Alicia Windwalker told the *Riverton Ranger* exclusively that Big Mike is the father of her son, Jason. Jason was born January 1, 1974. Constance Teton and Big Mike married on June 3, 1971, and Constance was stationed in Vietnam with the Army from July, 1971 through July, 1973. Alicia claims that Big Mike was leaving Constance, but told her he was afraid for his life, because Constance told him 'if she couldn't have him, no one would,' after she found out.'" He dropped the paper in his lap. "Wow."

Wes turned into the hotel parking lot. Raising his eyebrows, he said, "I hate to say this about a friend, but Constance doesn't sound like much of a grieving widow to me."

Patrick snorted. "Or act like one, either."

CHAPTER TWENTY-ONE: STOWAWAY

Susanne

Susanne was hopping, steaming mad.

The Brown and Flint caravan pulled to a stop at the motel in Lander. There was already three inches of fresh snow on the ground, and the weather reports were getting worse. If it didn't clear up soon, they'd be stuck here tomorrow, unable to even go look for Patrick. And she really needed to see him. The sellers hadn't been willing to extend the deadline past five o'clock, but they said they'd take a verbal offer. So, Susanne had made one. A much higher one. She had to tell Patrick, face-to-face., and she was really afraid he wasn't going to be happy.

And she hated driving the Suburban in this weather. She knew she should be happy that Patrick had agreed to trade in their bronze station wagon after it was stolen and treated roughly a few months before. The giant vehicle was like a boat, though, and she felt like she couldn't see things on the ground around it. She was paranoid of running into a gas pump or a small child.

But it wasn't the vehicle or the weather that had Susanne angry. No, she was upset because, at a gas stop in Riverton an hour before, she'd been inside paying when she saw a familiar lanky figure sneak back from the bathrooms and crawl into the rear of their Suburban, with Trish glancing around furtively and then tucking a blanket over him.

Brandon. Trish had somehow stowed Brandon away on their trip.

"Mama," Susanne had called. Mama Cat was in the snack aisle, holding a Snickers bar in one hand and a bag of Lay's Potato Chips in the other, looking between them like she was trying to decide which of her children to sacrifice. "Did you see that?"

Mama Cat ambled over to her. The woman wouldn't hurry if her tush was on fire. "See what, dear?"

"My not-yet-sixteen-year old daughter has snuck her boyfriend along on this trip."

"How did she do that?"

"I'm not sure how, but he's in the back of the Suburban, with the luggage."

Ever unruffled, Mama Cat sighed. "Oh, dear. Where does she think she's going to hide him once we get there?"

"I haven't the foggiest."

"What are you going to do?"

"What would you do?"

"I don't think I'm the one to ask. Look at how successful your daddy and I were in keeping our daughters from sneaking around with boys."

Mama Cat had a valid point.

With Leslie perched on one hip, Shelley poked her head between them. "What were you saying about your daughters, Mama?"

Mama Cat reached up and squeezed Shelley's cheek to hers. "That I have the two best daughters in the world."

Shelley kissed Mama Cat on the cheek before heading out to the vehicles.

Susanne snorted. "I think Patrick and I turned out okay."

"And maybe Trish and Brandon will, too."

Papa Fred came out of the men's room. "Are we ready?"

Susanne had decided to hold off confronting her daughter and the stowaway until Lander. But once they were there, she was letting the girl have it. She handed money to the cashier for her gas and her mama's snacks. "Yes, Daddy. Last stretch."

He grunted. "Come on, Kitty Cat."

The rest of the drive to Lander, Susanne had stewed until she came up with a plan. She'd confront Trish as soon as they parked, in case the plan was for Brandon to slip away somewhere in town. She needed to catch them red-handed, so to speak. And out of earshot from Perry and Matthew. From what she'd heard, Brandon had family all over Wyoming. He could have a whole slew of them in Lander.

So, here she was in Lander. At the hotel. It was time. She put the Suburban in park. Without turning around, she said, "Perry, Matthew, you two run along with the rest of the group. I need to talk to Trish alone."

"Okay, Mom."

"Yes, Aunt Susanne."

Perry opened his door and hopped out on one foot, then stood on his tiptoes and stretched back in for his crutches from the top of the luggage in the back end. He couldn't reach them. Matthew pushed them forward for him, then exited, too. He shut the door, and they joined the others.

"Okay, Brandon, you can come sit in the backseat by Trish now, where I can see you both."

There was a long silence.

"I saw you, Brandon. If it's not you, it's a serial killer hiding back there under a blanket, or we forgot to drop Ferdie at Ronnie's. Please don't tell me it's an ax murderer. Or that dog." She peeked in her rearview mirror.

Trish's face was as white as the snow outside.

There was a rustling sound in the back, then Brandon's head appeared behind Trish's in the mirror. He crawled over the luggage and plopped down beside her daughter.

Susanne kept her voice pleasant. "Which one of you wants to tell me what the heck is going on here?"

Brandon opened his mouth to speak.

Trish cut him off. "Brandon wanted to come see his cousins."

"How did you sneak him into this vehicle?"

"He parked at the Lindemanns'." The Lindemanns were their neighbors on the opposite side from Ronnie. "They're out of town for Christmas. Then he walked over. And, I, uh, helped him hide in the back."

"Why didn't you ask permission?"

"Because I knew you'd say no."

"You're darn right I would have said no. His mother let me know in no uncertain terms that Brandon is forbidden from seeing you. You've put me in a terrible position. Where does your mother think you are, Brandon?"

Brandon clasped his hands in his lap and rocked forward. "Um, up at a friend's cabin near Circle Park campgrounds. She'll never know, Mrs. F. It will be fine."

"No, it won't be fine, and yes, she will know, because I'm going right inside to call her and tell her."

"You can't do that, Mom!"

Susanne ignored her daughter. "Brandon, let's get you to your cousin's house. Whenever we find Dr. Flint and are ready to drive home, I can come get you."

"Uhhh . . ." Brandon's voice tapered out.

"Mo-om. No!"

Susanne didn't believe the cousin story for a moment, but it was time to call their bluff. She shifted the Suburban into reverse. "Which way? And, are they expecting you?"

Trish's head slumped forward.

Brandon wiped his hand across his mouth. "Maybe we should call them first."

"I think it's best if we just drive over there."

Trish scowled at her mother. "Fine. He doesn't have cousins here."

Susanne put the Suburban back into park. "And where exactly were you planning on him staying?"

"I have money, Mrs. F. I got it for my birthday. I can get a room."

"Fine. After we call your mother from the lobby." She turned off the engine. "You two, bring our luggage." She slammed the door and stalked into the hotel, reckless of the slippery conditions and kicking snow up to her knees with her moon boots.

When she got to the check-in counter, her daddy was standing by a tall stone fireplace with the group.

He handed her a key. "We're all checked in. Last three rooms they had. I hear you've got a little, um, situation." He wheezed out a laugh.

Susanne groaned. "Last three rooms? We've got an even bigger situation. Brandon was going to pay for a separate room."

Mama Cat said, "He'll just stay with us. That should be punishment enough for any teenage boy."

"Inspired idea. Thank you, Mama."

"I try." She patted her daughter.

"Now, I've got to call this boy's mother."

Half an hour and one phone call to an irate Donna Lewis later, the group congregated in the nameless hotel bar and restaurant. The décor leaned toward modern trashy, with velvet paintings of Elvis, Marilyn Monroe, and dogs playing poker. Susanne barely noticed. She hadn't had time to decompress after the butt chewing Donna had delivered to her. It wasn't Susanne's fault that Brandon was a sneak and Donna didn't supervise him. She sighed. But Trish's bad behavior was her responsibility, so she'd taken the woman's abuse. Now, she just needed a size extra-large glass of white zinfandel.

The hostess settled them into a U-shaped booth. The faux leather creaked as Susanne slid into the last spot at the adult's table. She wrinkled her nose. The whole restaurant smelled like nasty cigarettes and pungent salmon—a questionable choice land-locked in the middle of Wyoming in a blizzard—and it was even worse at their table. She looked under it and saw a few flakes of fish that had fallen from someone's plate. *Ew.*

Next to them at the kid's table with Perry and Matthew, Brandon and a pouty Trish weren't speaking to each other after a humdinger of a fight in the hall outside the Flint's room. Come to think of it, it had been a little too one-sided to call it a fight. More like Trish chewing his butt in much the same way Donna had chewed Susanne's.

As Susanne looked at the kids, she noticed a couple at a table on the far side of the restaurant. A beautiful Indian woman with two empty wine glasses in front of her, and a third, half full, to her lips, sat across from a companion, a man in his early thirties with sandy brown hair and a handsome face. Suddenly, the woman set her glass down and grabbed the man's hand, putting it to her lips. Susanne's cheeks flamed, because it wasn't just any man.

It was her husband.

"Where are you going?" Shelley asked. She was cradling Leslie in her lap with a bottle.

Susanne hadn't even realized she was on her feet. She didn't answer her sister. Her steps across the carpeted floor of the restaurant were quick and silent. When she was one table away from Patrick, she reached down and grabbed a water glass from a table as she passed by.

"Hey, that's mine," a woman said.

Susanne didn't hesitate. She walked straight to Patrick and emptied the icy contents over his head.

Patrick gasped and yelled. Jumping to his feet and brushing ice from his chest and lap, he looked around for his attacker.

His eyes met his wife's. "Susanne!"

She wheeled and marched back toward her family. Her heart was pounding so hard that she couldn't make out his words, even though she heard his voice behind her. She felt nauseous, yet somehow better. How could her husband have done this to her? Her Patrick? She'd always believed that she'd won the husband lottery. Handsome. A great provider and father. Loyal, loving, and kind. In fact, the only ongoing source of contention between them was his insistence they live in Wyoming, so far away from her family. And now, this? She would never have believed it if she hadn't seen it with her own eyes. With each step away from him, her rage transformed into something else, though. Sadness. By the time she reached the kid's table, tears were pooling in her eyes. She kept going toward her seat.

"Wait," Patrick said.

He grabbed her elbow. She jerked it away, whirling to face him.

"I said, 'Wait!'" He snatched up her hand and didn't let go, even when she tried to pull it away, too.

"Leave me alone," she hissed.

"Susanne, stop it. That wasn't what you think."

"What do I think?"

"That I was doing something that deserved a glass of ice water to the head. Listen, that was my co-worker, Constance Teton. She's drunk. Her husband died yesterday."

"And you have her at a hotel? And you're drinking together?"

"No. Look."

She resisted, but he tugged on her hand, and she looked back toward his table. Another man was on the side of the table Patrick had vacated. "Wes."

"Yes. Wes and I are staying here. He'd just run out to the bathroom when you saw us."

"But why is she here?"

"Because Wes and I got separated when he brought a patient to Lander while I was still working at Fort Washakie. She's been my wheels, and Wes invited her to dinner. I don't know why she grabbed my hand. She's not acting like herself. But you know me better than that."

Susanne's tears doubled. She did know him better than that. Why had she reacted like she did? And in front of her family. She wanted to crawl under the table.

"Hey, don't cry. I would have been upset, too. Just—well, I'm a good guy. I love you, and you need to trust me."

This time when he touched her arm, she leaned into his chest. He enveloped her in a Patrick-scented hug, all soap, leather, coffee, and the indefinable something that was uniquely him. She wiped her tears on his shirt.

"I'm sorry," she whispered.

"Me, too," he said. Then he lifted her chin. "And what the heck are you doing here?"

She stepped back from him but kept her hands on his elbows. "I had to make an executive decision today." She took a deep breath. "I raised the offer on the house." Susanne tensed, waiting for sparks to fly. Patrick was so cheap that she cut tags off all the new clothes for the kids so as not to raise his blood pressure. A few bucks on a pair of jeans was nothing compared to thousands of dollars on a house. "Another buyer is bidding against us."

Patrick's face paled, but, if he was mad, his voice didn't show it. "How much?"

She told him. "There's still time to withdraw the offer if we call Barbara now."

"Is this the house you really want?"

She gave him a half smile. "It really is."

"Okay, then."

"Okay? Really?"

He pulled her tight against him with his hand on the back of her head. "Really."

She leaned back to look up into his crystal blue eyes. "I have the papers for you to sign. We can do it now. We just need to drop them at the realtor's office on the way back."

He laughed. "Slow down. You just got here."

"*We* just got here."

"What do you mean?"

"Look around you."

He did, to discover his in-laws, niece, nephew, kids, and the group's plus one—Brandon. Throwing his head back, he laughed aloud. "What are you all doing here?"

Susanne put her arms around his waist. "We talked to a man on the

CB named Chuckles, and he said Gussie broke down and you and Wes were separated. We came to give you a ride home. And to confess to you I'd raised the offer on the house."

"Gussie is fine now. I don't need a ride home."

Her face fell.

"But this is great. We'll all be snowed in together." He waved to everyone. "Hello, you guys. I hate that you drove all this way, but I'm glad to see you."

He got an avalanche of greetings back. Before he could start a round of welcoming hugs, there was a crash on the other side of the restaurant. Susanne peered around Patrick's shoulder. Constance had knocked over her chair and was on her feet, fists clenched, leaning across the table at a woman standing beside Wes.

Susanne placed her hand on Patrick's shoulder. "Who's the other woman?"

Patrick glanced over. "Oh, no. That's Verna. The sister of Constance's dead husband. She's trying to get the police to arrest Constance for murder." He shook his head. "Come on. This could get ugly."

Susanne hustled after him, eyes glued to the two women. Watching the loud drama unfold with all the patrons turned to watch was like theater in the round.

"I can't believe you said that." Constance's voice was boozy, and she weaved on her feet around the table toward Verna. "To the paper."

"I didn't just say it to them. I called the police chief and told him, too. I told him all your secrets. The things Big Mike told me about you."

"How could you do that?"

"How could you kill my brother?"

"I didn't kill anyone, you bitch."

Constance lunged at Verna and caught her upside the head with a roundhouse. Verna was taller by a head and Constance was drunk, but Constance was younger, more fit, and had military training. Verna staggered back, then toppled over. Wes caught her before she crashed into the table behind them. Constance moved in, ready to pounce, but Patrick dove between Constance and her target. Susanne halted five feet away, mouth open. Women fighting, in public. As a Southern-raised woman, it was beyond her ken.

He grabbed Constance by the shoulders, shaking her slightly. "Stop it."

Constance's eyes were unfocused. "Did you hear her? Did you hear what she said to me? What she did?"

"I did."

"She has it coming. Whatever happens to her, she asked for it."

Patrick held firm. Suddenly, Constance relaxed and laid her head on Patrick's chest. A jealous rage reddened Susanne's vision, and she stepped so close to them she was almost pressing against Constance. She trusted her husband, but that didn't mean this woman's behavior was okay, whether drunk or not.

Constance looked down at Susanne without lifting her head. "Why are you staring at me?" Then recognition dawned. "You're the one who spilled your drink on Patrick."

Patrick tried to push Constance away, but she stuck like she'd Super Glued herself to him. "Let's not get all of us thrown out. The manager's on her way over."

Susanne saw a tiny woman with a name tag and a frown marching toward them. She couldn't understand what had taken her so long.

"I'm Patrick's wife Susanne." Smiling like a crocodile, she slid her hand between Constance and Patrick and shoved the woman back by her face. "And you're in my spot."

CHAPTER TWENTY-TWO: ENVISION

Patrick

Did *you find the trickster?*
The voice startled Patrick, but he knew who it belonged to and what it meant.

I don't think it's my place, he replied.

He shook off sleep and took in his surroundings. He was balancing on the edge of a deep ravine, snow gone. He tracked the other voice. Big Mike loomed on the other side of the ravine, larger than life, like a giant. The eerie glow still emanated from his chest.

Whose place do you think it is? Even though they were maybe fifty feet away from each other, it sounded like Big Mike was standing next to him, talking into his ear.

The police. Your wife.

Big Mike snorted. *You're the one I'm talking to in his dreams.*

Did someone murder you?

What do you think? Big Mike's image started to fade.

Patrick blinked. *I think you were poisoned.*

All that was left of Big Mike was a flickering light where his chest had been.

Patrick had questions for him. *Coyote Hunter, who killed you?* When there was no answer, he said, *But I'm an outsider here.*

As the light blinked out, Patrick heard Big Mike's voice like a whisper on the wind. *Sometimes people are too close to see the truth.*

Something shook his shoulder. He yelped and swatted, connecting with flesh. Soft flesh.

"Patrick, wake up. You're dreaming. It's okay." A woman's voice. His wife. Susanne. Susanne, in a hotel, in Lander. Not Big Mike. And he'd hit her.

"I'm sorry." He sat and pulled her into his arms. She didn't resist. "Did I hurt you?"

They laid back down with her head on his shoulder.

She stroked his hair. "I'm fine. What happened in your dream?"

But Patrick was so tired he couldn't form the words.

"Go to sleep," she whispered, and kissed his collarbone.

So, he did.

CHAPTER TWENTY-THREE: REBOOT

LANDER, WYOMING
TUESDAY, DECEMBER 21, 1976, EIGHT A.M.

Patrick

Patrick dumped a second mound of scrambled eggs onto his plate with an ice cream scoop. The restaurant looked less seedy in daylight, and the breakfast buffet seemed far removed from the drama served up the night before. Outside the window, the sun glinted off two feet of snow on the sidewalk, with even more piled on the edge of the street where a plow had been by. Two little boys were sliding down the mini mountain on their bottoms. Patrick smiled. The entire world looked good to him this morning. He'd enjoyed a rare night alone with Susanne, after they'd called Barbara to confirm their higher offer. Perry had stayed with his grandparents and Brandon, while Trish slept in her aunt and uncle's room.

Heaven.

In the wee hours of the night, Patrick had told Susanne all about Big Mike's death and the events over the last two days. She'd agreed with Wes that Patrick had to take his concerns to the police, even if she didn't like it. He'd also let her know about the patient meeting them at the clinic.

He'd left a sleepy Susanne soaking in the tub with a smile on her face and her promise to be down in five minutes before he and Wes had to leave for the clinic. "As long as you promise not to spend any more time with *that woman*," she'd said.

He'd laughed. "She's long gone."

"Good."

He'd kissed her, and for a heady moment, he'd been tempted to skip breakfast and be late for Mr. Gray Horse's appointment. But duty called, and he always answered. He'd pulled away. "See you in five."

Now, sitting alone at a table in the restaurant, he marveled at her. *My God.* He was so lucky in his marriage. Susanne was a beautiful, passionate creature. The way she'd gone after him last night, and how she'd put Constance in her place, even shoving her away from him? He loved that about her. Every broken coffee cup, every fiery word—she was amazing.

Then his mind did an abrupt shift on him. After he and Susanne had fallen asleep, he'd had a dream. A very vivid dream. It washed back over him. *Sometimes people are too close to see the truth,* Big Mike had said. *You're the one I'm talking to in his dreams.*

What did it mean?

"What are you talking to yourself about, Dad?" Perry asked. His tow-headed, freckle-faced son took a seat at the next table. Brandon and Matthew followed him, but Trish was nowhere to be seen.

Patrick shook off the dream. "Hey, buddy. Matthew. Brandon."

He got a few limp waves in return.

"Did you guys have a good night?"

Perry poured Fruity Pebbles into a plastic bowl. Patrick pretended not to notice he was eating junk. "It was awesome. We watched *Happy Days* and *Laverne and Shirley*."

Patrick groaned. "Does your brain feel mushy this morning? You probably lost a few IQ points."

The younger boys laughed. Brandon just looked nauseous. He avoided Patrick's eyes, watching the entrance as if willing Trish to appear. Or maybe planning his getaway.

"Good morning, Doc. My, aren't you glowing." Wes's coffee sloshed over onto the table. He set his plate down in the puddle, then mopped the edges with Patrick's napkin.

"Hardee har har. Did you ever get Constance to go home last night?"

"She wasn't in any shape to drive. I let her sleep in your bed."

Patrick's eyebrows shot up. "That was brave."

"The woman snores like a diesel engine then gets up earlier than a hen in a coop full of roosters. I didn't get a wink of sleep." He smoothed his mustache, which looked like he'd slept on it funny. "She accidentally got her purse switched with Verna's last night, so she doesn't have keys to her car. She called that Riley fellow to bring her spare set. He should be here any minute."

"Great." Patrick had assured Susanne Constance was gone. Not good. Maybe their paths wouldn't cross. "You look a little rode-hard and put up wet."

"Yeah, Constance got in the bathroom first. I haven't had a chance to shower."

"Now that you mention it, I thought something smelled funny."

Wes grinned. "I was thinking. Maybe we could ask Mrs. Doc to return Verna's purse and pick up Constance's from her, while we're at the clinic this morning?"

"Constance can't do it?"

Wes cocked an eyebrow at him. "Only if you have a death wish for Verna."

"Fair point."

Wes swallowed another bite. "Constance was asking about you and Susanne this morning."

"What about us?"

"Personal questions. About your relationship. I told her you were tighter than Farrah Fawcett and Lee Majors."

"Why, thank you. I've always been told I favor him."

"I was really thinking more that Mrs. Doc looked like Farrah." Wes flashed a toothy grin.

"Seriously, though, I don't understand Constance's fascination with me. It's strange. I need to tell Dann about it, along with everything else."

"Don't look now, Doc, but she's in line at the buffet."

Patrick didn't look. He didn't want to do anything that attracted her attention. Dang it, Susanne would be here any minute and see Constance, too.

Wes lowered his voice. "In my humble opinion, after you call the police, you need to stay away from her, Doc, and get the heck back to Buffalo. Don't forget, you're an outsider here, and one stirring up trouble with a big fat stick. You wouldn't want someone taking another shot at you, not with your family here."

Patrick couldn't argue about staying clear of Constance. At least until she got through this *whatever-it-was*, grief reaction, or need for rescue, or crush. But he felt an obligation to Big Mike that was hard to explain. He'd never met the man. He'd never even treated him. But he'd found him in the parking lot, so he was *almost* his patient. For Patrick, the doctor-patient relationship was a sacred bond. Just like he never gave up trying to save a patient, he never gave up trying to figure out what had happened to them, even in the hardest of cases. He questioned himself and everyone else. Because cause of death mattered. Saving people mattered. And maybe, if he knew what had happened to a deceased patient, he could save the next one.

It was no different with Big Mike. Maybe he felt it even more strongly since he was the only one who seemed to care, and because in a crazy way, if he could trust his dreams, it was almost like Big Mike had picked him out to ask for help in finding his killer. So, yes, Patrick was an outsider, stepping into relationships and customs that he didn't understand. But maybe that made him the perfect person to figure this out, as long as he kept his family safely out of it. What better way to honor the dead than by someone caring enough about them to do what was inconvenient, or even foolish in the eyes of others, to figure out what had happened?

"I hear you. How about when we get to Fort Washakie, I borrow Gussie to go see Dann in person, since their offices are there. If you don't mind doing the tetanus shot without me."

"Fine with me."

"Are these seats taken, boys?" Constance was suddenly beside them, looking as fresh as Wes looked stale.

"Uh . . ." Patrick said, about to object.

Constance set down her plate and took a chair. Patrick bit the inside of his lip. From behind him, Riley appeared and took the empty fourth seat at their table.

"Good morning," Wes said.

The man nodded, one side of his smile tight from the edge of his scar.

A young woman with black hair wound into a high bun was busing tables near them. She did a doubletake at Riley and hurried over. "Dr. Pearson. Hello."

Who the heck is Doctor Pearson? Patrick was just about to acknowledge the woman, assuming she'd made an error on the name, when Riley rose from his chair.

He glanced at Patrick, then back at the woman. "Hello, Veronica. How's that cut healing?"

Riley. Riley Pearson. *Posing as a doctor?*

"Great. Thank you so much. I don't think I'm even going to have a scar."

"Glad to hear it."

"Well, thanks again. I have to get back to work."

With his eyes down, Riley took his seat.

"Doctor Pearson?" Patrick asked.

"I never told her I was a doctor."

Constance patted Riley on the shoulder. "I told you he helps out any way he can. He does great work, and the patients love him. I'm hoping he'll go to nursing school one day."

"Well, you guys be careful. That could get the clinic shut down. Or keep Riley out of school."

She shook her head. "People around here are just grateful for the help. We appreciate Riley."

Riley's non-scarred cheek blushed. "It's the least I can do. I wouldn't be here if you hadn't given me great care in Vietnam. Anytime I can help other people, I feel like I should."

"Well, good for you, Riley. Maybe I can write you a recommendation letter, if you'd like." Patrick could relate to Riley's feelings and admire them. But he thought they were downplaying the risk.

Riley gave a noncommittal shrug.

Patrick picked up his plate, eager to get away before Susanne arrived. "I've got to get moving."

"But I just got here." Constance tugged at his jacket and pouted. "Will I see you later?"

Wes took Patrick's hint and stood. "Sorry. We have to get to Fort Washakie before we head back to Buffalo."

Constance brightened. "Oh?"

"Um, yeah. We have a patient meeting us there." Patrick turned, throwing a, "Bye," over his shoulder, then bumping into his wife.

She head-pointed at the table where Constance and Riley were still sitting. "Already finished eating breakfast with your *friends?*"

"Morning, Mrs. Doc." Wes made a face at Patrick.

Susanne's voice was dry. "Good morning, Wes."

"Meet you at the car?" Wes said to Patrick.

"See you there." Patrick saluted with two fingers. In Susanne's ear, he whispered, "I ate before them. They just showed up."

"I thought she'd be gone," Susanne whispered back.

"Me, too."

"Join us, Mrs. Flint?" Constance's voice was brittle, like a frozen rose petal.

"Thanks, but I'm going to eat with the boys." Susanne smiled at Perry, Matthew, and Brandon.

Trish slid into the empty chair at the kids' table. "This is my seat."

Brandon jumped to his feet. "Um, you can have my chair, Mrs. F."

Trish crossed her arms over her chest. "You're not going anywhere, Brandon. Sit."

Brandon's face flamed. "Don't talk to me like that."

Trish snarled, "Sit. Down."

"Trish." Susanne looked embarrassed.

Brandon's eyes went blank. "You know what, Trish? I don't need my mom to tell me not to see you anymore. I've made that decision all on my own." He turned on his heel and beelined for the exit.

"Get back here," Trish called after him.

When he didn't stop, she raised her voice. "Brandon, don't you walk out on me." As he disappeared, she jumped to her feet and chased after him.

Patrick shook his head at his wife. "Where did she learn to act like that?"

Susanne put the back of her hand to her cheek. "I'm praying it's hormones. But whatever it is, it's going to make Donna Lewis very happy."

He laughed. "Ouch. True."

She pulled him aside. "I got a call from Ronnie a few minutes ago."

"Is there a problem?"

"Ferdie ate a bag of raisins last night. She took him to the vet. Doctor Crumpton."

"That dog. How much did it cost us?"

"Aren't you even going to ask if he's all right?"

"If he was dead, I'm assuming you would have led with that information."

"They think he'll be fine. Although, apparently, raisins can be toxic to dogs."

"I didn't know. And, again, I ask you, how much did our free dog cost us this time?" Ferdinand had racked up sizable vet bills in his short life. A rattlesnake bite the previous summer. A fight with a raccoon. And now he could add raisin poisoning to the list.

"Since you're in a good mood, I think I'll keep that between Ferdie, Ronnie, and me."

Patrick grinned. He leaned over and whispered in her ear. "I had a nice night, Mrs. Flint."

She harrumphed.

"This is almost over, okay? Listen, here's a thought. Why don't you come with me this morning?"

She sighed. "I should really stay here. In case Brandon and Trish make up."

Patrick saw his daughter and her former boyfriend in a one-sided discussion on the sidewalk outside the restaurant. Trish may have been doing all the talking, but Brandon seemed to be having the last word. Leaning against the Suburban with his arms crossed and facing away from her, he looked totally resistant and disengaged.

"Okay. The group seems to be getting a late start anyway. And Wes needs a favor."

"What's that?"

"Someone to run Verna's purse to her."

"Who?"

"Constance's sister-in-law."

"The one Constance got in a fight with last night?" Susanne snorted. "Does she live near here?"

"Somewhere in Lander."

"How am I supposed to find her?"

"Phone book? Driver's license? I don't know."

Susanne flapped her hand. "I'll figure it out."

"Sorry. There's a hot tub here, though, if anyone wants to get in it. Then maybe you could bring me lunch at noon and we can all get on the road?"

"I'm not sure everyone will want to stay."

"Well, a carload could go ahead. Or I can ride back with Wes if you'd rather."

"What do you prefer?"

He smiled and whispered in her ear. "To be with you. Always to be with you."

She finally smiled back. "Fine. Noon. At the health center. But if she knows what's good for her, Constance won't be there when I come to pick you up."

CHAPTER TWENTY-FOUR: BUST-UP

LANDER, WYOMING
TUESDAY, DECEMBER 21, 1976, EIGHT THIRTY A.M.

Trish

Her dad and Wes walked out of the hotel, heading toward where Trish was trying to talk sense into Brandon.

"What's my dad doing?" Trish wrapped her arms around herself. It was so cold outside the tears were freezing on her cheeks. "Is he following me?"

Brandon wasn't even shivering. He also wasn't speaking to her.

Her dad nodded at them as he went by. "Trish. Brandon."

Wes said, "Hey, kids."

"Where are you going?" Trish shouted at her dad's back.

He didn't break stride. "Fort Washakie. We have a patient coming in."

Wes unlocked Gussie and ducked his long body in. He leaned across and pulled up the lock on the passenger side.

"What about us?" Trish said.

Patrick stopped with his hand on the door to the Travelall. "Talk to your mom. She's got a plan." He got in and shut the door behind him.

"Great," Trish said, kicking up clouds of snow. "Now what are we going to do?"

Brandon didn't respond, just kept leaning like a statue against the wall.

As the Travelall pulled out, Constance and a scar-faced man came out of the hotel and walked toward them as well. Trish couldn't believe it when her dad told them he worked with Constance, not that Trish had met her or anything. Only seen her across the restaurant. The woman was movie star gorgeous. Like she seriously could have been a model or actress instead of a nurse. Sometimes adult choices made no sense to Trish. But getting in fights at restaurants seemed more like something one of the girls at Trish's high school would do. Trish's mom had been super pissed at Constance last night, too—something to do with Trish's dad—which made Trish even more curious about the woman. Her dad told them Constance's husband had died a few days ago. Maybe that was why she'd lost it.

Trish kept her face down, pretending like she wasn't watching but straining to hear every word out of the woman's mouth.

The man with the scars had a funny way of talking out of the side of his mouth. "Are you involved with him?"

Constance put a hand to her chest. "Wes? No!"

"You know who I mean."

"Oh, Patrick. Isn't he perfect? We'll see." She made a zipping motion over her lips.

"He's also married."

"She's kind of mousy, don't you think? Not a match for him. And he doesn't wear a wedding ring."

A funny noise burbled from Trish's throat before she could stop it. How dare that woman talk about her mother like that! Luckily, neither Constance nor the man seemed to notice the sound or Trish.

"I don't think you can trust him."

"Don't be a spoil sport."

He growled. "People will talk, Constance."

"People have always talked about me. Let them say whatever they want."

The two kept talking, but they'd walked out of Trish's ear shot. Constance got into a Jeep Cherokee, and the man into a beat-up truck with fuzzy dice hanging from the mirror.

Trish's jaw dropped. She turned on Brandon. "Were they talking about my *dad?*"

Brandon broke his silence. "What do you think? She was all over him when we got to the restaurant last night. Your parents got in a fight over her. And then that guy she's with was eavesdropping on every word your dad and Wes said this morning before she got all flirty and invited herself to sit with them."

Confused, Trish's face puckered. Her dad was old. Why would a woman like Constance look twice at him? "How do you know all that?"

"Because I pay attention to things other than myself, unlike somebody else I know."

Trish's mouth dropped open. "Are you talking about me?"

Brandon pushed off the wall where he'd been leaning. "You think everything is about you. This time, it is. You know how worried I am about my cousin Ben, and you haven't even asked about how he's doing in juvie, not even once."

"He kidnapped me!"

"He protected you."

"I know. And I tried to help him. I do care how he's doing, Brandon."

"Ben's just another example. I honestly don't think you care about anything but yourself." He walked back into the hotel, leaving her with a scream still on her lips and her fists balled.

CHAPTER TWENTY-FIVE: WARN

Patrick

"I think our patient beat us here." Patrick reached into the back seat for his doctor's bag.

An old man was sitting cross-legged and alone on the snowy sidewalk outside the clinic, his back ramrod straight and his eyes closed. There were no vehicles in the parking lot.

"Looks like it." Wes parked near the front door.

Patrick hurried out and over to the man. "Good morning, sir."

He opened his eyes, then inclined his head slowly. When he raised it back up, he stared at Patrick.

"Are you here for treatment?"

The man swung his legs under himself and climbed to his feet nimbly. Pulling up on the baggy leg of his overalls, he displayed a heavily-bandaged unshod foot and leg. The toes were a little blue from the cold.

"Aha. I'll bet you're here for a tetanus shot."

A thumbs-up indicated the affirmative.

Patrick was starting to think the fellow was mute, but his hearing seemed fine. He smiled at him. "Just give us a moment to get set up, and we'll get you taken care of." He looked over at Wes, who was unlocking the door. Patrick waved an arm toward the entrance. "Come on in."

The man walked inside with no trace of a limp. Patrick followed him. The clinic was toasty warm compared to the day before. Wes flicked on the lights—they had power—and lifted the phone receiver.

"Dial tone," he said, grinning.

"We're off to a good start, then. How about I feed the boiler while you get our patient set up? Then I'll run my little errand and be back as quick as I can."

"Sounds like a plan."

Wes was escorting the man into an exam room by the time Patrick set his bag down and headed for the boiler. The small room was filled with tall stacks of wood. *Riley*. Patrick opened the boiler. The bottom was filled with live coals. He cross-hatched several logs over them, then crouched and blew on the coals until the logs caught fire. Standing a few feet away, he surveyed his work with satisfaction. Things were back to normal at the clinic, and it felt good.

When Patrick was on his way back to the lobby, Wes called for him from the door of the exam room.

"Hey, Doc. Before you go, could you come bless my work?" He lowered his voice. "Tough old bastard made mincemeat out of his legs. I can't believe he didn't want to come in yesterday. But I think it will be okay if I clean it up pretty aggressively and you write him a script for a megadose of antibiotics."

"Let me grab my bag." Patrick detoured for his doctor's bag and joined the other two men in the little room. He stuck his hand out to the patient. "We didn't meet officially. I'm Dr. Flint, from Buffalo."

The man nodded, and they shook hands.

"Do you mind if I take a look at your wounds?"

He gave Patrick another thumbs up.

Patrick leaned over to get a closer look at the man's foot and ankle. It looked like he'd gotten them wrapped in barbed wire and then torn himself free. "Goodness. I'd hate to see the other guy in this fight."

The man grinned.

Wes interjected. "Old rusty barbed wire. I'm cleaning him up, giving him a tetanus shot, and suggesting antibiotics. Anything else, Doc?"

"Do you have diabetes, sir?" Patrick asked.

The man shook his head.

"What kind of antibiotics do we have onsite, after the break in?" Patrick asked Wes.

Wes blanched. "I hadn't even looked."

Patrick waved him off. "I've got the good stuff in my bag. Could you write me a scrip for Amoxicillin, and I'll sign it in a minute?"

"Sure thing, Doc."

Patrick unclasped his old-fashioned bag. He popped the hinges open and peeked inside. His bottle of Amoxicillin was visible, but his attention was diverted by a piece of paper that hadn't been in the bag the last time he'd opened it. He frowned and pulled it out. In block printing someone had written STAYING HERE WILL BE BAD FOR YOUR HEALTH. DOCTOR GO HOME. He stared at the note, perplexed— black marker, maybe the same as on Big Mike's forehead. Maybe the same as the note on his desk. When was this put in his bag, and by whom?

A knock on the exam room startled him. Still holding the note, he went quickly to the door and cracked it open. "Yes?"

Constance shot him a bright smile. Her hair hung iron straight in front of her shoulders. "What did I miss?"

Patrick shoved the note behind his back. "Uh, Constance, what are you doing here?

CHAPTER TWENTY-SIX: RESOLVE

Patrick

Patrick was discombobulated. To say he hadn't expected Constance in the clinic today was an understatement. Yet there she was, acting like today was any other normal day, not two days after her husband's suspicious death, or one day after she'd drunkenly gotten in a fight with her sister-in-law and spent the night in Lander.

He'd ducked out of the exam room as quickly as he could, making an excuse about having to run back into Lander, not wanting her to know he was on the way to tell Dann his suspicions about her. Then he'd hustled to the police station. He wanted this done, to turn over his information to the proper authorities and leave Big Mike in good hands.

As Patrick turned off the ignition to the Travelall he looked out the window. At first all he noticed was the thermometer bungee-corded to the arm of the side view mirror. It made him smile. Then Dann walked past him, heading out from the police department building into the parking area.

Patrick leapt from the car, slipping and catching himself on Gussie's door. "Officer Dann."

"Can I help you?" Dann sounded pleasant until he recognized Patrick. Then his eyes narrowed.

"Yes. I was coming in to update you on some developments with Big Mike's case."

"Can this wait? I'm on my way to the north end of the reservation."

"I don't think so. I'm leaving. To go back to Buffalo."

Dann brightened, smiling. "Good."

"Excuse me?"

The officer crossed his arms. He had on only a light jacket over his uniform. Patrick felt silly in his heavy, quilted coat. "Fine. I'll give you a minute. But that's all."

Cars were driving by on the road in both directions, and a very young Indian couple walked past them toward the building, holding hands.

Patrick raised his brows and tilted his head toward the couple. "Is this private enough?"

"We're fine."

Easy to say when you hadn't been shot at in a parking lot the day before. "Uh, okay. I wanted to let you know that Lander Hospital lost the urine sample I sent in for testing."

"That's a shame. They're understaffed and underfunded. It's an epidemic around here."

"It's more than that. They said they never received it, even though my co-worker Wes dropped it off with them yesterday. It seemed awfully suspicious."

"Don't go looking for a problem where there isn't one."

Patrick shoved his hands in his pocket. He wished he'd worn his gloves. "What about the marking on Big Mike's forehead? And the shot at me?" He hadn't even told him that someone cut Constance's brakes, but he didn't want to cloud the issue. When Dann didn't answer, Patrick hurried on. "I think there's a better-than-even chance this was murder. That Big Mike was poisoned. If the urine sample had been tested, I could have proved it."

"You thinking something isn't the same as evidence."

Patrick opened his mouth, ready to argue, but Dann held up his hand.

"Listen, Dr. Flint. This reservation already has enough problems.

We don't need a scandal over one of our tribal council members *maybe* being murdered. It's bad for the eastern Shoshone. Bad for all the Indians here, and the non-Indians, too."

"But what if it *was* a murder?"

"We've already covered that, Doctor. "If" and "maybe" are just speculation."

Patrick stomped his feet in place for blood flow. "Did you search the Teton residence? I bagged and labeled all the food and beverages Big Mike had the morning before he died and left them in the refrigerator for you, in case they contain strychnine."

"It's not a crime scene."

"But it might be." Patrick looked around. The only other people in the parking lot slipped into a car and started the engine. "Look, I've been trying to avoid saying this directly, but you're giving me no choice. Have you looked at Constance for this?"

Dann scowled. "Dr. Flint, I've really got to go." He started walking at a brisk clip toward his BIA truck.

Patrick hurried after him. "Constance didn't want me to do the sample. She was one of the only people that knew it went to Lander. Then it went missing."

"That's not evidence."

"Her own sister-in-law suspects her. And I know Constance stands to inherit a lot with his death."

Dann stopped for a moment. "And who do you think will inherit if Constance goes to prison?"

Patrick frowned. "I don't know."

"Verna." Dann resumed walking.

That did put a different spin on things. But there was more he needed to tell Dann. "The newspaper reported that Big Mike cheated on Constance and had a child. I was with Constance yesterday when a woman with a child confronted her about money."

Dann stopped beside his truck. "Alicia?"

"I—I'm not sure."

"So Big Mike owes someone money, and you think Constance killed him for it? Seems to me under that logic, if she was a killer, she would have gone after the person he owed it to."

Patrick sucked in a breath. He was getting nowhere with Dann. He tried another tact. "Constance has been acting weird."

Dann laughed. "If this were a contest for the worst excuse for evidence you've given me so far, that one would take the cake."

Patrick shook his head, refusing to give in. "She's not grieving. She's . . . flirty."

Something flickered across Dann's face. *Finally, I'm getting through to him.* "What do you mean? With who?"

"Um, with me. Touchy. Too close. Saying things that she shouldn't. So much so that my wife blew a gasket at her last night."

Whatever emotion had passed across Dann's features was gone, leaving behind a sardonic smile. "Again, not evidence. And a bit egotistical, if you ask me."

"Fine. Don't believe me. But Wes—you remember Wes, from Buffalo, who was also at the clinic?" Dann nodded, so Patrick continued. "He said she was asking about my relationship with my wife last night. He's the one that suggested I come tell you this."

Dann turned away from Patrick, his hand on the door handle. "I'll talk to her."

"Thank you. There's something else." Patrick set his doctor's bag on the pavement, opened it, and retrieved the note. He handed it to Dann. "I found this in my bag this morning."

Dann read it, turned it over, pursed his lips. He waved it in the air. "Did you see who left it there?"

"No."

"What would you propose I do about it? It's not a criminal matter."

"But someone shot at me yesterday. And now this note."

"Someone took a shot yesterday. Lots of shots are taken every day around here. But this is evidence of . . . something, so I'll keep it." He folded the note and put it in his pocket. "Now, is that all?"

A frustrated rage burned in Patrick's gut. He thought about his altercation with Eddie and the weird encounter with Manning and Elvin but decided not to mention them. Dann hadn't cared about anything he'd said, and he wasn't going to care about them either.

In a tight voice, he said, "Do you want me to have the Lander Hospital test another sample?"

"It's not your place. If we want one, we'll order it. You go on back to Buffalo, like that note suggested. We don't need a meddling doctor on the reservation. Sometimes bad things happen when people go sticking their noses in other people's business."

The blood rushed from Patrick's face. It felt like a threat. It sounded like a threat. So much so that he had a disturbing thought. *Had Dann been the one who left the note in his bag?*

But Dann smiled. "And I don't want anything to happen to you, Dr. Flint. Thanks for coming out." He let go of the door handle and took Patrick's hand, shaking it without Patrick participating. Then he drove away, south.

Hadn't he said he was headed north? Maybe Patrick had misheard him. But he hadn't misheard the dismissal of his information and theories or the threat against him.

Dann wasn't going to do squat about Big Mike's death.

Patrick got back in Gussie and pounded the steering wheel. For all Dann's resistance and his words about protecting the Eastern Shoshone, he was forgetting that something bad had already happened to one: Big Mike Teton. No one on the reservation had done right by the man about his death. Maybe Dann truly felt his duty was to the living. Or maybe he was a crappy cop, or worse. Patrick thought again about Big Mike's words in his dream, when he'd talked about being too close to see. This had to be what he meant.

But Patrick knew where his own duty lay. With his patient. With Big Mike, who had asked for his help—he was convinced of it. And that meant he owed the man his best attempt to determine what killed him. If he could figure that out, he believed he could do a lot more good for the Eastern Shoshone than Dann gave him credit for, too.

He glanced at his watch. He had time for one last try. If he couldn't get a urine sample done without more evidence, then he needed something else to hand to Dann.

He pointed the big vehicle toward the T-ton Ranch.

CHAPTER TWENTY-SEVEN: RESCUE

Perry

The Flint's new-to-them Suburban glided down the hill of the residential street like an oversized toboggan. Susanne yipped.

"Woo hoo," Perry yelled.

There were no curbs in the neighborhood, and the Suburban wooshed smoothly into a front yard, finally coming to a stop five feet from a mailbox.

His mom let out a shaky breath. Then she wagged a finger at him. "Don't distract me when I'm driving. Especially when there's a problem."

Perry made a zipping motion over his lips.

Trish sniffed. "You could have killed us."

His mom ignored Trish and squinted at the numbers on the mailbox. "At least we crash landed at the right house. Perry, can you take this to Miss Teton while I get the car on the road?"

"Why me? I'm on crutches." He knew why. It was because Trish's face was so swollen that it looked like she'd been stung by a hive of bumblebees.

"This from the kid that's doing so good he tried to chisel himself out of his cast yesterday? Just do it."

Perry sighed heavily. She had a point, but no reason to make this easy on anyone.

"And check her name before you give it to her. Make sure we're at the right house."

"I don't know her name."

"I told it to you already. You've got to listen to me. It's Verna Teton. Call her Miss Teton."

"Miss Teton."

"Right."

Climbing down from the tall vehicle, he took the purse from his mom through her open window, and used one crutch to cross the yard. The snow was deep, so he kicked a trail, the purse banging against his leg as he went. A man came out the front door with another purse in his hand. He kept his head hunched down into the collar of his parka and didn't even respond when Perry said, "Hey." He walked past a little car parked in the driveway and out to the street, disappearing from Perry's view.

"Whatever." Perry trudged on to the house.

Before he could ring the bell, a woman came to the door. He definitely recognized her. She'd been the one in the cat fight with the woman who was flirting with his dad last night. Down the street, an engine started.

"Whatever you're selling, I'm not buying." She pushed the door like she was going to close it in his face.

Perry held up the purse. "Are you Miss Teton?"

The door stopped. At first her face puckered with confusion, then she nodded. "Yes. What are you doing with my purse?"

"You left this at the hotel last night."

"Right. Who are you?"

"Perry Flint."

"Flint. Is your dad the doctor?"

Perry nodded.

Miss Teton reached for the purse. "Thank you."

"You're welcome."

The woman's face spasmed. Her neck arched, and her eyes went wide and panicky.

Perry didn't know what to do. Was she sick? He'd seen a scary movie once where a woman was possessed by a demon, and she'd looked exactly like Miss Teton did now. Not that he was supposed to have seen it. He'd been sleeping over with his buddy John, and they'd had a babysitter. A college girl. She'd met her boyfriend at the movie, and, since they were over eighteen, they'd sworn him and John to secrecy and escorted them in. In the movie, a priest and a scary dude did an exorcism on the demon lady. He'd been scared of demons ever since, and he never wanted to see another scary movie.

Holy cow, he hoped Miss Teton wasn't being possessed by a demon now. He backed up a step. "Um, are you okay?"

After a few seconds, her weird expressions and neck movements stopped. "I . . . I don't know. I don't know what happened."

"Are you sick? Maybe you should go see my dad." Or an exorcist. He shuddered.

The woman nodded, then her face contorted again. She clutched the door frame. Perry took another step backwards, wanting to make a run for it. He peeked into her house. It was dark. A large cross hung on the wall behind her. A cross was good, wasn't it? Her fit lasted longer this time.

When it ended, she said, "I—I think I need a ride to the hospital. Is that your mom?"

"Yes."

She shot out the door so fast, Perry slipped and nearly fell as he was turning around to follow her. It wasn't until she stopped for another attack of whatever-it-was that he caught up with her. He passed her and knocked on his mom's window. She cranked it down.

"Miss Teton's sick or something. We need to take her to the hospital."

"What?" His mom looked confused.

Verna walked up behind Perry. "Something very bad is happening to me, and I need your help."

CHAPTER TWENTY-EIGHT: REBUFF

Patrick

Out at the T-ton Ranch, Patrick parked the Travelall by the barn, relieved not to see any other vehicles. He knew Constance was at the health center, but he'd been worried about Eddie. He struck Patrick as someone who played all night and slept until noon—definitely not the kind of guy with a day job—so he considered his absence a stroke of good fortune. And if Eddie showed up, Patrick would just claim to have left something at the ranch house when he'd stayed over.

Just as he was about to get out of Gussie, Patrick realized he didn't have his doctor's bag. *Dammit.* A fluttering in his chest made him laugh at himself. He was worse than a woman and her purse about that bag. Normally he was reliable about keeping tabs on it. He'd had it with him when he was talking to Dann. He went back through his actions. He'd set it down, taken out the note, and given it to the officer. And then what? He remembered Dann putting the note in his pocket but didn't remember picking up the bag.

Groaning, he pictured what he'd done. Or what he hadn't done, rather. He'd been so upset when Dann blew him off that he'd forgotten to pick his bag up when he left. It had to be on the ground in the parking lot, unless someone had taken it. For a moment, he considered going back and getting it. But then he had a better idea. He switched on Wes's brand-new CB. If he could reach Susanne and ask her to get it, that would save him a trip. She had to drive right past the station to get to the health clinic anyway.

It took him a minute and a false start or two, but he found and pressed the mic key. He guessed he needed a handle. It came to him like a bolt of lightning. "This is, um, Sawbones. Come in Papa Fred, if you're out there."

Almost immediately, Papa Fred's voice came through the speaker, loud and clear. "This is Papa Fred, Sawbones. What's up?"

In his excitement, Patrick fumbled the mic.

"Are you there, Sawbones?"

"Sorry. I, um, yeah, I'm here. This is Patrick."

"I know your voice, son."

"I left my medical bag at the police station in Fort Washakie. In the parking lot actually."

"Doesn't sound like the brightest move you've made lately."

"It wasn't. Can you ask Susanne to pick it up for me? Maybe even call the station before someone steals it, and ask for it to be brought in and held at the front desk?"

"I can ask her, but I can't make her do anything. Never have been able to."

Patrick grinned. "Roger, that. We're in the same boat."

"Uh huh," Papa Fred said, a smile in his voice, too. "Anything else?"

"That's it."

"All right then. We'll see you at noon."

"Thanks."

"Over and out."

"Over and out." Patrick hung up the CB, feeling hip and capable. Not enough to get a CB of his own, but still, it had been pretty handy.

He decided to start by checking to see if the labeled items he'd left in the refrigerator were still there. If someone had gotten rid of it all, it would further his theory that the food had been laced with strychnine. To Dann's point, it wasn't evidence per se, but it was still an important piece of information to collect.

Patrick knocked, then tried the front doorknob. The door was unlocked, like to almost every house out in the country, and he let himself in. It still smelled like the hamburger filling for the tacos Big Mike had made two days before, only what was once probably appetizing was now slightly rotten and stomach-turning, despite the fairly cool temperature inside the house. The quietness screamed at him. It felt spooky to be here searching for clues as to whether a friend and co-worker had murdered her husband, and he wished he'd brought his revolver. But that was tucked in his doctor's bag, too.

"Okay, Big Mike. I'm at your place. If the trickster was here, now's the time to help me find him."

He didn't expect an answer, and he didn't get one, but he still felt silly talking to a dead man.

In the kitchen, he opened the refrigerator, and cold air flooded out. That's when he realized that the house was a little warmer than the day before. The power was back on here, too. Staring into the refrigerator, he frowned. The paper bag wasn't there. He rummaged around to be sure, but it was definitely gone. He backed away, bumping into the table. Constance had been with him all day yesterday and last night, but she had come by the house to change clothes before work that morning. Maybe she'd thrown it out then, possibly innocently. He lifted the lid on the kitchen trash can. A foul odor blasted him in the face.

"God." He put the back of his hand over his nose.

The trashcan was full to the brim, but the labeled brown paper bag was not inside it. Or, he didn't think it was since the trash on top included empty wrappers for cheddar cheese, sour cream, and hamburger. Those were from Big Mike's tacos, so the paper bag would have to have been above them. He could only be sure if he emptied the can and dug down below, though. The thought disgusted him. It didn't seem worth it.

The front door to the house opened, shooting his pulse rate up. "Patrick? Are you in here?"

It was Constance.

Patrick squeezed his eyes shut and coached himself. *Act natural.* "In the kitchen."

But Constance was already in the room with him by the time he got the words out. "What are you doing here?"

"Um, I can't find my bag. I thought maybe I left it here."

"Why didn't you just tell me that at the clinic?"

"I hadn't realized it then. What are you doing here?"

The look on her face said she didn't believe him. He wouldn't have either. "Looking for you. I had a feeling you'd be here."

He kept the surprise off his face. "Oh?"

"Dann told me you went to see him."

Anger surged through Patrick. And something else. Uneasiness. "I did."

"And you told him you thought I murdered my husband."

"That's not what I said."

She stepped so close to him that he could smell the alcohol still seeping from her pores from the night before. Her pupils were dilated. "Sounded a lot like that to me. And now you're here, snooping. I don't get it. I thought we were friends." She spat the last word.

Patrick stepped around her, giving himself a clear path to the door. No point lying anymore. "Why didn't you want that urine sample done on Big Mike?"

"This again? I already told you. Big Mike would have hated it. It's not our way." She hugged herself, suddenly more forlorn than angry. "You *do* think I killed him."

"I never said that."

"But you have questions."

"I just told you my question."

"More questions, then."

Outside, Patrick heard an engine as a vehicle passed the house. Constance didn't react to it.

He cleared his throat. "A few."

"Spit them out. Let's get this over with."

"Why would someone write BETRAYOR on his forehead?"

"How should I know? Maybe it was political. His campaign to pass hunting regulations was viewed by some as a betrayal of his people. Maybe it was Alicia, since she's had to raise his bastard child on her own. Hell, maybe it was Eddie, since Big Mike had threatened to report the poker club to the police. Or Joshua, in revenge for Big Mike killing his dogs—they used to be best friends, you know, so there's a lot of history there."

"I didn't know that."

"Of course you didn't. You're not part of this community. But the bottom line is, I don't know who wrote it or why. All I know is I didn't. You were with me. You know that."

Patrick was with her, but she could have done it before they ever left the clinic the day Big Mike died. For that matter, she could have written the note Patrick found on Big Mike's desk or the one in Patrick's bag. There was no point in confronting her with all of that, though. She wasn't going to admit it.

"I understand."

"Patrick, I know it's unlikely he just keeled over dead. In my heart, I believe this was an accident. A horrible accident that he messed up somehow with his own poison and killed himself instead of a coyote. And that's not something you can learn from a urine sample. Whatever the reason he's dead, the end result is the same. He's gone." She paced the length of the kitchen, then whirled around. A fringed leather handbag swung out on a long strap from her shoulder. She stopped it with her hand. "And I can prove I didn't do it, anyway."

"How?"

She walked into the front room and took a book off a shelf. A heavy, gilded King James bible. "Come in here."

He walked over to her.

She pulled a travel agency envelope from the bible's pages. She handed it to him, and he turned to read it in the light from the window. WIND RIVER TRAVEL AGENCY, LANDER, WYOMING.

"What's this?"

"A ticket from Denver to Chicago."

"I don't understand."

"I was leaving him. Not killing him. Leaving. And I was going to file for a divorce. Think about it. Why would I spend the money I didn't have on an expensive plane ticket to get away from him, if I was going to kill him and didn't need it?"

Patrick was growing more confused by the second. Until he'd read the article in the Riverton paper and been the subject of Constance's unwanted attentions in the last few days, he would've sworn that Constance and Big Mike had a good marriage. Plus, from his perspective, her plan to leave him made her an even better suspect. What would she get in a divorce? A helluva lot less than she would if Big Mike died. He kept that thought to himself, though.

He didn't move. "I see."

She glared at him. "Why does this matter to you anyway? You didn't even know my husband."

He wasn't about to tell her about his dreams or visions or whatever they were. "Because when an unexpected death happens on my watch,

I feel responsible, I guess. For justice. Black and white, right and wrong."

"You want black and white, right and wrong?" She ripped her shirt up and over her head.

He averted his eyes, afraid she was making a play for him. "Constance, I can't—"

"Look at me. See these bruises?"

Reluctantly, he swung his eyes back to her torso. She was wearing a milky white lace bra over small, nut-brown breasts. Her ribs showed, but so did the ridges of her muscular abs. The woman was athletic. And *bruised*.

His attitude toward her quickly turned clinical as he surveyed her injuries. Black bruises. Green ones. New ones. Old ones. Big and small.

She laughed, a bitter sound. "You know what these are right?"

"I'm sorry." His voice was calm, soothing, empathetic. "I'm pretty sure I do."

She nodded. "Fist marks. This was the last straw. I put up with him cheating on me and having a child with another woman, but not this. He wasn't a nice person when he drank. And, yes, he drank a lot more than I said. Lying about how nice he was is a bad habit for me. We can't ruin the mighty tribal council member's reputation, after all. I wasn't going to lie about this, too."

Anger pounded on his chest from the inside. He remembered the row of whiskey bottles in the pantry. Alcohol was no excuse for domestic abuse. In his eyes, only the worst of men took advantage of their size and strength by beating women and children. "Did you report this to the police?"

The look she gave him was patronizing. "Do you really think anyone would help me here? Far worse is done every day."

Patrick walked across the room to the window. Yes, domestic abuse and alcohol problems went hand in hand with poverty, and the reservation was a prime example of that. He'd seen it firsthand in the clinic. The funds for police were even more limited than the funds for health care, too. That didn't make it right, though. He felt his lips move and stopped himself, finishing a thought aloud instead. "But surely someone knew."

"Eddie. Riley. No one else. Big Mike was smart and political. And I hit back—I can fight, I promise you that."

"His bruises. The scratches. Was that you?"

She lifted her chin. "Yes. I made sure he knew he would never get away with it again. But I didn't kill him. I wanted away. I wanted a divorce. I told him so."

"He knew you were leaving him?"

"He knew I wanted to."

Patrick was flabbergasted. This turned everything on its head. If Big Mike had known Constance was leaving him, he could have been desperate. Maybe he really loved her. Maybe he was afraid of what other people would think, that it would ruin him. His problems with alcohol, self-control, and violence added to those things might have pushed him over an edge. Enough to kill *himself*. Suicide by strychnine wasn't common since it was a ghastly way to go, but it wasn't unheard of, especially in someone who wanted to punish himself. Nor was it unusual for a suicide victim to seek medical help when it was too late. Big Mike poisoning himself wasn't outside the realm of possibility.

He became aware that Constance had come to stand behind him. Turning and resting against the windowsill, he faced her.

"I wanted—want— a good man." She swallowed, and her shoulders dropped a few inches. "Like you."

Constance pressed her bare stomach and barely covered breasts against him, her eyes nearly level with his. Quickly, she reached her hands up and around his neck, trapping him between her and the window.

He put his hands up, dropping the travel agency envelope, afraid to touch her, unable to get away without it. She was all skin, breasts, hair, and hands. "Constance, I—"

"Shh." She tipped her chin, bringing her lips in line with his.

He twisted his head away, roughly pulling his body aside at the same time. "I'm married."

Constance didn't let go. She wasn't only nearly as tall as him, she was nearly as strong. "But you don't have to be."

With both his hands, he reached behind his neck and grabbed hers, pulling them apart. As he put space between them, she clamped her hands around his wrists.

"I *am* a good man, and I love Susanne. Besides, what makes you think the kind of man you could make leave his wife is a *good* man? You want someone better than that. And I hope you find him someday. That he treats you like you deserve. But I'm not him."

"Then why don't you wear a wedding ring?"

He frowned. "I got it caught on something once and nearly lost a finger. I don't need to wear a ring to know I'm married and love my wife."

Constance froze. The flame in her eyes died out. Then she scrambled for the shirt she'd tossed on the floor. "I need out of here." She pulled the shirt over her head, struggling to get her arms through the long sleeves.

"Away from here, your house?"

"Here, this place. This whole damn place." She stormed to the door, calling over her shoulder. "Lock up when you finish tossing my place. I want to keep people like you out next time."

CHAPTER TWENTY-NINE: NOSE

Kinnear, Wyoming
Tuesday, December 21, 1976, 10:30 a.m.

Patrick

Patrick scooped the travel agency envelope from the carpet. He was still standing in the Teton living room holding it, trying to pick his jaw up off the ground, when he heard the sound of a vehicle outside again. Doors slammed, then he heard loud voices. At the window, he saw a Dodge pickup and the familiar figures of the Mannings, Joshua and Junior. The neighbors.

Junior put down the tail gate to his truck, and Joshua dragged and hefted something off of it. Joshua marched toward the ranch house, his arms around a furry beast. As he got closer, Patrick could see it was a black and white border collie, and that it wasn't moving. Joshua tossed it on the front stoop. The dog landed with a heavy thud.

Patrick threw the door open. "Hey, what did you do that for?" His eyes were drawn to the dog like it was magnetized. Its tongue was hanging out and body stiff, obviously dead.

"Dr. Flint," Junior said. He lifted a hand and cut his eyes away.

Patrick drew in a breath, paused, then said, "How's that baby, Junior?"

"She's great, sir. Thank you."

"Glad to hear it."

Joshua strode back to Patrick, facing him across the carcass of the dog. "Not that I can figure out what business it is of yours, but this animal was a state champion herder. My best by far, and a great dam. She was the most valuable animal on my property. And she died a horrible death, treated like a rat. She didn't deserve that."

Patrick was surprised to see tears in the rancher's eyes. "No, she didn't."

"If Big Mike weren't already dead, I'd kill him again myself. You hear me?" Joshua jabbed a finger toward his dog. "He deserved to die like my dogs did. He had it coming to him."

The words reverberated in Patrick's head, familiar. He had no reply for Joshua. The careless poisoning of a dog was tragic. So was Big Mike beating Constance. Both were punishable offenses, but that was a matter for the legal system, not angry neighbors. At least, that was the way it should be.

Joshua turned on his heel and stomped back to his truck. Patrick watched the Manning men drive away. He toed the stiff dog off the stoop as gently as he could. Should he bury it? Or at least get it away from the house where it would attract predators? Before he could take any further action, the phone rang. After the eighth ring, he closed the front door and followed the sound into the kitchen. The caller was determined. He picked up.

"Teton residence. This is Patrick Flint." Only silence answered him. "Hello? Is anyone there?"

A man cleared his throat, then, in a raspy voice said, "Dr. Flint. I wasn't expecting you."

"Who is this?"

"Officer Dann."

Having just learned that Dann had ratted him out to Constance, he couldn't keep the irritation out of his voice. "Can I take a message? Constance just left." Patrick set the travel agency envelope on the countertop and opened drawers, one after another, looking for paper and something to write with. He found aluminum foil. Silverware. Cooking utensils. Knives. But no junk drawer and no paper and pen.

"Care to explain why you're there?"

"I left some things here after she put me up the other night. Had to pick them up so I can get out of town."

The snort from the other end of the line sounded skeptical.

"And thanks a lot for telling her I suspected her. She chewed me out, good."

"Sorry. I didn't have any idea you'd be going straight to her, not after the things you said to me."

"It wasn't like that. She had a lot to say, by the way."

Dann's voice sounded interested, unlike earlier. "Anything I should know?"

A lot, Patrick thought. But Dann had minimized his concerns about Constance before. He'd also potentially pointed a murderer at Patrick. Would bringing up Constance's bruises and her ticket to Chicago do any good? He decided it didn't matter. He had to tell Dann. It was just the right thing to do.

"She showed me bruises all over her torso and claimed Big Mike beat her."

"I'd heard rumors of that."

Well then why hadn't you done anything about it? He fought to keep the anger from his voice. It wouldn't help to drive Dann away. "And she has a plane ticket to Chicago, that she claimed she booked before any of this happened. She said she was leaving Big Mike."

"She should have left him long ago."

Something in the way he said it gave Patrick pause. After a moment, he added, "The Mannings showed up here a minute ago. With another dog that they claim died of strychnine poisoning. They blame Big Mike."

"Yes. They called me."

"Joshua said Big Mike deserved to die, and that if he wasn't already dead, he'd kill him again himself. I know I talked mostly about Constance earlier. But there are other people besides Constance with motive. Means and opportunity, too, I'm sure."

"True. But I'm beginning to have my own doubts about the Black-hawks, based on new information."

The Blackhawks. Constance *and* Eddie. Patrick froze with his fingers on the final drawer pull. "What do you mean?"

"You know how we were talking about Verna this morning? How she called Constance out, and their altercation last night?"

"Yeah."

"Well, I just got a call from the hospital in Lander. Verna's in inten-sive care there, and they suspect strychnine poisoning."

Patrick sagged into a chair at the kitchen table. Another possible strychnine case, and it just so happens to be Big Mike's sister. It couldn't be a coincidence. "Is she going to be okay?"

"You tell me."

"Depends on the dose, and how quickly they were able to treat her. Symptoms usually start about fifteen minutes after ingestion."

"You'll have to ask your wife to be sure, but I think she started convulsing at nine-thirty this morning."

"Susanne? What does she have to do with this?"

"She's the one who took Verna from her house to the hospital."

Patrick pulled at the neck of his shirt, which suddenly felt too tight, even though he hadn't buttoned the top button. *Of course.* He'd asked Susanne to return Verna's purse. So, she would have had a reason to be at Verna's house. Verna was lucky Susanne was there. "Okay. But what does that have to do with Constance? She was at the clinic, then here at her house."

"Doesn't mean she didn't do it. Or have Eddie do it for her. Every motive you listed earlier for Constance—they're the same for Eddie, and then some." Dann paused, then dropped his voice. "Constance and I, we were going to get married."

Dann was Constance's former fiancé. Patrick felt his eyebrows shoot up his forehead. "Oh?"

"It didn't work out. I cheated on her. I was young and stupid, but Eddie put me in the hospital for it, and he got put away for a while because of it. My point is that he's a scary guy, and he fights her battles, even though they don't always get along. One of them could even have put poison in something Verna ate before your wife found her. But they could have done it anytime. There's no expiration date on strychnine is there?"

"None." Dann was right. Patrick's head was spinning. It was like every new fact expanded the possibilities instead of contracting them. "Is there anyone else who would want Verna dead?"

"Just about anyone who knew her had reason to dislike her. She was unpleasant, but not someone you'd kill without a darn good reason."

"Like trying to get you arrested for murder."

"Like that."

CHAPTER THIRTY: FLEXING

Susanne

The Fort Washakie Health Center building was stucco and obviously old, but sturdier and nicer than Susanne had expected for a clinic on an impoverished reservation. *So impoverished that my husband feels he has to volunteer here one weekend a month.* Not that she was resentful, except for maybe a little. She'd be less unhappy about it if the femme fatale clinic manager wasn't making passes at her husband. She took a deep breath, let it out, then did it again.

She knew she was an hour and a half early, but after taking Verna Teton to the hospital, she was rattled, and she needed to see her husband. Verna had been so seriously, violently, and inexplicably ill. What would have happened if they hadn't taken her purse to her? She could have died in her living room, with no one even knowing she was sick. Susanne had been afraid she would die en route. That they all would, since it had been hard to keep the Suburban on the road with Susanne's eyes glued to Verna. Every time Susanne had spoken to her, it triggered another episode. Verna would spasm—face in a rictus, chin smashed, the tendons in her throat like the long toes of chicken feet, her neck and back arched. How Susanne had wished Patrick was with them.

Luckily, they'd made it, and the emergency room staff had triaged Verna to the front of the line and straight into an exam room. Susanne and the kids had left, since there was nothing else they could do for the poor woman, but Susanne had felt horribly guilty about it. She didn't even know a friend or relative to call for her. The woman at reception had promised she did and would make the calls herself.

When she'd gotten back to the hotel, Susanne hadn't wanted to stick around, couldn't just hang out at a hotel with all this nervous energy inside her. Everyone else was ready, too, and she suggested a drive out north near the clinic. *Doing something* was always the right suggestion for her daddy. No one else put up any objections. Perry couldn't get in the hot tub because of his cast, her sister and her family were already out from their soak, and Brandon and Trish were both refusing to do anything that might lessen the misery they were inflicting on themselves and the group. Within fifteen minutes—a record for Catherine and Shelley—both vehicles were on the road. Brandon even sat with Perry in the back seat this time, Trish in the front beside Susanne. Of course, the silence in the Suburban was deafening. Matthew had made the right call squeezing into the Cadillac. How could Brandon and Trish make not speaking to each other so loud?

So here they were, in Fort Washakie, at the clinic. She squeezed her hands in her lap, then released them. Her daddy parked beside her, their car noses pointed in toward the clinic.

She put her arm on the seatback. "I'll be back in a moment. I'm just going to let Patrick know about the change of plans."

Trish and Brandon didn't respond. Susanne sighed. This was going to be a long, long day.

"Okay, Mom," Perry said.

She smiled at her sweet son. Had he grown an inch since yesterday? And lost a few of his trademark freckles? His face and belly were slimming up, too. Maturity was coming for him. Her heart contracted. She wasn't ready for him to grow up. Especially if he was going to act like Trish as a teenager. "Thanks, Perry."

When she'd shut the door, she turned to the other vehicle and tapped on the front passenger glass. Her mama rolled down her window.

Susanne crouched beside the car. "I'm just running in to update Patrick."

"Okay, sweetheart."

Her daddy's deep voice reverberated comfortingly in her chest, like she'd always loved. "Forgot to tell you earlier. Patrick left his doctor's bag in the parking lot at the police station and needs us to pick it up."

It wasn't like Patrick to be forgetful. And in a parking lot? Totally out of character. "He called?"

"Hailed me on the CB. Gave himself a handle. Sawbones." He wheezed and laughed.

Will laughed, too. "Sounds like him."

"It does." Susanne smiled and patted the door frame. "Roll this window up before you freeze to death."

Her mama saluted. Susanne trotted off with one hand holding her coat collar up around her throat. She pushed open the door with the other hand.

The tiny waiting area was gloomy and humid, in stark contrast with the dry, sunny skies and snow glare outside. It also didn't smell like the other hospitals Patrick had worked in. At those, she was always assaulted with an institutional smell of disinfectant and floor wax. Here, she just smelled wet boots, people in need of a shower, and the dusty odor of old adobe. But the voice that greeted her was familiar.

"Mrs. Doc, you're early." Wes's tall, thin body loomed in the dim light toward the back of the waiting room.

"Hi, Wes. It's been a crazy morning, and our plans were flexible, so we changed them. Is Patrick here?"

Wes shifted a file to his other hand and his weight to his other foot. He stroked his mustache. Susanne thought it made him look a little like Mark Spitz. "No, he ran out to," he lowered his voice, "drop by the police."

Susanne's head tilted to the side. Hadn't he radioed her daddy that he'd left his doctor's bag there? That suggested he'd been there and gone. But maybe only a few minutes ago. "Do you expect him back soon?"

"Truth is, I expected him an hour ago."

"Oh." Unease crept into her gut.

"Can I pass a message to him for you?" When she didn't respond, he snapped his fingers. "Earth to Mrs. Doc. I've lost you."

"Sorry. Like I said, it's been quite a morning. What did you say?"

"Can I pass a message along for you?"

"Sure. Thanks. We've decided to take a drive until he's ready to go."

"Anything up?"

Spying the radiator in the corner, she walked to it and let it warm her backside. "Well, we went to return Verna's purse."

Before she could tell him the story, he cut in. "Did she give you Constance's handbag? She's been threatening to go get it herself all morning." Sotto voce he added, "And none of us want that."

"Constance is here?"

"She was. She's out running an errand—God, I hope she didn't go to Verna's—and then she's coming back."

"But her husband just died. Isn't she grieving?"

"She said working is better for her than sitting alone in their house." Wes walked over to the radiator and held his hands above it.

Or she had used this as another excuse to chase after Susanne's husband. Susanne trusted that woman like she would a snake in a nest full of eggs. "She didn't go with Patrick, did she?"

"No." Wes patted her shoulder. "Nothing to worry about there, Mrs. Doc."

Easy for him to say. He wasn't married. Plus, men didn't understand women. Not like other women did. There'd been no defeat in Constance's eyes last night. "Sorry. I don't like her."

"She's not that bad."

The radiator suddenly felt too hot, and she moved out of its range. "Apparently, I'm not the only one."

"Probably not."

The door opened. Two teenage boys stumbled in, one supporting the other.

"Can I help you?" Wes said, instantly at attention.

"He wrecked his dirt bike," one of the boys said. "Hurt his arm bad."

The other boy was cradling his right arm, using his hand to support his elbow. He groaned.

"Come on in." Wes pointed to an open door behind him. He turned to go with them.

"Are the phones working?" Susanne called after him. She was dying to call the real estate agent and find out if the sellers had accepted their offer. If they had, she and Patrick needed to drive in and sign the offer on their way back into Buffalo.

"They are. Help yourself." Wes shut the exam room door behind him.

The phone sat on a desk across the room. Susanne went to it and dialed the long-distance number. There was no way she was making a collect call. As it rang, she pulled a five-dollar bill from her purse and put it under the base of the phone.

"Buffalo Real Estate. Thunder across the plains for your own mountain view of heaven on earth." The young, female voice held a hint of boredom and embarrassment.

"Hi. This is Susanne Flint. Are Steve or Barbara there?"

"No, Mrs. Flint. They're both out with clients. Is there something I can help you with?"

"My husband and I made an offer on a house yesterday, and I was calling to check the status. We're traveling and can't be reached by phone."

"Oh, that gorgeous place on Clear Creek. I heard the doctor was looking at it." *And his wife.* "No word yet. Sorry."

Her disappointment was sharp. "Well, I'll call again later. And we should be home tonight."

"'Tis the season for holiday travel. Goodbye."

"Thank you. Bye." Susanne hung up the phone.

Wes plopped into the desk chair with a pencil and a patient file. He started scribbling in it. He muttered, "I think the numbskull in there broke his elbow."

Susanne started to bid him goodbye and leave, but then she remembered Verna. "I almost forgot to tell you. We had to take Verna to the emergency room this morning."

He lowered his pencil. "Oh, no! What was wrong with her? She's a pill, but that's not something you can treat with medication, as far as I know."

"I have no idea. She just started having the most violent seizures."

Wes's face puckered like he'd sucked a lemon. "Seizures?"

"Yes."

"What did they say was wrong with her?"

"I don't know. They wouldn't tell me anything, since I'm not family."

Wes pushed his file aside. "That's a crazy coincidence."

"What do you mean?"

"Big Mike had seizures before he died, too."

Patrick had told Susanne he thought Big Mike had been poisoned, but he hadn't mentioned seizures. "Oh my gosh."

"Patrick thinks Big Mike died from strychnine."

"And now Verna, too."

"It may be unrelated. But it's really strange."

Susanne pressed her fist against her mouth. "That poor woman. So, she's going to die?"

"Maybe it's not poison. Or maybe she got a nonlethal dose."

"I'll pray for her." Susanne closed her eyes and sent a quick silent prayer to the man upstairs. *Dear God, please help Verna survive this.* She couldn't believe they'd been there, at the same place and maybe even the same time as someone was poisoning another human. She decided to tack on praise, hoping God would take it as a suggestion for continued favor. *And thank you, God, for keeping the kids, Patrick, and me safe. Amen.*

She opened her eyes. "Do you think I should go to the police about this?"

"Not unless you saw something or somebody that would help them. But if you did, be warned. In general, the Indians on the Wind River Reservation aren't eager for what they consider outside interference, so you might not get a warm welcome."

"Patrick mentioned that." Susanne shook her head. "But I didn't see anything."

"There you go, then. You're off the hook. But are you sure you don't want me to just drive Patrick back to Buffalo with me? You're going to be in the car an awfully long time today."

Susanne shook off the bad news about Verna. "Thanks, but we're good."

He nodded. "Gotta get back to my patient."

She waved, turning to exit and he went back to the exam room. There was no way she was leaving Patrick here after coming all this way to get him. Especially with Constance on the prowl and sniffing around Patrick.

CHAPTER THIRTY-ONE: DISCOVER

Patrick

After hanging up the phone with Dann, Patrick looked at his watch. It was eleven o'clock. He needed to get back to the clinic to meet Susanne and their family. If he left the T-ton Ranch now, he'd have time to see a few patients before leaving at noon, too, if he was needed for it. But again, he saw Big Mike's face. Not the face of the dead man on the table at the clinic, but the live one from his dreams, and he felt a renewed sense of duty.

He scanned the kitchen. Was there anywhere else in the house he should look? Even though it wasn't new to him, his eyes landed and stayed on the glossy blue travel agency envelope he'd set on the counter-top. Opening it, he leafed through the documents, then frowned. The first document was the itinerary. The second was a ticket to Chicago in Constance's name. The third was another ticket to Chicago. But the name on it was John Doe.

"What in the hell, Constance?"

There was no way she had a real "John Doe" in her life. Was this just a way of getting a ticket that anyone could fly on? He'd flown on a ticket from Dallas to Austin once that was in Susanne's name. The airlines didn't check identification, so it hadn't mattered that he was fifty pounds heavier, eight inches taller, and not a woman. But who could Constance intend this one for? Not Big Mike, if she was leaving him.

Did Constance have a boyfriend already? Elvin's insinuation about Constance at Dairy Land came back to him. She could have booked the ticket like this in case Big Mike found it, to keep the guy's name a secret from him. But what about the way she'd been coming on to Patrick—was that fake? He snorted. While he didn't have any interest in her, he didn't like being played either. Giving her the benefit of the doubt, maybe she'd been seeing someone when she made the reservation, but they'd broken up since then.

Or maybe she intended this for me, and she showed me the tickets to gauge my reaction. But she wouldn't have had time to get the tickets since he'd arrived. He'd been with her practically nonstop, at least during the hours a travel agency would have been open. His breath caught. Except when she left him at the hospital, heading for the automobile repair shop and the funeral home. She could have ducked into a travel agency. Purchased a ticket then. God forbid she'd been interested in him all along and had bought it before Big Mike died, before Patrick even arrived in Fort Washakie, if it was for him.

Whatever the reason, Patrick's interest in looking around was re-piqued. Not to try to figure out the identity of the person Constance intended the ticket for, per se. But to search for something that would prove whether Big Mike was murdered, and whether Constance was the one who did it, especially since Verna had likely been poisoned, too. Because, if Constance did it, she had a lot of incentive to get rid of anything even slightly suspicious.

This might be the last chance for anyone to find anything at the ranch.

The barn would be next, he decided. He placed the tickets, itinerary, and envelope back on the counter, then slipped out the front door. That's where Big Mike would have kept his infamous dog-killing strychnine. He stomped snow down to make a path to the old white wooden barn, intersecting the trail of another set of human footprints that wound around ten feet from the building. He studied them, suddenly feeling less alone, but unable to tell anything from them. Was someone here, watching him? He listened intently, heard nothing. *I'm being paranoid.* Most likely, these tracks were from Constance or Eddie feeding livestock that morning.

Returning his attention to the barn doors, he found them secured with a heavy padlock. *Damn.* But when he lifted the lock, it fell open. A ruse, but not an unusual one. From a distance, it appeared locked to deter would-be thieves. Patrick unfastened the latch and hung the lock back on it.

Wind-blown snow was a fine sandpaper against his skin. He slid the doors open and peered into the dark interior. From somewhere nearby, a coyote howled with the wind, followed by the excited yips of a pack. Patrick hurried inside and sneezed. The barn was segmented. Six stalls —three to a side—with aged wooden slat fencing, each stall filled with hay to the top rails. More lofts groaned with hay above on both sides of the building, with a floor-to-ceiling opening down the center of the barn. On the near end of the stalls was tool storage. The roomy center aisle held two tractors parked one in front of the other. And on the far end of the barn, behind the last row of stalls, was the feed and tack.

The tool area was his first stop. It was crowded with farm and ranch implements of all types, a few new ones but mostly wooden-handled older items. Shovels. Axes. Sledgehammers. A post hole digger. Smaller tools like screw drivers, hammers, and wrenches. Jar after jar after jar of nails, screws, nuts, bolts, and fasteners.

Patrick didn't see anything resembling poisons, so he sidled around the tractors and headed for the feed area. Wooden pallets lined the floor there, with bags of cattle and horse feed stacked on top of two of them. Fertilizer was on a third. And, on a fourth, he found pesticides. The sight of the chemicals electrified him like jumper cables to a dead battery, and his heart pounded madly. He moved in close, crouching and scanning the names on the sacks, looking for strychnine, rodenticide, or any brand names that suggested the killing of furry pests.

Nothing.

He turned in a tight circle. This felt like the right area, and Big Mike had the stuff at one time, recently. It had to be here. His eyes lit on a work bench at the far side of the partitioned space. On one end was a cubby holder with jars of pills and potions. He hurried over and read labels. Bute. Ivermectin. Penicillin. Epinephrine. They were names he recognized as vet medicines for cattle and horses. A baggie filled with syringes and droppers. Nothing suspicious. He was about to give up when he saw a green plastic tub with the words GOPHER GONE emblazoned across it on the far end of the space.

Bingo. Patrick scooted down to it for a closer look.

CHAPTER THIRTY-TWO: DEADEND

Trish

"The rest of the group is going to visit Sacajawea's grave," Susanne announced, as she backed out of the parking spot at the clinic. "We're dropping by the police station."

Trish stared at her lap, vaguely aware of the blur of snow-covered pastures in her peripheral vision. "Why?" Not that she was interested in Sacajawea's grave. That was her dad's kind of thing, not hers. This ride was living hell, and she just wanted to go home. To be out of this car where Brandon sat right behind her, hating her. Where she could call Marcy. Marcy would understand what a jerk Brandon was being. She'd let Trish cry or yell or scream as long and hard as she needed. When Trish felt better, they'd make popcorn with extra butter and plot out the all-important post-break-up moves.

"Your dad was there and left his doctor's bag."

"Is he leaving with us from here then?" *Please oh please oh please, God.*

"I don't know. I think he has to go back to the clinic first. But, no matter what, we need to find him and tell him our plans."

Trish sighed deeply, all the way to her toes. She heard Brandon make a sound like a snort from the back seat. She wanted to flip him off, but she also wanted him to change his mind and be her boyfriend again. Her hand stayed in her lap, twitching like a dying fish.

Susanne didn't react to Trish's sigh. "Mr. Braten thinks Verna might have been poisoned."

"You mean Wes?" Trish tried to think of a reason she cared about what had happened to a woman she didn't even know. Her tough girl attitude slipped, though. She cared a little. Maybe more than a little. The woman had been in their car, after all, which had been horrible and scary, and Trish felt bad for her.

"Mr. Braten to you kids."

Even though he'd always told Trish to call him Wes. Her mom could be such a pain with her old-fashioned rules. It was like she didn't even realize it was going to be 1977 in a few *days*.

Trish closed her eyes as a wave of guilt hit her. After she'd gotten away from the men who had kidnapped her up in the Bighorns, she'd promised God and herself that she'd be nicer to everyone and even go to church. Thinking about that took her mind to Ben and her fight with Brandon, but she pushed those thoughts aside. She'd been doing better— being nicer—until lately. She didn't know what it was that had made her so irritable. It wasn't all the time. Just every couple of weeks. Something just came over her and everything bugged her, and she couldn't control her mouth. She knew she'd been awful to Brandon earlier. And maybe to everybody else. It had been so embarrassing, though. Her whole family had heard what Brandon said to her. But they'd also heard what she had said to him. Tears welled up in her eyes, and she turned her face to the window.

Brandon was right. She'd been a beast.

She clenched her fists. She would do better. She would. Starting right now, and then maybe people would like her again. Which brought her back to what her mom had been saying about that woman who she really did feel bad for. That Verna had been poisoned. And Verna was the same woman who'd had a cat fight in the restaurant last night with the woman who was after Trish's dad.

Wait a minute—the woman who was after Trish's dad. *What was her name?* "Could that Connie woman have done it? They had a major fight last night."

"Connie?" Susanne said. "You mean Constance?"

"Yeah. Her."

Her mom's voice was tight. "I don't know. The police will have to figure it out."

Perry flopped over the front seat, his chin in his hands, his elbows dangling. "Or it could have been that guy I saw there."

"What guy, where?" Susanne asked.

"I didn't see a guy," Trish said.

"The one leaving right when I was walking up to the house."

"I was trying to get the car unstuck," Susanne said. "I didn't see him."

I was crying, because the love of my life had just broken up with me, so I didn't either.

Susanne put on a blinker then turned into the police station parking area. "What did he look like Perry?"

"Um, I don't know. I didn't see his face. I wasn't really looking. It was kinda hard getting across that yard in my cast."

"Okay." Susanne grabbed her purse and opened the door. "I'll be back after I check on your dad's bag. And hopefully talk to your father."

"This is a police station?" Trish looked out the window. They were at a small, nondescript metal building surrounded by prairie and blowing snow. "It's in the middle of nowhere."

"We're in a town. It's not nowhere."

Perry said, "How did Dad get here?"

Susanne hopped out of the car but leaned back in. "What do you mean?"

"It's just that there are no other cars here besides police cars."

Susanne looked around, then frowned. "Wes's big green monster should be here if he is."

"Gussie." Perry smiled. "Cool car."

Trish didn't want to stay in here with her dopey brother or the painful presence of her ex-boyfriend. "I'm coming with you."

She leapt down from the Suburban, and the wind almost knocked her over. Even with the sun out, she was colder than a lizard in Alaska. She'd left her coat in the car, but she wasn't going to make an idiot of herself going back to get it. Hustling, she caught up with her mom just in time to run inside the police building behind her.

Which is why she was able to hear her mom loud and clear when the first person she saw inside was Constance.

"Son of a bitch," Susanne muttered.

Trish's mom *never* cussed, but who could blame her? If her mom knew what Trish had overheard Constance saying to that guy outside the motel, she'd be even more pissed. "Isn't he perfect," she'd said, when the guy had asked if she was involved with Trish's dad. Then, "She's kind of mousy, don't you think? Not a match for him. And he doesn't wear a wedding ring." And she'd giggled. *Giggled. So rude.* Like it was all some kind of joke instead of other people's lives. Her mom's and dad's. And hers.

Trish moved closer to her mom and grabbed her elbow in a show of support.

Constance was sitting on a brown leather couch in a small waiting area, her legs crossed, one-foot swinging. She glanced up and saw them. "Mrs. Flint. Hello."

Susanne nodded. Trish refused to look at Constance.

A door opened, and a dark-eyed man with a mustache like Wes's stuck his shaved head out. "May I help you?"

"She was here first." Susanne sounded stiff and cold.

The man said, "We've already helped her. She's waiting to talk to Officer Dann." His voice was high pitched, and his teeth were yellow and crooked.

"I'm here looking for my husband's doctor's bag."

The man nodded. "Big leather case, right? Someone brought it in earlier. Said it was left in the parking lot. I'll get it for you."

"Wait. Is my husband here? His co-worker said he was coming by."

"What's his name?"

"Patrick Flint."

At the same time as the officer was shaking his head and saying, "He's not here, Mrs. Flint," Constance was nodding and smiling. The man ducked behind the door, leaving it ajar.

Constance studied her nails. They were short and unpainted. "He left here a long time ago. When I last saw him, he was still at my place. The T-Ton Ranch. If you drive fifteen miles out 132, you can't miss it. On the left." She looked up and gave Susanne a mean smile with no teeth.

Susanne's arm tensed in Trish's hand. After her crazy cussing outburst earlier, Trish was afraid to see how her mom would react to this.

The man appeared holding her dad's doctor's bag. "Here you go."

Susanne took it from him. "Thank you," she said, before walking outside with a calm look on her face.

As soon as the door shut behind them, Trish said, "I can't believe her."

Susanne's face went to full-on snarl in an instant. "I can't believe your father."

"Um, Mom, there's something I need to tell you. Something Constance said."

"What?" Susanne wheeled around.

Trish repeated Constance's words to her.

Her mom's face turned red and splotchy.

Papa Fred's Cadillac pulled up beside them. Sacajawea's grave must not have been all that exciting, since they'd only been gone ten minutes.

Papa Fred rolled down his window. "Where next, Tootie?"

Susanne pasted a smile on her face. She never liked other people to know she was upset. "An excursion to the T-ton Ranch. Follow me."

CHAPTER THIRTY-THREE: DEFEND

Patrick

Outside the barn, an engine noise started, grew louder, and then went silent. Patrick backed away from the work bench. If Constance had returned, he didn't want to be caught snooping, again. And if Eddie was out there, well, that was even worse. He already hadn't felt comfortable around Eddie, but since the encounter at the funeral home and the suspicions Dann had voiced, he wanted even less to do with the man. He exited the barn at a trot, checking in all directions for one of their cars. He didn't see them, but he did see a snowmobile. It looked like the one he'd seen Riley on before. He exhaled with relief and closed the barn doors.

He tramped over to the house, glancing at his watch. Eleven fifteen. Time to lock it up, like Constance had asked him to, and get back to the clinic. But nature called first. And not the kind he could do against the side of the barn. He'd just use the guest bathroom before he left. It wasn't like he hadn't already been in the house. Returning wouldn't make his intrusion any worse.

He toed the snow off his hiking boots, which were now damp—water resistant and water repellant were not the same thing, and they needed another good coating of Scotchgard—and went inside. The house was still eerily quiet, save for the low hum of the refrigerator. With the heat off and then recently on again, there was a mild scent of burning dust. He switched on a light in the hallway from the kitchen to the guest bathroom, then stopped. Something looked different than when he'd been in the kitchen earlier. He looked around, but he couldn't put his finger on it.

Shrugging, he walked down the hall and into the bathroom. Just before he entered the door, it hit him. He hadn't seen *anything*, and he had left the travel agency documents and envelope on the kitchen counter. Someone had been in here. Someone had moved them.

"Hello?" he called out. "Constance? Are you home?"

Maybe she'd parked her Cherokee out of sight. With no trees for miles he wasn't sure where that would be, but it wasn't his ranch. He didn't know the place. She could have parked behind the house for some reason.

But she didn't answer him.

He swallowed down a lump in his throat. His heartbeat was an accelerating drumroll in his ears. Holding his breath, he walked back into the kitchen. "Hello? Is anybody here?"

Still no answer.

He hurried into the bathroom and back out again as soon as he was done. He got the creepy feeling of another human presence as soon as he reached the kitchen. "This is Patrick Flint. Is somebody in the house?"

From the living room, a man's voice said, "Where's Constance?"

Patrick jumped sideways into one of the kitchen table chairs. There hadn't been anyone in the living room when he'd entered, had there? "Who's there?"

A rocking chair creaked. Footsteps approached. Patrick couldn't just cower in the kitchen like a child, so he walked to intercept the person. When he exited the dining room into the living room, he nearly ran into Riley coming from the other direction. The man was in jeans and a sweater, his snowsuit hanging on the coat hooks by the door behind him. He looked grim, but then he always did with the mask of scarring immobilizing his face.

Patrick put his hands up and laughed. "Riley. You scared me to death. Constance just left. I came in to use the bathroom before I locked up and got out of here, too."

Riley stood, like a slab of granite. "I talked to her."

"Oh?"

"She's upset."

"Yeah. I think the police want to question her about Verna."

"That won't happen."

Patrick returned to the kitchen and leaned his butt against the counter. "I don't know. Dann sounded like he meant it."

"Justin Dann." Riley snorted from the doorway. "The man is smitten with her."

"Really?"

"She doesn't return his feelings, of course. But they dated in high school."

Patrick crossed his arms across his chest and his legs at the ankles. "That explains a lot," he said, drawing the word "that" out extra-long.

"A lot of what?"

"Oh, just some weird feelings I got around the two of them together. And from Dann separately."

"He was probably just jealous."

"Of what?"

"Oh, come on, like you're not after her, too."

Patrick dropped his arms and pulled away from the counter. "I'm not. I'm married. Happily married."

"I saw you earlier. Through the window. Constance with her clothes off." Riley went to the refrigerator and got out a bottle of beer. He opened a drawer and withdrew a bottle opener. His tone never changed. "Want one?"

The conversation felt surreal. Patrick had to clear up the misunderstanding. He worked with Riley. And Constance. "Sure," he said. Then, "Listen, that wasn't what it looked like. I swear."

Riley pulled another beer from the refrigerator. "These were Big Mike's favorites." He popped the tops, dropped them in the trash, then put the bottle opener away in the drawer.

"I don't think Constance is in control of her actions right now. Grief does funny things to people."

Riley walked up to him, holding the new beer. "I hated Big Mike, too." Then, instead of handing Patrick the beer, he cracked him over the skull with it.

Patrick's vision went black, and he felt himself crumpling. He tried to catch the edge of the counter, but his world tilted, and his hand missed. A field of black blossomed with shooting stars. Then his head hit the floor, and there was nothing.

CHAPTER THIRTY-FOUR: SURVIVE

Patrick

Patrick groaned as he tried to move his arms. They were stuck somehow, so he rolled his neck, eyes closed. What had happened to him? The blank space in his head filled quickly with images. Riley. The beer bottle. His vision fading away. He gasped and tried harder to move first his arms and then his legs but failed. His head swam. He wanted to clutch it, to hold it still. Warily, he opened his eyes.

At first, all he saw was wavy lines of color, like an old television with the rabbit ears out of whack. Then his brain and his eyes connected, and he saw a face. Riley Pearson's face. The hideous burn scar. His eyes, cold, black, and flat. A green plastic tub on the table beside him, with the words GOPHER GONE across it, and a mason jar of milky liquid beside it, lid off. The travel agency envelope and documents peeked out from underneath the tub. Looking down, he saw his wrists tied together to one of the arms of a kitchen chair with what appeared to be a shoelace. He leaned forward. His ankles were restrained in the same way, and his hiking boots had no laces.

"We already both know I'm better at this than you. Write me a rec for nursing school—what a joke. You're not half the doctor I could have been." Riley's voice sounded like it was far away. "I hate weasels like you who used your *privilege* to get out of Vietnam."

Too late, Patrick looked back up and saw the needle as Riley expertly injected it into a vein in his left arm.

Jerking his whole body and popping his arms straight at the elbows, Patrick fought to get away from the needle. Riley had obviously dealt with large animal injections before, because, after sticking the needle in, he released the plunger so that Patrick's movements didn't pull the needle back out. Patrick bucked in the chair, but the syringe stayed in place. He wrenched his upper body to the left as hard as he could. The chair teetered over, then crashed to the floor.

The fragile arms busted away from the old chair on impact, and Patrick's wrists were freed from it but still bound. Dazed, he was desperate but not quick or agile. He kicked his legs out, and that shoelace slid down the intact chair leg. Riley launched himself onto Patrick's side. He pushed the plunger down in the syringe. Patrick rolled violently to the right toward the cabinets, slamming Riley's head into a cabinet door. Riley lost contact with the plunger again.

"Argh," Patrick yelled.

Adrenaline and terror were giving him back some of his strength. He exploded upward, dumping Riley's body to the floor, then flipped to his hands and knees with the syringe dangling from the inside of his elbow joint. Awkwardly, he scrambled away. Without the chair arm, the shoelace was loose around his wrists, and he pulled his right hand free. He tried to get a foot out of his other restraints, but his boots were too bulky. He kicked one off—something he couldn't have done if they were laced—and was about to try again when Riley bellowed and swam across the floor to grab Patrick's ankles. Patrick kicked at the man but couldn't break his hold.

Riley pulled him backwards. From his position on his rump, Patrick dug his fingertips and nails into the grooves between the old plank floorboards, clinging to the floor as he kept kicking. His kicks broke the shoelace, liberating his ankles. It helped, but it wasn't enough to shake Riley's viselike grip. What Patrick needed was to get the needle out of his arm. He knew what that syringe contained. Gopher Gone. Strychnine. Every nanosecond that passed was another chance for Riley to finish injecting the poison, and for the poison already in Patrick's body to do its damage.

In order to get the syringe out, though, Patrick would have to stop kicking and let go of the floor with his right hand. When he did, he knew Riley would be on him like a grizzly on a wounded elk. He would have one shot at this, and not much of one, and it had to be soon. It had to be now.

Patrick released his right grip on the floor as he stilled his feet and ducked his right shoulder under, lifting the left shoulder at the same time. His left hand came loose from its grasp on the floor, too. He was all-in. Riley grabbed his ankles and jerked Patrick toward him. Shoving his right hand below his chest in a sort of push-up as he slid backwards toward Riley, Patrick found the fat plastic syringe with his left hand. Careful not to knock it off and break the needle in his arm, he grasped its base and ripped it outward. Riley pounced on his thighs. For a split second, Patrick thought about jamming the needle into Riley's shoulder as he came at him, but too much could go wrong. He had to get rid of the needle. Just before Riley landed on Patrick's upper body, Patrick rolled over and threw the poison and its applicator as far across the room as he could. It hit the floor and skidded under the refrigerator.

Riley hissed in his ear. "It won't do you any good. I had three times as much in there as I needed to kill you."

Patrick struggled to get out from under Riley's weight. Riley was lighter, but Patrick was pinned like a turtle on his back and still foggy from the blow to his head. To his surprise, though, Riley released him, hopping to his feet like a cat. Patrick propelled himself quickly backward and away, ramming into the wall where he sat, stunned, while Riley caught his breath and eyed him like Patrick was a coiled rattler, poised to strike.

His mind raced to catch up with all that had happened and what it meant. Strychnine. Riley had injected him with strychnine. Head and neck seizures would start in about twenty minutes. Spasms would spread to every muscle in his body, until he would be in nearly continuous convulsions that would worsen at the slightest stimulus. The convulsions would progress, increasing in intensity and frequency until his backbone would arch and stay that way. His death would come after two to three hours, from asphyxiation caused by paralysis of the neural pathways that control breathing, or by exhaustion from the convulsions.

He needed his medical bag. In it, he kept phenobarbital, an anti-seizure med, along with valium. The more his anxiety ramped up—and how could he not be anxious when he'd been injected full of poison?—

the worse his seizures would be. He definitely needed the valium. And muscle relaxants, which were in there, too. He had no idea how much of the poison Riley had pumped into him. If he'd managed to inject a lethal dose, Patrick might not have a chance anyway. But he couldn't think like that. The meds from his bag could help him, possibly even save him.

If he had the bag. Which he didn't. Because he'd left it on the ground in the parking lot of the police station. *How could I have been so stupid?* He remembered his CB call to Papa Fred, asking him to have Susanne bring it with her from the police station to the health clinic. If she'd even picked it up yet, she was half an hour away. And he was that far or more from a hospital. Not that anyone was going to be taking him to one. He was alone here, except for Riley. All he had left was prayer.

He sent up a quick one. *Dear Heavenly Father, thank you for the wonderful life I've had with my wife and children. I'd like to keep living it. Please help my body resist this poison. Please send help. Amen.*

Riley said, "Your lips are moving. Only crazy people talk to themselves. Or at least that's what I've heard."

Patrick's mind leapfrogged back to seeing Riley talking to himself. He hated that they had that in common.

Riley sat in one of the remaining chairs. He crossed his arms and leaned back with a slight smile pulling at the scar on his face. "You were running off with her to Chicago. I saw the tickets. John Doe. I'll bet you think you're so clever. But you're married. And you would have just hurt her. I couldn't let that happen. No one is allowed to hurt Constance. No one."

Patrick touched the needle mark in his arm. He wished he could burrow into the skin and claw the poison out. "No, I wasn't. I'm not."

"I know you're not anymore. You're not going anywhere."

"You don't understand. I thought she killed Big Mike. I went to Dann to tell him I thought she did it. She made a pass at me, trying to get me to change my mind. I never touched her." His heart was racing. Was it fear or the poison? Strychnine was a convulsant *and* a stimulant, used in prior centuries for recreational purposes and as an athletic enhancer, before people got smart to how lethal it was. And now stimulation was bad for Patrick. He needed away from Riley, from any and all agitation. He had to get out. Get in Gussie. Drive like mad for the hospital. Like Big Mike had done, and hope it did him more good.

Big Mike. The dead man in his dreams had been right. Patrick should have worked harder to figure out who the trickster had been, before he had the chance to hurt Verna. And Patrick.

Riley dropped his arms, his fists clenched. "You turned her in to the cops?" Spittle flew with his words. "I should have done this sooner. *No one* gets to hurt Constance. Not you, not that bully of a husband or his crazy sister, her alcoholic parents, or her user brother."

He heard a car engine outside. What was Riley talking about? Had Riley killed Constance's parents and Eddie? "Did you poison Eddie?"

Riley's grin was maniacal. "Not yet, but he's next." He checked his watch, then saluted Patrick. "I'll be going now. No sense getting caught before the job is done. Or ever."

"Constance will hate you for this."

"She'll never find out." He wiped down the two beer bottles with his shirt. He winked with the eye embedded in scar tissue. "Fingerprints." After he threw them away, he grabbed the travel agency documents, the bucket of Gopher Gone, and a handful of syringes from the counter. "Have a nice life, doctor. What's left of it."

Then he walked out. Out of the room, and out of the front door to the house.

Patrick squeezed his temples. Time to make a run for it in Gussie. Or should he call an ambulance? His head hurt so bad. Then he had an idea, and he scrambled to his feet, fighting off waves of dizziness and nausea. Medicine cabinet. Constance ran a health clinic, had access to medications. Maybe she had what he needed. It was worth a minute or two to find out. He crashed down the hall toward the master bath.

CHAPTER THIRTY-FIVE: CONFRONT

Kinnear, Wyoming
Tuesday, December 21, 1976, Eleven-thirty-five a.m.

Susanne

"You're talking to yourself, Mom. Like Dad," Perry chirped from the back seat.

Susanne goosed the accelerator. Fence posts and barbed wire on either side of the road blurred. She was nearly snowblind without her sunglasses, which were God knows where. The Suburban hit a bump and caught air, then landed in a pothole that shuddered the frame. The tank-like vehicle bounced out and sledded across the packed snow. It didn't slow Susanne down a bit.

Trish made a show of righting herself in the passenger seat. "You're going to run us off the road and get stuck. And there's no one around to help."

Ahead less than half a mile and closing, Susanne could see the T-ton ranch headquarters. A sprawling one-story house. An old white barn with a dark roof. A smaller house, like the kind built for a ranch fore-man. *Good. I'm almost there. Brace yourself, Patrick.*

When she'd turned off the main road, she'd had no idea how far it was from the ranch entrance to the buildings, but fueled by her rage, she hadn't even cared. She would have driven to Canada and back to confront her husband. How dare he? How dare he act like he was single? With her entire family tagging along to bear witness to his betrayal. And then he'd topped it all off by lying to her about it, too. If the Suburban could get there faster by flying, she'd roll down the windows and start flapping her arms. That's how badly she wanted to light into her husband.

She glanced in the rearview mirror. It was too bumpy to tell whether Papa Fred and crew had kept up with them. "Is Papa Fred still back there?"

"Uh, let me look," Brandon said.

Susanne was mildly surprised to hear his voice. She'd been so upset with Patrick she'd forgotten Brandon was even with them. Or that he and Trish had been making things uncomfortable for everyone earlier. But it made sense for him to look. Brandon was more agile than Perry, who was hampered by his cast. She glanced in the rearview mirror.

The older boy turned around and knelt in the seat. "He's there, but, like, way back."

"Thanks."

The road flattened and smoothed as they neared the house. She took a moment to scan the area. It was barren, like most of this Godforsaken state. No trees, no animals. Just wind, snow, and rocks, big and small. In the distance, more of the same, and no neighbors that she could see. She'd go stir crazy from the isolation if she lived out here. A cry welled up in her as she thought about where she did live, and where she wanted to live, but she swallowed it back. The house. The house on Clear Creek that she thought she and Patrick would build their future in. If he was cheating on her, all of that was just a fantasy. Real only in her mind, going poof in reality.

The Suburban careened around a curve and into the parking area in front of the buildings, coming in hot on Wes's green Travelall. The long vehicle lost traction. Trish squealed. Susanne gripped the steering wheel tight with both hands and let off the gas. The tires found their grip again, but then she jammed on the brakes, sending them into a fast slide sideways toward the house.

"Jeez, Mom. Watch out," Trish shouted, her voice high and strained.

A man in a white snow suit jumped out of their way from the front steps of the house. Susanne had a fleeting impression of a hideous scar on his face and wide eyes. But that was all. She was too focused on trying to stop.

"Is that the guy who was asking Constance about your dad this morning, Trish?" Brandon's excited voice was close to Susanne's ear.

Trish was bracing her feet against the floorboard. She had one hand on the ceiling and the other gripping the armrest. When the Suburban finally came to a stop, she flopped against her seat. Then she leaned toward the windshield. The scarred man made eye contact with her before walking toward the smaller house.

Trish nodded. "Yeah, it's him. I wonder what he's doing here with Dad."

Perry bounced in the back seat. "I think it's the same guy I saw leaving the sick lady's house. Verna's house."

Susanne could care less about anyone but Patrick. "I'm going in to talk to your father. Alone." Leaving the keys in the ignition, she wrenched the door open and bounded out.

Before she slammed the door, she heard Trish say, "Like any of us wants to be in there for *that*."

Knowing that Constance was at the police station, Susanne didn't bother knocking when she reached the house. She threw the door open so hard it banged on the outside wall. "Patrick Flint, I know you're in here. Your girlfriend told me where to find you. Get out here so we can talk."

She stepped inside before he could answer. Her eyes had trouble adjusting from the snow glare to a room with no lights. She flicked the switch by the door, revealing a living room painted a dark green with a big gray stone fireplace on the far side. She had a quick impression of Army memorabilia and Indian blankets as she marched through.

"Patrick?"

She heard footsteps. Running. Then Patrick appeared in the far door to the kitchen. He lurched against the countertop, one hand holding his head. His bloody head.

"Patrick." The word came out on a rush of air. All thoughts of him and Constance, all her anger vanished. He was hurt.

He took a giant step toward her, catching himself on the dining room table. "Help me."

"Your head. What's wrong?" She ran to him and grabbed his elbow.

"Dizzy. Concussion. No meds here. My bag. Did you bring my bag?"

"Your duffel?"

"No, my kit. My doctor's bag."

"Oh, yes. It's in the Suburban." She stared into his eyes, trying to figure out what had happened to him.

"I need it. Fast. I've been poisoned, with strychnine. We don't have much time. Get it for me."

Susanne's brain felt like it would explode, but she whirled and ran as fast as she could for the car without another word. When she burst from the house, waving her arms, she found Perry outside the vehicle, standing by the rear driver's side door. "Your dad's medical bag. Get it. Hurry."

Perry leaned into the backseat. She heard him describing the bag to Brandon, who dove into the third seat. By the time she reached them, Brandon had handed it out to Perry.

Her son said, "What's wrong, Mom?"

"Your dad's been poisoned." She grabbed the bag and fled back into the house.

Behind her, she heard Perry shout, "Like Verna?"

But she didn't have time to answer him. She had to get to Patrick.

CHAPTER THIRTY-SIX: RESCUE

Perry

Perry turned back toward the Suburban. It only took him a second to put two and two together. He screamed at his sister. "Trish, that's the guy who poisoned Verna and now he's poisoned Dad." He pointed after the scarred man, who was now helmeted and getting on a snowmobile. "We can't let him get away."

The snowmobile engine revved. The man shot a glance at them. Had he heard Perry? Probably not with the wind as loud as a freight train. Inside the car, Trish scrambled across the front seat into the driver's side. Perry almost shouted to ask her what she was doing. She didn't have her license yet, and their parents would be really mad if she drove without permission. But that didn't seem to bother her. She started the Suburban's engine.

All of a sudden, the snowmobile went flying across the yard, toward the gap between the house and the opposite side of the barn from where it had been parked. The Suburban shot forward like a cannonball, t-boning the snowmobile. It smashed through the wall of the barn, and the whole front half of the Suburban disappeared as it pushed the machine and its rider inside.

"Trish," Perry shouted.

After a second that felt like an eternity, Brandon jumped out of the back seat.

"Is Trish okay?" Perry yelled. He was torn between running to help his sister and going after his mom and dad.

"I think she's fine." Brandon pushed through some siding to Trish's window. Perry heard him shouting at her.

Papa Fred's Cadillac pulled to a stop where the Suburban had been a moment before. His grandfather jumped out first, then his uncle.

Perry called out, "Be careful. There's a man in the barn who poisoned my dad. And Trish may be hurt."

Papa Fred paused. "Is your dad okay?"

"Mom's with him."

Papa Fred nodded, then ran after Uncle Will toward the barn. Just then, there were loud scraping noises, and the Suburban backed out, with boards gaping like broken teeth around it.

Brandon held up a pitchfork. "I've got him."

Uncle Will ran into the open side of the barn after Brandon. Papa Fred detoured to the Suburban to check on Trish. Uncle Will grabbed a long-handled ax. Then he and Brandon disappeared from view.

Trish was going to be all right. Perry didn't care if the bad guy was hurt or not. His mom and dad needed him most now. He turned and crutched toward the house. He hit a slippery patch, where he teetered until a blast of wind splatted him hard on the concrete steps. There was a loud crack as his casted ankle hit the corner of the bottom step.

Pain shot through Perry's ankle. The cast had split in two, from top to bottom, right through the hole he'd pounded with the chisel and mallet the day before.

CHAPTER THIRTY-SEVEN: AID

Patrick

The windows rattled in the grip of the wind.

"I've got your bag." Susanne was out of breath, but she ran to Patrick's side. He was sitting on the couch, and she kneeled in front of him, putting the bag in his lap. "What can I do?"

Patrick ripped it open with shaking hands. He'd already calculated the dosage for valium, phenobarbital, and ibuprofen. A telltale tightening in his jaw and neck started. *Am I imaging the symptoms because I'm scared?* "Water. Hurry. *Hurry.*"

Susanne jumped up, knocking into the coffee table and sending a few hardcover books to the carpet. She ran into the kitchen, where Patrick heard a cabinet slam shut and the tap water running. He opened the different bottles and amassed the pills in his hand. As fast as Susanne was moving, she couldn't go back in time, and that was what would have helped him most. To never have been poisoned in the first place. His jaw and neck went hard again, and he was certain now that this and the agitation he was feeling was the stimulant effect of the strychnine. The convulsions wouldn't be far behind.

"Here." Susanne was back, handing him a glass.

Water sloshed over the edge and down the side onto his hand. He put the small handful of pills in his mouth and gulped the entire glass of water.

"Now what?" Susanne said.

Patrick felt the first seizure start. His neck stiffened, his face grew tight and spasms rolled over it.

"Patrick," Susanne screamed. "Patrick, oh my God, Patrick." She put her hand behind his head to support it.

What felt like an eternity passed, then the seizure ended. Immediately, Patrick jumped to his feet. "This isn't going to be pretty. But you've got to ignore it and get me to the hospital."

Susanne slipped her arm around his waist. "Lean on me. It's slippery outside."

They exited the house, almost tripping over Perry prone on the ground.

His face was pinched and concerned. "Are you okay, Dad?"

Susanne didn't pay any attention to the child at their feet. "Where's the Suburban? I have to get your dad to the hospital in Lander right now."

"Over by the barn."

"We'll take Gussie." Patrick fished the keys from his pocket and handed them to Susanne. "I don't know how much longer I have before another seizure."

CHAPTER THIRTY-EIGHT: UNITE

Perry

As his mom and dad climbed into the Travelall, Trish ran to Perry's side. "What's going on?" She was out of breath, and her cheeks were bright red, matching the blood on her forehead.

Perry pushed up on one elbow. "Mom's taking Dad to the hospital." He tried to keep his voice steady, but it cracked. His dad had told him it would start changing soon, but he didn't think that was the problem.

Trish broke away at a run. Over her shoulder, she shouted, "Get up. We've got to follow them." Her voice was swallowed up by the wind, but he could read her lips.

He rolled onto his side, tried to stand, and fell back. "I can't. I think I broke my ankle again. Or at least my cast."

Trish spun like her horse Goldie around the barrels, returning to crouch beside him. Blood dripped onto the snow and his cast. Perry shivered. The snow had melted into his clothes, turning him into a human popsicle.

"Come on." She wrapped an arm around him. "Good thing you're a shrimp."

For once, he didn't argue. He could gripe her out after he was in a car with the heater going full blast.

Before she could help him up, Papa Fred's shadow fell across them. He grunted. "We'll be following your parents into the hospital just as soon as I call the popo to come get our hostage."

"Okay," Trish said.

From the barn, Brandon and Uncle Will emerged, marching toward Papa Fred's car with Riley hopping on one leg between them, his shoulders hunched, his face down, and his wrists behind his back. A long piece of rope was dragging the ground like a tail.

Trish hoisted Perry up. "We'll be in the Suburban."

Perry stood on one foot while she handed him his crutches. Blood rushed to his ankle and foot, and they throbbed like he was pounding them with the stupid mallet he'd used a few days before. He kinda wished he hadn't done that now.

Papa Fred went into the house.

"Hurry," Trish whispered in Perry's ear.

He crutched after her, but she beat him to the Suburban, then turned with her hands on her hips.

"Come *on*." She helped him into the passenger seat, then ran around to the driver's side. She was like a wild-eyed linebacker rushing the quarterback. Faster than he could say supercalifragilisticexpialidocious, she'd started the engine and the heater and thrown the dented Suburban into reverse.

"What are you doing?" Perry asked. At least there were no strange sounds or smoke coming from the engine, so the Suburban was probably okay.

"You think I'm going to sit here and wait on the cops to come for that murderer when Dad's been poisoned? We have to get to Lander. People die from this. Dad could *die*."

Her words made his stomach hurt. He didn't want to think about what it would be like if their dad died. It would be bad. The worst. Clutching his belly, he drew in a deep breath. "Shouldn't we get Brandon to drive? Since you don't have a license, and all."

His sister ignored him. She pressed the accelerator. The tires spun uselessly for a moment, then caught, and she turned around in one speedy perfect arc. Perry looked out the window and saw Uncle Will and Brandon yelling at them and waving, but then the Suburban was flying in the opposite direction, toward Lander, and their dad.

CHAPTER THIRTY-NINE: SURVIVE

Patrick

Big Mike loomed over Patrick, his face enormous and eyes squinting. *"Pull it together, Dr. Flint. More folks than just me are counting on you now."*

Had wild horses stampeded over his body? It sure felt like it. Patrick prodded his neck, identifying the most painful spots. *"What happened to me?"*

"You survived. You found the trickster, and you brought me justice. You're a man of honor. Thank you."

Patrick tried to remember what he had survived, but he was fuzzy on the details, other than it somehow involved Riley and was the reason he felt so damn bad. *"There's no need to thank me. I was just doing my job."*

"Which too few people do." He pulled an eagle feather from his breast pocket and put in on a table near Patrick's head. *"Now I can die a second time."*

"Don't people only die once?"

"You'd think so, but, if that's true, why was I here with you?" He winked.

Noises pulled him away from Big Mike. His vision flickered, faltered, and disappeared. He opened his eyes to a blurry cluster of faces. They came slowly into focus but the room behind them was still just a kaleidoscope. Perry. Trish. His in-laws. But the face he saw first and the gaze he held was his wife's.

Weakly, he smiled at her. "We've got to quit meeting like this." It seemed like only yesterday he'd woken in the Buffalo hospital after succumbing to giardia, although it was months ago. Hers had been the first face he'd seen then, too. The first and only girl he'd loved, the first and only face he wanted to wake up to.

Her return smile was stiff. "I'm glad to see you returning to normal." She kissed his forehead, then moved across the room to let everyone else poke, prod, and hug him for themselves, positioning herself by a chair at the window, with a blank-screened TV on the wall over her head.

"You had us scared," Papa Fred said.

"You nearly died, Dad," Perry added, sitting on the edge of the bed.

"I feel like it," Patrick said. He started to ask what had happened to him, but it came back to him in a rush. Riley. The beer bottle to his noggin. The needle, with a solution of strychnine. Fighting his way free, jerking the needle from his arm. Searching for remedies in Constance's empty house, with no luck. Susanne showing up with his bag. Taking the meds. The nearly out-of-control drive into Lander, half of it in a delirium as seizures racked his body, until, finally, blessedly, he must have lost consciousness, because his memories ceased until this moment. He'd survived strychnine poisoning. Gratitude washed over him, and he mouthed, *Thank you, God.*

"I know you're going to be okay," Trish said. She was standing behind Perry, her hands on her brother's head. "Your lips are moving. You do realize you don't have to talk to yourself in a room full of people, don't you?"

His eyes stayed on his wife. She was upset. Really, really upset. Was it the after-effect of fear? Or something else? He wished his brain was working better. The hours and days before Riley had attacked him were like a scratched record. He could hear the words, but he couldn't understand them. Whatever was bothering her, he wanted to deal with it, to get back to good, and he couldn't with a room full of people in their way. A thick-middled nurse in white hose, shoes, and dress bustled in to take his vitals and replenish his IV, followed by a hospital kitchen worker quickly in and out with a pitcher of water and his doctor stopping by on rounds. Patrick wouldn't have the privacy he needed with Susanne any time soon.

The very young doctor with short black hair and a large flesh-colored mole by his nose lifted one of Patrick's eyelids and shined a light in his eyes, then repeated the process on the other side. Patrick couldn't tell if he was Shoshone or Arapahoe, but he was definitely Indian. "You were right on the edge of a fatal dose. But you're doing well. Good thing your attacker wasn't precise in his measurements."

Patrick pursed his lips. "He tried to give me three times as much. I just managed to pull the needle out before he succeeded."

Perry bounced the bed as he readjusted his position on it. "Holy cow, Dad, that's intense."

"How's Verna Teton?" Patrick asked.

The doctor clipped the pen light to the breast pocket of his white jacket. "She made it. She had an even lower concentration of strychnine in her blood than you. But hers was in her stomach. From a cup of coffee, according to reports from the police."

"And Riley Pearson? What happened to him?"

Perry grinned. "Trish rammed him with the Suburban so he couldn't get away. Brandon held him until the police could come. With a pitchfork."

Papa Fred made a "hmm" noise. "And Will grabbed an ax and helped."

"The police have Riley now," Susanne added. "In a cast. Trish broke his leg when she t-boned him."

"Wow."

"And Perry has a new cast, too." Susanne ruffled Perry's hair.

He ducked. "Stop it, Mom. I'm not a baby."

Susanne lifted her hands up in front of her. "Sorry."

"What happened to you, bud?" Patrick asked.

Trish didn't give Perry a chance to answer. "He fell and broke his cast off. And it's his own fault because he'd been trying to break out of it all week, and he'd weakened it."

"Thanks, Trish," Perry muttered.

"We'll talk about that later, son. And where is Brandon, the pitchfork-toting boyfriend?" Patrick winked at Trish.

She turned away to face the window. "He's not my boyfriend anymore."

Susanne put her hand on Trish's shoulder. "He rode home with

Wes, as soon as the doctor let us know that you were out of the woods. Shelley and her family crammed in with them, too."

The doctor moved toward the door. "We'll release you tomorrow if you continue to improve."

"Thank you."

The doctor nodded and walked out, his gait brisk.

The nurse huffed at Patrick. "We've been humoring you, but this is far too many people in your room, Dr. Flint."

"Can my wife stay?"

"One person only, and please try to rest."

"It's okay, I have to take care of a few things." Susanne picked up her things from the chair, putting the purse strap over her shoulder and coat over her arm. She kept her eyes averted from his.

"When will you be back?" he asked.

"In the morning. I'll let you get a good night's sleep. Come on, everyone."

Susanne herded the family to the door after more hugs, kisses, and good-natured prodding.

Perry was the last to leave. "When I come back, can you sign my cast?"

Still reeling from Susanne's abrupt departure, Patrick longed to muss the boy's hair, but those days were over. "Only if you promise to leave it on this time."

His son crutched his way out, smiling, but making no promises.

The empty room fell deathly quiet. The hallway beyond was silent, too, and dark. He swung his head to face the window, where the blinds were open. Night had fallen. He'd lost a whole day. More than a day. He knew the nurse was right—he should rest. But Patrick wasn't sleepy. In fact, he was agitated. He hated the chilliness from Susanne. His memories were flickering in and out but lying here thinking wouldn't bring them back any faster. All inactivity would do is make him recycle. About Susanne, and with wondering what was wrong. About Riley, and what the man had done. About Big Mike's senseless death. And Verna's close call, like his own.

Verna. She would probably still be in the hospital, too. He could check on her. He wanted to see for himself that she was okay and commiserate with her over their similar near-death experience. The nurse had urged him to rest, but no one had told him he couldn't get up.

He sat and let his head adjust. The dizziness and a wave of nausea made him feel like he'd drank a six pack of Coors, but then he remembered it was from a bottle to his skull. Standing slowly, he tested his balance, letting a head rush pass. Wobbly, but functional. He grabbed the IV stand. It would have to come with him. He rolled it along beside him a few steps. A breezy feeling on his behind gave him pause. Open-back hospital gown. That wouldn't do. His jeans were out of the question. He spied a stack of hospital gowns. If he put one on opening to the front, it would cover his southern exposure. Struggling into it, he ended up with his IV line running up the sleeve and out the bottom of his top gown, but his modesty preserved.

After he shuffled to the door, he realized he didn't know Verna's room number. But Lander's hospital was one story. A small hospital broken into even smaller wards. She was likely to be on his hall. He peeked out the door. The hall was empty, not that he needed to hide from anyone, per se, but it was a good bet that his adventure would be discouraged if he was seen. His room was at the far end of a hall. Good—he could check all the rooms on his wing in one sweep. If she wasn't there, he'd come back and rest.

He pulled his door mostly closed behind him. The wheels of the IV stand squeaked. The sheet vinyl flooring was icy cold on his bare feet. He hadn't checked the time, but it seemed late. Well past the dinner hour. As he made his way down the hall, he stuck his head in doors and scanned faces, most of them showing every sign of being asleep, except for an elderly woman watching *The Price is Right* without the sound on.

She gathered her saggy skin into a grimace and shouted, "I need a bed pan."

He couldn't help feeling like he should do something for her. Occupational hazard. "Can you reach the phone to call the nurse?"

Her eyes flitted away. "I guess so."

He waved to her and moved on. Ahead on the left, he heard voices coming from a room. Not on a TV, but in real life. A man, a woman, and another woman, he decided. Light streamed into the hallway from their room. When he stood in the doorway, a man's wide back blocked his view of the patient inside, but he recognized the uniform—tribal police—and the man's profile—Dann.

"Officer?" he said.

Dann looked over his shoulder at Patrick. Patrick caught a glimpse of Constance seated in an upright recliner. Faux leather, like the ones in Buffalo, placed in the rooms so visitors could catnap while patients were resting. His interaction with Constance at her house the day before came flooding back over him like a tsunami. How she caught him snooping. Her revealing Big Mike's abuse and her plans to leave him to go to Chicago, then taking off her shirt and pressing herself against him. His reaction, and her angry departure. He groaned aloud before he could stifle it.

He acknowledged her with a nod. She nodded back.

Dann took a step toward him, hand out. "Dr. Flint. You're awake. You and Verna had us worried."

Patrick shuffled forward and shook Dann's hand.

Verna's voice was weak and thready. "Come in Dr. Flint. Come in so I can thank you."

Patrick's cheeks burned. He'd wanted a private chat with Verna in dim lighting. He hadn't bargained on a group conversation that included Constance, under interrogation-worthy lights, when he was nearly unclothed. Just like Constance had been last time he'd seen her.

He advanced the IV stand toward Verna, wobbling like an old man and sounding like he needed a squirt of WD40. "Verna, I was looking for you. I'm so glad to see you alive and well."

"Thanks to your son and wife."

"That's what I hear. Thank God for lucky timing."

Constance stood, smoothing a calf-length corduroy skirt that she was wearing over boots. She looked different, somehow. Unlike the clinic manager he was used to. "I'm sorry for what happened to you, Patrick. I had no idea about Riley. None."

"Thank you." Patrick didn't doubt it, but he hadn't come here to talk to her. Dann's presence, though, was fortuitous. "Dann, there are things Riley told me that you need to know. He confessed to killing Big Mike and poisoning Verna, which is no surprise, but he went further than that."

Constance put a fist over her mouth.

"What else did he say?" Dann said.

"That Eddie was next, and he hinted he may have had something to do with the death of Constance's parents. Does that make any sense?"

Constance sank back into her chair. Elbows on her knees, she lowered her face into her hands. Her back heaved, but she didn't make a sound.

"Constance?" Dann said. He moved closer to her and laid a hand on her back. A very affectionate hand that kneaded her shoulder.

She raised a tear-streaked face. "Riley had just moved here. My parents died in a car wreck. I never had any reason to think it was anything but an accident. They were both drunk. Nothing new there. But, but . . ."

"He said no one is allowed to hurt you." Patrick leaned some weight on his IV stand. He was starting to feel tired.

She wiped her eyes with both palms. "I told you that he credits me with saving his life in Vietnam?"

"Yes."

"While he was in my care, I talked to him. Told him he was a survivor and could make it through anything. Sometimes he was combative and negative. He accused me of not being able to relate. So, I shared what it was like growing up in poverty and the harsh conditions of the reservation as the daughter of two alcoholic parents."

"And he remembered."

Dann kept his hand on her shoulder. Not that Patrick was timing it, but the gesture had gone past affection and support to intimacy. Maybe Riley was right and Dann's feelings for Constance were still there.

"Yes."

Verna barked, "I was wrong about you. I'm sorry."

Constance dipped her head at Verna. "It's okay."

"If I'd have known my brother was beating you, I could have helped." *So Constance had told Verna about the abuse.* "Our father used to beat on our mother, and Big Mike swore he'd never do that to a woman. I'm ashamed of my brother."

"It's fine, really."

Verna turned to Patrick. "She's invited me to live with her. To share the ranch. Can you believe that? And she's giving Big Mike's life insurance to his son Jason."

Dann cut in. "We've convinced her to offer to fill Big Mike's spot on the tribal council. To continue his work on hunting regulations."

"You're not going to Chicago?" Patrick said. She had told him that she was only leaving the reservation to get away from Big Mike. With him gone, there was no need to leave her home, he supposed.

She nodded.

"That's good for the people around here."

Dann's eyes shone as he gazed at Constance. "Very good."

Constance picked lint off her shirt. "If I can serve on the council, I can continue some of the work Big Mike was doing. Important work that

I agree with. Plus, there's so much other work to do. At the clinic, I see firsthand how alcohol, domestic violence, and poor diet are impacting our children, like they did me. I'd like to change that."

Patrick swayed, rolling the IV stand a little with him.

Constance's sharp eyes picked it up. "You need to get back in bed, Patrick." She stood again. "Your body has just been through a trauma, and it needs rest to recover. I'll get you back to your room."

The last thing Patrick wanted was any time alone with Constance. "No, I'm fine. I can make it on my own."

Dann said, "Let me just finish up with Verna."

She nodded. "I'll meet you back here in a minute." To Patrick she said, "Are you forgetting I'm a trained nurse and medic? Besides, I need to talk to you for a moment."

That was exactly what Patrick was afraid of.

CHAPTER FORTY: FORGIVE

Patrick

S ummoning all his strength and ignoring the fuzziness in his head, Patrick moved ahead of Constance, weaving down the hall like a drunken draft horse trying to outrun a thoroughbred. Determined, but uncoordinated and ineffective. Constance moved smoothly ahead of him when he paused at his door.

She pushed it open. "You don't have to be scared of me, you know."

He beelined for his bed without responding.

"Stop. We've got to get your double gown off so it doesn't interfere with your IV line."

"I can do it after you leave."

She put her hands on her hips. "Patrick. I'm not going to take my clothes off again. Or ever. I was upset earlier. I don't know what made me act that way, but I haven't been my best. I'm better now. Really. And I'm not taking no for an answer on this."

He sighed. His body ached with tiredness. "Okay."

Constance walked up to him. She untied the front of the top gown. Patrick swallowed hard. He just wanted this moment to be over,

Constance to leave, his head to be on the pillow, and his eyes to be closed.

Susanne's voice cracked like a whip. "So, this is what you do when I tell you I'm leaving for the night."

Constance jumped away, and Patrick fell against the inclined head of the bed. The IV stand teetered.

He caught it with one hand. "Susanne. You're back."

"Surprise," she said through gritted teeth. "And here I thought I was coming with great news. But 'congratulations, honey, we got the house' just doesn't have quite the same punch when you're sneaking around with her."

"I wasn't—"

"I was just going," Constance said.

"It looked more like you were just undressing my husband."

The room swayed. Patrick didn't know how much longer he could stand up. "She's a trained medical professional."

"So are the nurses who work for *this* hospital. And yet Constance just happens to be the one in here doing a good deed."

"I went down to visit Verna, and Constance and Dann were there. I wasn't feeling good. She insisted on getting me safely back to my room." He pointed at his chest. "I was stuck in this double gown. That was all."

"Right."

"I swear."

"That's not what she made it sound like yesterday at the police station."

"What?"

Susanne turned on Constance. "And it's not what my daughter told me she overheard you saying to the man who tried to kill my husband."

Patrick felt like he was watching a handball match, from the center of the court, with a player aiming for his head. "Susanne, I don't know what you're talking about."

Constance was shaking her head and opened her mouth, but Susanne spoke first. "Riley asked you if you were involved with Patrick, and you said, 'we'll see,' right in front of Trish. And you said I was mousy and not a match for Patrick."

Patrick turned to Constance. "Is that true?"

She bit her top lip. "I'm sorry. I've already told you, I wasn't myself."

Susanne barreled on. "Then at the police station, you insinuated to me that you and Patrick had been out at your ranch house together. Alone."

Patrick's brain couldn't take much more. He held up a hand. "Only because she walked in on me. I'd gone out to search for evidence that she killed Big Mike, after Dann didn't seem inclined to follow up on my suspicions. Of course, I was wrong, and look what happened to me as a result." He swayed like a sapling in the wind, and both women rushed forward. "I think I need to get in bed."

"I've got him," Susanne snapped.

Constance backed away. Susanne untied Patrick's top gown and slipped it off, then held the IV stand while he lowered himself onto the bed. She adjusted his gown and pulled the covers over him, her movements still rough and jerky.

Constance smoothed her sweater. Then she squared her shoulders and took one step toward Susanne. "I'm sorry. I've been having a tough time. You're married to a good man. I tried to latch onto him, I admit it. But he wouldn't let me, and I was jealous of you. Of your relationship. I was wrong."

Susanne sniffed and looked at Patrick.

He didn't want to rub salt in Constance's wounds—she *had* been having a hard time. Her pain didn't make her actions right, though, and he wanted even more to reassure his wife. "That's all that happened, Susanne," he said quietly. Then to Constance, "My wife is the most beautiful woman I've ever seen, and I'm lucky to have her."

"I'm sorry. You're right." Constance looked at her feet. "I'll be going."

"You said you needed to talk to me." Patrick pressed his hand to his temple. "Is there anything else?"

She paused. "I just wanted to apologize. And to tell you that Riley admitted he'd left the notes and marked up Big Mike's face."

"Thank you."

"Dann probably wonders what's happened to me." She walked to the door with her chin held high.

"Constance, who was the other ticket for?"

She didn't look back. Didn't stop. But her voice was clear from the doorway. "Anyone I could convince to go with me. Anyone so I wouldn't be alone." Then she was gone.

Susanne's eyes clouded. She turned to Patrick, and her voice had a defensive edge. "Don't expect me to just stand by when some woman makes a play for you. You're my husband." Her voice cracked. "And I love you."

He reached for her hand, and she let him take it. "And I love you. It works both ways, though, you know. If some guy tries to steal you away, he'll have a battle on his hands."

"No one could ever steal me away from you."

"Or me from you."

She sat on the bed. "No person, maybe, but sometimes it feels like all your . . . stuff . . . steals you away from me one minute, one hour, one day at a time."

"What do you mean?"

"Well, the Fort Washakie Health Center comes to mind as an example. You picked coming here over me."

"Not over you. It wasn't like it was a choice between us or the clinic."

"No, but I told you I needed you."

His heart sank at the hurt in her voice. She had told him that. "I'm sorry. I really am. Maybe if you really, *really* need me, you could exercise veto rights. Tell me, 'Patrick, I need you to be here,' instead of staying silent and getting hurt. Speak up, veto, get what you need."

She gave him a grudging smile. "That would work."

He weighed her need for his presence versus the pressing health needs of the patients in Fort Washakie. "It's a different kind of need, but they needed me here, too. I can do some good here, for a lot of people."

Susanne rolled her lips in, then said, "I'll grant you that, and I'm proud of you for caring so much. But I have to ask, after how it's gone, how do you feel about this good deed trip now?"

He snorted and pulled his gown loose where it was caught under his thigh and cutting into his shoulder. "Like no good deed goes unpunished."

"So, does that mean you're done with Wind River?"

"I didn't say that. No pain, no gain."

She shook her head, but she was smiling, and her eyes were clear and sparkling again. "I guess I wouldn't know who you were if you'd have answered me any differently. But can I at least request no more Constance outside work?"

"Absolutely." Patrick put the back of her hand to his lips. "And I know what I want for Christmas."

"I hope it's a house on Clear Creek."

He shook his head. "A new wedding band."

She lifted his left hand. "For the finger you don't want to get ripped off?"

"The same one."

"Patrick, you don't need to put a ring through your nose or around your finger to prove you're mine."

"I don't want you to feel threatened or like I'm not committed to you."

"It's your actions I care about. A ring won't make me feel more married. But the house on Clear Creek will."

"We got it, huh?"

"We did."

He smiled. "More room for your family to come visit."

"If they'll ever come back after this trip."

"I'm sorry about that."

They locked eyes for a moment. He hated that he'd had any part in ruining the visit from her family that'd she'd been looking forward to for so long.

Then Susanne laid her head on his shoulder. Her voice was wry when she spoke. "Actually, believe it or not, my mother and sister said they took a family vote and have declared this their most exciting Christmas ever. They're already making plans to come back next year."

Patrick threw back his head and laughed. It hurt, but it was worth it.

***

Next up: There's more **Patrick Flint** and family in *Sawbones*: https://www.amazon.com/gp/product/B083TZBCQS. When a killer threatens his family before their testimony in a capital murder trial, Patrick Flint will do anything to keep them safe.

Or you can continue adventuring in the *What Doesn't Kill You* mystery world:

> *Want to stay in **Wyoming**? Rock on with Maggie in*
> **Live Wire on Amazon** *(free in Kindle*
> *Unlimited) at*
> *https://www.amazon.com/dp/B07L3RYGII7/*

> *Prefer the **beginning** of it all? Start with Katie in*

Saving Grace *on **Amazon** (free to Kindle Unlimited subscribers), here:* *https://www.amazon.com/dp/B009FZPMFO.*

*Or **get the complete WDKY series** here:* *https://www.amazon.com/gp/product/B07QQVNSPN.*

***

And don't forget to snag the **free** *What Doesn't Kill You* **ebook starter library** by joining Pamela's mailing list at https://www.subscribepage.com/PFHSuperstars.

For my mom, who loves me despite myself, is always the most fun person in the room, and epitomizes the concept of "spit fire."
And for Eric, who also loves me despite myself, is sometimes one of the most fun people in the room, and epitomizes the concept of "intensity."

OTHER BOOKS BY THE AUTHOR

Fiction from SkipJack Publishing

The *What Doesn't Kill You* Series

Act One (Prequel, Ensemble Novella)

Saving Grace (Katie #1)

Leaving Annalise (Katie #2)

Finding Harmony (Katie #3)

Heaven to Betsy (Emily #1)

Earth to Emily (Emily #2)

Hell to Pay (Emily #3)

Going for Kona (Michele #1)

Fighting for Anna (Michele #2)

Searching for Dime Box (Michele #3)

Buckle Bunny (Maggie Prequel Novella)

Shock Jock (Maggie Prequel Short Story)

Live Wire (Maggie #1)

Sick Puppy (Maggie #2)

Dead Pile (Maggie #3)

The Essential Guide to the What Doesn't Kill You Series

The Ava Butler Trilogy: A Sexy Spin-off From *What Doesn't Kill You*

Bombshell (Ava #1)

Stunner (Ava #2)

Knockout (Ava #3)

The Patrick Flint Trilogy: A Spin-off From *What Doesn't*

Kill You

Switchback (Patrick Flint #1)

Snake Oil (Patrick Flint #2)

Sawbones (Patrick Flint #3)

Scapegoat (Patrick Flint #4)

Snaggle Tooth (Patrick Flint #5)

Stag Party (Patrick Flint #6): 2021

The What Doesn't Kill You Box Sets Series (50% off individual title retail)

The Complete Katie Connell Trilogy

The Complete Emily Bernal Trilogy

The Complete Michele Lopez Hanson Trilogy

The Complete Maggie Killian Trilogy

The Complete Ava Butler Trilogy

The Complete Patrick Flint Trilogy #1 (coming in late 2020)

Nonfiction from SkipJack Publishing

The Clark Kent Chronicles

Hot Flashes and Half Ironmans

How to Screw Up Your Kids

How to Screw Up Your Marriage

Puppalicious and Beyond

What Kind of Loser Indie Publishes,
and How Can I Be One, Too?

Audio, e-book, and paperback versions of most titles available.

ACKNOWLEDGMENTS

When I got the call from my father that he had metastatic prostate cancer spread into his bones in nine locations, I was with a houseful of retreat guests in Wyoming while my parents (who normally summer in Wyoming) were in Texas. The guests were so kind and comforting to me, as was Eric, but there was only one place I wanted to be, and that was home. Not home where I grew up, because I lived in twelve places by the time I was twelve, and many thereafter. No, home is truly where the heart is. And that meant home for Eric and me would be with my parents.

I was in the middle of writing two novels at the time: *Blue Streak*, the first Laura mystery in the What Doesn't Kill You series, and *Polarity*, a series spin-off contemporary romance based on my love story with Eric. I put them both down. I needed to write, but not those books. They could wait. I needed to write through my emotions—because that's what writers do—with books spelling out the ending we were seeking for my dad's story. Allegorically and biographically, while fictionally.

So that is what I did, and Dr. Patrick Flint (aka Dr. Peter Fagan—my pops—in real life) and family were hatched, using actual stories from our lives in late 1970s Buffalo, Wyoming as the depth and backdrop to a new series of mysteries, starting with *Switchback* and moving on to *Snake Oil* and *Sawbones*. I hope the real life versions of Patrick, Susanne, and Perry will forgive me for taking liberties in creating their fictional alter egos. I took care to make Trish the most annoying character since she's based on me, to soften the blow for the others. I am so hopeful that my loyal readers will enjoy them, too, even though in some ways the novels are a departure from my usual stories. But in many ways they are the same. Character-driven, edge-of-your-seat mysteries steeped in setting/culture, with a strong nod to the everyday magic around us, and filled with complex, authentic characters (including some AWESOME females).

I had a wonderful time writing these books, and it kept me going when it was tempting to fold in on myself and let stress eat me alive. For more stories behind the actual stories, visit my blog on my website: http://pamelafaganhutchins.com. And let me know if you liked the novels. I have three more in my hip pocket, waiting to be written if you want them: *Snaggle Tooth*, *Scape Goat*, and *Strike Out*.

Thanks to my dad for advice on all things medical, wilderness, hunting, 1970s, and animal. I hope you had fun using your medical knowledge for murder!

Thanks to my mom for printing the manuscripts (over and over, in its entirety) as she and dad followed along daily on the progress, for letting me use her beautiful real name, and for loving me despite myself.

Thanks to my husband, Eric, for brainstorming with and encouraging me and beta reading the *Patrick Flint* stories despite his busy work, travel, and workout schedule. And for moving in to my parents's barn apartment with me so I could be closer to them during this time.

Thanks to our five offspring. I love you guys more than anything, and each time I write a parent/child (birth, adopted, foster, or step), I channel you. I am so touched by how supportive you have been with Poppy, Gigi, Eric, and me.

To each and every blessed reader, I appreciate you more than I can say. It is the readers who move mountains for me, and for other authors, and I humbly ask for the honor of your honest reviews and recommendations.

Thanks mucho to Bobbye and Rhonda for putting up with my eccentric and ever-changing needs. Extra thanks to Bobbye for the fantastic *Patrick Flint* covers.

Patrick Flint editing credits go to Rhonda Erb and Whitney Cox. The proofreaders who enthusiastically devote their time—gratis—to help us rid my books of flaws blow me away. My gratitude goes to Anita, Caren, Karen, Kelly, Misty, Ginger, Lanier, Tara, and Pat.

SkipJack Publishing now includes fantastic books by a cherry-picked bushel basket of mystery/thriller/suspense writers. If you write in this genre, visit http://SkipJackPublishing.com for submission guidelines. To check out our other authors and snag a bargain at the same time, download *Murder, They Wrote: Four SkipJack Mysteries*.

ABOUT THE AUTHOR

Pamela Fagan Hutchins is a *USA Today* best seller. She writes award-winning romantic mysteries from deep in the heart of Nowheresville, Texas and way up in the frozen north of Snowheresville, Wyoming. She is passionate about long hikes with her hunky husband and pack of rescue dogs and riding her gigantic horses.

If you'd like Pamela to speak to your book club, women's club, class, or writers group, by Skype or in person, shoot her an email. She's very likely to say yes.

You can connect with Pamela via her website
(http://pamelafaganhutchins.com)
or email (pamela@pamelafaganhutchins.com).

PRAISE FOR PAMELA FAGAN HUTCHINS

2018 USA Today Best Seller
2017 Silver Falchion Award, Best Mystery
2016 USA Best Book Award, Cross-Genre Fiction
2015 USA Best Book Award, Cross-Genre Fiction
2014 Amazon Breakthrough Novel Award Quarter-finalist, Romance

Patrick Flint Mysteries

"Best book I've read in a long time!" — Kiersten Marquet, author of
Three Reluctant Promises
"A Bob Ross painting with Alfred Hitchcock hidden among the trees."
— Scott Westerman, author of *Motor City Music*
"A very exciting book (um... actually a nail-biter), soooo beautifully
descriptive, with an underlying story of human connection and family.
It's full of action. I was so scared and so mad and so relieved... sometimes
all at once!" — *Tara Scheyer, Grammy-nominated musician, Long-
Distance Sisters Book Club*
"Well drawn characters, great scenery, and a kept-me-on-the-edge-of-
my-seat story!" — Caren Luckie, Librarian

What Doesn't Kill You: Katie Romantic Mysteries

"An exciting tale . . . twisting investigative and legal subplots . . . a char-
acter seeking redemption . . . an exhilarating mystery with a touch of
voodoo." — *Midwest Book Review Bookwatch*
"A lively romantic mystery." — *Kirkus Reviews*
"A riveting drama . . . exciting read, highly recommended." — *Small
Press Bookwatch*
"Katie is the first character I have absolutely fallen in love with since
Stephanie Plum!" — *Stephanie Swindell, Bookstore Owner*
"Engaging storyline . . . taut suspense." — *MBR Bookwatch*

What Doesn't Kill You: Emily Romantic Mysteries

"Fair warning: clear your calendar before you pick it up because you won't be able to put it down." — *Ken Oder, author of* Old Wounds to the Heart

"Full of heart, humor, vivid characters, and suspense. Hutchins has done it again!" — *Gay Yellen, author of* The Body Business

"Hutchins is a master of tension." — *R.L. Nolen, author of* Deadly Thyme

"Intriguing mystery . . . captivating romance." — *Patricia Flaherty Pagan, author of* Trail Ways Pilgrims

"Everything about it shines: the plot, the characters and the writing. Readers are in for a real treat with this story." — *Marcy McKay, author of* Pennies from Burger Heaven

What Doesn't Kill You: Michele Romantic Mysteries

"Immediately hooked." — *Terry Sykes-Bradshaw, author of* Sibling Revelry

"Spellbinding." — *Jo Bryan, Dry Creek Book Club*

"Fast-paced mystery." — *Deb Krenzer, Book Reviewer*

"Can't put it down." — *Cathy Bader, Reader*

What Doesn't Kill You: Ava Romantic Mysteries

"Just when I think I couldn't love another Pamela Fagan Hutchins novel more, along comes Ava." — *Marcy McKay, author of* Stars Among the Dead

"Ava personifies bombshell in every sense of word. — *Tara Scheyer, Grammy-nominated musician, Long-Distance Sisters Book Club*

"Entertaining, complex, and thought-provoking." — *Ginger Copeland, power reader*

What Doesn't Kill You: Maggie Romantic Mysteries

"Maggie's gonna break your heart—one way or another." *Tara Scheyer, Grammy-nominated musician, Long-Distance Sisters Book Club*

"Pamela Fagan Hutchins nails that Wyoming scenery and captures the atmosphere of the people there." — *Ken Oder, author of* Old Wounds to the Heart

"I thought I had it all figured out a time or two, but she kept me wondering right to the end." — *Ginger Copeland, power reader*

OTHER BOOKS FROM SKIPJACK PUBLISHING

Murder, They Wrote: Four SkipJack Mysteries,
by Pamela Fagan Hutchins,
Ken Oder, R.L. Nolen, and Marcy Mason

The Closing, by Ken Oder
Old Wounds to the Heart, by Ken Oder
The Judas Murders, by Ken Oder
The Princess of Sugar Valley, by Ken Oder

Pennies from Burger Heaven, by Marcy McKay
Stars Among the Dead, by Marcy McKay
The Moon Rises at Dawn, by Marcy McKay
Bones and Lies Between Us, by Marcy McKay

Deadly Thyme, by R. L. Nolen
The Dry, by Rebecca Nolen

Tides of Possibility, edited by K.J. Russell
Tides of Impossibility, edited by K.J. Russell and C. Stuart Hardwick

My Dream of Freedom: From Holocaust to My Beloved America,
by Helen Colin

FOREWORD

Snake Oil is a work of fiction. Period. Any resemblance to actual persons, places, things, or events is just a lucky coincidence. And I reserve the right to forego accuracy in favor of a good story, any time I get the chance.

Made in the USA
Columbia, SC
15 December 2020